CACTI WOMEN

A Novel

Sandra Sydell

ISBN: 13:978-154-4241296
ISBN: 10:1544241291

Cover photographer: Harvey Mendelson

for Julie, Jodie, Brian, Greer and Sam
my amazing family

Acknowledgements

I am sincerely grateful to ...

Toby Katz for editing the original manuscript, Toni Eubanks, my friend and professor, for her words of encouragement and editing while I attended her Creative Writing Class at SMCC, Gerry Newbanks for editing the proof and a special shout out to Sarah Vogt for reading and editing the completed book.

My daughters, Julie and Jodie, and my son-law, Brian, for cheering me on. My grandchildren, Greer and Sam, for their help with my computer questions and their encouragement.

My parents, Freda and Marvin Schwartz (in spirit) who always supported and encouraged my endeavors. My brothers, Bob Schwartz and Michael (in spirit) Schwartz for being on this life journey with me. My 'kissing' cousins, Fran Mesnick, Barbra Hill and Joyce Bregman, for their love and support. My dear friends, Carol Leibow, Raven Stone, Sharon and Harvey Mendelson for always being there for me.

The Spiritual Chat Group, led by Joni and Tony Gatto, for creating a nurturing environment as we shared and explored our mystical and higher self.

Kathy, owner of the former Emily's Café, for her encouraging words and delicious breakfast.

Zak, Doran, Ivy, Hannah and the friendly staff

at Snooze, a Scottsdale breakfast café, for their Wednesday morning hugs and tasty gluten-free blueberry pancake.

Ashley and her brother, Coby, at The Corner, a Scottsdale restaurant, for cheering me on as I typed away on my laptop while I worked on this book.

May, Manager, and Becca, Izzy, Barry and the staff at Wildflower Bread Company at Sonoran Village for their positive energy while I enjoyed breakfast.

Bina Bou, Qigong and Tai Chi instructor, where I learned simple mindful exercises that engaged and uplifted my body, mind and spirit.

LaVerne Henson, former owner, at Curves for her support and comradery, as I exercised for wellness.

Marla Leigh, owner/beautician, for her great haircuts and kind words as I pursued the completion of this book.

Linda Cramier, officer manager at Scottsdale Fashion Square Management Office, who always insisted that I could figure it out - my many computer questions, and I did!

And I am especially thankful to . . .

The Creator, within and without, that loves us unconditionally.

Introduction

In her Manhattan apartment, Kari Silverman, an established attorney, looks at the boxes of her deceased Gramma Sera Golden's possessions. These boxes have been cluttering her living room for more than a week.

Kari lifts one of the boxes to move it out of the way, and the bottom pulls apart, scattering her grandmother's belongings onto her area rug. She picks up the items: a beige fabric jewelry box filled with colorful gemstone jewelry, a collection of angels and assorted crystals, old photos, tarot decks and a weathered journal. She places each item carefully on her chrome and glass dining room table.

Remembering her grandmother's passion for things spiritual, she sighs loudly and thinks that she is not into this metaphysical stuff. She feels she does not have time for her spirituality, let alone her *lessons*. She remembers hearing her grandmother say, "Everything is a lesson here on this planet. This is like a big school. We are here to experience, to learn and grow, and as we grow, we help others do the same. We are all connected. There is more here than the physical eye can see."

She thinks her grandmother certainly marched to a different tune. She was a spiritual teacher and a medium, for she saw and heard entities, as she called people that had died or were from another dimension. She was an avid reader of occult books such as Tarot, Astrology and Numerology. She did tarot readings for her friends and her clients, but, Kari was not interested.

Kari scanned her living area with its custom contemporary furniture and abstract artwork. She was comfortable with the luxuries, her coveted job at the prestigious law firm. She worked hard and rarely had time to think about anything "other than her work" - let alone her spiritual nature. She picks up a large deep purple amethyst crystal and touches its rough spiked edges.

She remembers her grandmother telling her, "We are imperfect here in this dimension. Yet, we strive to perfect ourselves, to evolve as we connect to the Divine Source." Kari admits to herself that she still doesn't understand what she was talking about.

A strand of her thick red hair falls onto her face. She pushed this aside as she thinks it's amazing that we are related for we are so totally different.

She picks up the journal for it has aroused her curiosity and glides her manicured fingers across its worn cover.

She pictures her grandmother seated at her little black desk writing in the journal. She held the journal for a moment, not sure if she wanted to read what was inside, then decided why not and opened it.

A folded note fell out from the journal onto the dark wood floor. The outside of the note is addressed to her. As she opens the note, she sniffs her grandmother's perfume. The floral fragrance lingers in the air sweet and vibrant. Kari thought it's still hard to believe that she is gone. She opens the note.

Dearest Kari,
Now that you found my journal, I hope you will read it. Some of my lessons and strange occurrences may be hard for you to understand. Keep an open mind. Play with the tarot. It will teach you.
I love you,
Gramma Sera

Kari swipes a tear as it slides down her cheek. She takes the journal to her favorite chair near the crackling fire in her fireplace and begins to read.

my personal journal

Sera Golden

1
strange and magical moments can appear

The year was 1946, World War II had ended, and my father, a soldier, returned to our home town, Cleveland, Ohio. The mock air raids with shredded paper falling from airplanes were over; the rag men shouting, "paper-rags," from their horse drawn carts gone. My world was my family and my friends. I was eight years old.

I felt different. I felt that I didn't belong in my present family, even though I was surrounded by my loving parents, my brother, aunts, uncles, and cousins. My family lived on the first floor of a two-story apartment building. My maternal grandparents lived next door. My mother had five close siblings.

Many times I looked at my hands and thought my skin should be darker. I often wondered why my skin was this light color. I had a dream that I rode inside a streetcar, all alone to the end of the line, where my dark-skinned family met and welcomed me. I remember the warm loving feeling. Over time I forgot about this dream and drifted into school, friends, day to day life, until strange things began to happen that I could not ignore.

One strange thing happened after a dance. It was a Sadie Hawkins dance (where girls ask boys to dance) at my high school. I had just moved to another area of the city and missed my school and classmates.

I called my Aunt Betty to see if I could sleep over Friday night as their house was near my high school. She agreed. I loved my large bellied aunt. I nicknamed her Spaghetti Betty, for there was always a big pot of delicious homemade spaghetti sauce cooking on her stove top for her Italian husband. My aunt and uncle owned one car. My uncle worked nights, so I would have to take the bus from the dance back to their house. I was used to riding buses for I was too young to drive.

On Friday, I took the bus to my aunt's house. After spaghetti dinner, I changed for the dance: a coral sweater set, gray gabardine skirt, white ankle socks, and of course, Murray Bender brown loafers with shiny new pennies in the front flaps. I hurried along the long street past the small look alike houses to the bus stop. I felt the warmth of the still lit May night.

The steps seemed steep as I climbed into the empty bus and sat on the worn upholstered seat. About ten minutes later, the bus stopped in front of my school. I ran down the long gravel drive and opened the heavy door of the building.

It felt good to walk through the familiar corridors, and I could not wait to see everyone. I walked to the auditorium. The large room was transformed into a big dance floor, folding chairs outlined the sides of the room. The darkened room had a silver ball hanging from the ceiling that threw different colored lights onto the dance floor. The jitterbug music blasted through the speakers. The boys sat on one side of the room and the girls on the other.

It took me a moment to gather my courage and then I went over to one of the boys and asked, "Would you like to dance."

He said, "Yes." He was tall and nice looking. I didn't know the boy because most of the boys were from another high school.

I said, "Thank you." He was a good dancer. Nevertheless, I never danced with him again.

I looked around the room and made eye contact with one of the girls from my class. She came over to where I was standing and asked, "How is your new school?"

"Great," I replied. "About three times as big as this one."

"Wow, how did you find your classrooms?"

"It took me several days to learn the building and not go down the wrong corridor. I thought more of the girls I knew would spell be at the dance. I was looking forward to seeing them. You're the only one here that I know from our class."

She answered, "Most of the girls I talked to were not interested. They didn't want to ask the boys to dance. They thought that they would have to ask a boy to dance every dance. I tried to explain that only a few dances are Sadie Hawken's dances. The other dances are normal where a boy would ask a girl to dance."

A boy tapped her shoulder. "May I have this dance?" Off they went. I didn't see her again.

Another classmate, Jim, came up to me and asked, "Sera, do you want to dance?"

"Sure," I said, and we danced to a slow-motion song. He was a good dancer and we danced several dances together.

Several other boys I had never seen before asked me to dance. Before I knew it, the auditorium lights came on and off to signify that it was the last dance. Then all the lights were on.

"Do you want a ride home?" asked one of the boys I danced with.

"No. Thanks." I was not comfortable going with him, besides, I planned to take the bus back to my aunt and uncle's house.

There was a handful of students left as I made my way through the empty corridors out into the cool night. The hall clock showed 8:55 pm. My loafers crunched through the gravel driveway scattering the small stones. I hurried across the deserted Mayfield Road to the bus stop.

The soft wind blew my shoulder length auburn hair as I stood and waited for the bus. The streetlight illuminated my thin silhouette. Across the street, the school's lights glowed in the dark. Cars flashed by me on the rural road in both directions as students left the dance. Suddenly it was very quiet, too quiet. I had assumed the bus would be there. I forgot to look at the schedule.

I began to worry. Where is the bus? It should have been here at 9:00 pm, because the bus ran on the hour. I looked at my watch and saw that is was 9:15 pm. Little tremors pricked me as I realized that the bus wasn't going to arrive. I felt alone and tired.

Worrisome thoughts nagged at me. I should have taken the ride offered me. Why didn't I do that? How am I going to get to my aunt and uncle's? It's too dark and too far me to walk. What am I going to do?

Engrossed in my frenzied thinking, I suddenly stopped - aware of energy next to me. I looked down at my left side and there was a large dog with reddish fur. I couldn't believe it! Where did this dog come from? How long had the dog been there? I didn't feel the dog was harmful, quite the contrary, as I looked again at its furry silhouette. The big dog didn't look up, just stared straight ahead as if someone had commanded him to sit and stay. I knew deep within me that this dog was there - to protect me.

"Oh! No!" I shrieked, as the school lights across the street turned off, and the large brick building disappeared into darkness. Panic seized me. I saw two headlights; a lone car was driving down the darkened school drive. I ran as fast as I could across the street, up the drive in the path of the car. The car stopped, and the front passenger window went down. I could see a mom, dad and their daughter, who I didn't know in the car.

The words flew fast. "Can you take me to my aunt and uncle's house? I thought the bus stopped here." My eyes felt moist.

"Of course, we'll take you. Climb into the back," said the compassionate mother.

I sighed softly as I opened the rear car door. Before I stepped inside, I looked across the street for the dog and gazed around the area. The streetlight cast its yellowish glow on the lone bus stop sign. Where did he go? Who was he? I wondered.

It was much later that I realized that I am protected and need to be open and accept strange and magical happenings in my life, such as the appearance of the protective dog.

At twenty-one, I fell in love, and married an attractive charismatic man, Marcus Golden. He was two years older than me. We met at a single's dance, had mutual friends and similar desires. I think we both were ready to get married, have children and live in Suburbia. In those days, most of the women I knew never went to college. We were destined to be homemakers. It was the 50's generation.

Marcus and I had fun together during our courtship. We liked being with each other or out with friends. We both worked and saw each when we could. I think we enjoyed the courting and making out. What we thought was love was probably infatuation. After we married and were living together, everything was totally different. I saw too many sides of my husband that I didn't like such as nastiness, impatience and ego. I used to think instead of saying "Yes, I do, I should have said, "No I don't."

My young husband was nervous, high-strung and a workaholic. He worked in the family dry cleaning business six days a week. If I wanted to see him, I would work my job and help in the store as well.

We grew up in an era where the husband worked, and the wife took care of the children and the household. Marcus had role models such as

Frank Sinatra, Dean Martin and other macho men. My television role models were Harriet from Adventures of Ozzie and Harriet and Margaret from Father knows Best. These television shows depicted middle-class families, and how they acted and dealt with the standards of the times. We were young, naïve and engulfed with work, family and friends.

Three years later, at twenty-four, my dream to have a child came true. I had twin daughters, Abby and Tracey. I became engrossed in motherhood, trying to survive both emotionally and financially. I didn't have a clue as to who I was as a person.

After the girls were born, my husband, Marcus, became less interested in me. He had a new job as a salesman that required traveling and staying in other cities. He was home on the weekends. We began to drift farther and farther apart.

It was 1972. I was in my middle thirties. I was drawn like a spiritual moth to a light bulb. I felt something was missing in my life. I explored my dreams, my intuition and began self-observation. I attended metaphysical classes on self-improvement, self-awareness, took yoga classes and studied various religions. I read as many self-empowering books as I could. I intuitively knew there was more to this life than the physical, and I wondered if I could connect with my spiritual side.

Open to unusual happenings, I encountered another strange thing after a yoga class. Let me explain what happened. My cousin Dawn called, "Do you want to take yoga at the YWCA? I think the exercises would be beneficial and good for my back."

"Of course, it's something I've wanted to do."

The class was taught by a young energetic woman. Thirty students filled the auditorium, and after a month, it dwindled to four students. My cousin and I were the only ones left who arrived for the last class.

The instructor asked, "Do you want to walk next door to the Carmelite Catholic Monastery after class."

I looked at my cousin and we both said, "Yes," in unison. We followed her, across the church's plush green lawn to a beautiful courtyard.

She pulled open a rather heavy wooden double door into the large church. My cousin and I had never been in a church before because we were Jewish. We nervously glanced at each other before we walked into the impressive building.

Once inside, we followed her down the long passageway between the empty wood pews. I felt my arms go around my body, behind my body, and my hands grasp each other. What is happening? Why were my hands in this odd position?

I stared at the altar for a moment as I passed it and continued toward the vestibule. The instructor opened the heavy door, and we were back out in the sunshine. I felt my hands return to their usual position hanging down at my sides.

"Do you know anything about the Carmelite nuns?" I asked the instructor.

She answered, "Yes, I read it was 1794, sixteen

French Carmelite nuns clothed in their white mantles with their hands bound at their backs boarded carts that took them to Place du Trône Renversé, where the guillotine awaited them. They were killed because of their religious beliefs."

Was I one of these nuns in a previous life? Does the mind and the body give us insight into our past lives? I think I was open to this belief and felt this was possible, and yes, I believed that I was one of the nuns in that lifetime. As I connected with my inner awareness, it revealed my past life memory through my senses, such as when I thought my skin should be darker when I was only eight years old. I probably was a different color, a different entity in that lifetime.

My spiritual quest continued. I sought my inner path through meditation and reading all I could from authors such as: Ken Keyes, Richard Bach, Louise Hays, Paramahansa Yogananda and Elizabeth Haich. My husband, Marcus, was not interested in my pursuit. He was more interested in gambling, drinking and playing the macho man, which demanded a submissive wife.

It was the 70's, the feminist movement was in full force. The feminists challenged us submissive women to participate in our lives, to speak up and get out from behind our comfortable aprons. I resonated with this movement. I wanted to break out of my passive role, my comfortable cocoon, not only for me, but for my daughters as well. I was chipping away at the very essence of who I thought I was. I was following my inner guidance, which was taking me on a journey of self-discovery.

At this time, I experienced another strange phenomenon after I returned home from a self-awareness class. I suddenly felt tired and climbed the stairs to my bedroom to lie down. I felt the softness of my comforter under me as I stretched out on the bed. Within seconds, I felt an intense energy and saw in my inner awareness a brilliant current of white light travel through my physical body from my feet upwards. My body, as well as the bed, shook with a tremendous force as this energy moved throughout my body.

Then my rational mind kicked in. Was this white light the end of me? Somewhere I had read that people were drawn to a white light when they were dying or were in a near death experience. The minute I thought this worrisome thought, the light energy stopped. I lay there thinking. What was that all about? What connected with me?

The more I thought about it. I knew that this energy had changed me; changed my vibration to a higher frequency, so I could communicate with the Other Side, where we reside as spiritual beings with a light body instead of a physical body. We are connected to our astral body, whether we know this or not. The Other Side, or other dimension, is about two feet away, yet it could be a thousand feet away, as we are unable to see this dimension with our human eyes.

I felt different, changed – more connected to everyone and everything. I wanted to learn more and more about my spiritual side and seemed guided to do this. I began to see auras, energy fields that encircle us. I became aware of white or vivid colors surrounding people. I even saw white translucent human faces with their upper torsos floating in the air above some people. I thought these to be their guides as they didn't resemble the person.

After this strange shaking episode, I became interested in learning about the seven chakras, especially the sixth chakra or third eye chakra.

The word 'chakra' is derived from the Sanskrit word meaning 'wheel,' translated from Hindi, it means 'Wheel of Spinning Energy.' The chakra system originated in India between 1500 and 500BC and is referenced in the Vedic scriptures, the spiritual literature of the ancient Indian cultures.

The chakras regulate the flow of energy throughout our electrical meridians that run through our physical body and connects our spiritual body to our physical one. It is a vertical power current inside you that moves from the base of the spine all the way up to the crown of the head.

Each chakra is a different color and relates to a different part of our body. The third eye or sixth chakra, an indigo color, expands our inner vision, intuition and wisdom.

I wondered if I could open my third eye chakra. I stared into my bathroom mirror at the center of my forehead for several days. Nothing happened, or so I thought until a blemish about the size of a dime appeared in the center of my forehead above my eyebrows. I stared at it. It stayed open for several weeks and then healed and disappeared.

I felt that my third eye had opened. I knew I was opening more and more to my inner awareness.

Some evolved individuals see the third eye as an actual eye reflected back at them in their inner vision.

2
listen to your intuition

While I pursued my spiritual studies, I ignored my deteriorating personal life. My husband, Marcus, was out-of-town quite a bit on business, and when he was home, we had little to say to each other. Our seventeen-year-old twin daughters were busy with their friends. I wanted to find something creative to do, something to challenge myself. I decided to take an art class at a local women's college. After I passed the college entrance exams, I signed up for the class. This was a big step for me as I was moving out of my comfort zone.

The art class was taught in the art wing of the college. The first day of class I arrived early. I walked around the building until I found the right entrance. It led to a large vestibule. The walls were surrounded by impressive oil portraits. I stopped to study them before walking into the art room. Many times, after this day, I would linger to admire these large Rembrandt style portraits, each set in a gold ornate frame. The instructor, Sister Kathleen, had painted them, including a self-portrait, obviously painted when she was much younger. She was an accomplished artist.

Class had been in session several weeks. I walked into the art room, found a table and settled in. Sister, an imposing figure in her black and white habit, walked over to me and in her soft raspy voice said, "Come with me. I want to show you something."

I followed her tall, stooped frame to a table high bookcase where she kept her private collection of art books. Her long-knobbed fingers shook as she pulled out a vintage book. I realized that it would be difficult for her to paint. She managed to open it. As she turned each page, I viewed the dark opaque photographs of magnificent paintings, obviously painted by master artists.

She found the page she wanted. An artist had painted a young woman with long dark hair, her slim nude body skimpily draped in a cloth. Sister suggested, by pointing to this woman, and then looking back at me, that there was a resemblance between us. I jerked my head away without noting the artist's name for I was caught off guard and felt uncomfortable with her implication. Did Sister believe in reincarnation? Probably not. She most likely saw a similarity between us through her artist's eyes.

Later, after much thought, I felt I was that model in that lifetime. I had opened to the idea that I had lived before and would probably live again after this incarnation: this lifetime in this dimension.

Our next class assignment was to paint a self-portrait using acrylic paint. We had several weeks to complete this project in class. I ambitiously bought a large canvas around four feet tall and brought it to class. I wanted to challenge myself by painting my whole body that was reflected at me in the full-length mirror. Most of my classmates chose to paint their faces and upper torsos.

After my painting was finished, I stood back and critiqued it. I noticed that my body was painted in fluid strokes in an abstract free style. My face, however, was painted in a very different style with smooth careful strokes. I stared at my rigid lifeless face. I could see that my emotions were hidden behind this blank mask.

How long have I been this way? I felt sad at this revelation and vowed to bring my emotions back to the surface. I realized I had suppressed my emotions in my marriage and in my life.

Our last class assignment was to set up a still-life arrangement, and then paint it. This finished oil painting would represent a large portion of our class credit. Sister brought in many textured fabrics in a variety of patterns and colors, objects of all sorts and piled them onto one of the large wooden tables. She instructed us to select our items.

Along with my classmates, I dug through the overflowing pile to make my selections. I picked up a small gold-plated statue of a slender woman seated on a carved concrete bench. Her meditative gaze beckoned me. The gold woman was dressed in a long gathered antique dress with a scoop neckline, short capped sleeves, and a thick book was clutched in her left hand. Hard to tell what era she was from, and if I had to guess, I would say ancient Greece or Rome. There was a quiet elegance about her.

I searched through the pile and chose several purple textured and orange woven fabrics that I thought would complement her and carried everything back to my table. I positioned the statue and moved the colorful fabrics around her until I was satisfied with the way the still-life looked. I placed the canvas on the wooden table easel. I was excited to begin this project. Using a large brush to begin the underpainting, I spread a thin coat of white acrylic paint mixed with water over the blank canvas.

I took a break as I waited for the canvas to dry and walked around the art room and glanced at the other student's paintings. It was fun to observe that each of the artists had their own distinctive style. Chatter would occasionally drift through the air. Snow had chalked the large windows. It felt warm inside the art room.

Back at my worktable, I took my thin paint brush, dipped it into purple acrylic paint on the palette, studied the still-life and started sketching. I worked carefully on the many folds in the statue's dress and completed the drawing.

The bell rang. It startled me. I had run out of time. I panicked. I knew I would not be able to finish this painting by the next class. I had not started to paint in oil which takes longer to dry than acrylic paint.

With much trepidation, I walked over to Sister and asked, "Could I . . . could I take my still-life items home and work on this project over the weekend? I'll never be able to finish this painting by the end of the class on Monday."

She looked into my pleading eyes, thought for a moment and said, "Okay, write the items you're taking with you on this sheet."

"Thank you." I signed out the items, collected everything and rushed to the door before she could change her mind.

On the way out of class, I casually remarked to Beth, one of the other art students, "Sister let me take my still-life items home. I'll work on this project over the weekend."

"Are you kidding?" Beth replied shaking her prematurely white hair. "Sister never lets anyone take anything out of the art room!"

I blinked and decided to let the remark go. Outside I packed all the art things into my trunk and drove home. December's white snowy glaze dwindled into darkness around my house. I turned on the inside lights as well as the outside lights. I heard my shoes hit the floor tiles as I walked through the short hallway into the attached garage. I unlocked the trunk of my car, and pulled out the bagged art supplies, canvas, and took everything upstairs.

I was excited to tackle this project. My husband was out of town and my daughters were sleeping at a friend's house. I smiled to myself that I could paint all night if I chose to. I ate a quick dinner as I was eager to start painting.

The fourth bedroom in the house was a den/guest room. The existing outer wall had been cut out and a wooden railing installed to give the room an open feeling. I liked looking down at the contemporary living room below.

I turned on the ceiling light with the dimmer

switch. I moved a table near the floor easel and covered it with an oil cloth. I positioned the fabrics and the statue until I was satisfied with the way everything looked. I opened the individual oil containers, put a dab of color next to the other around the palette. As I filled a little tomato paste can with turpentine, I smelled its strong distinctive aroma and turned away. I placed the canvas on the floor easel, stood back and studied it. I was pleased with the sketching and that it was finished.

I began to paint. Occasionally a car drove by. The heater went on and off disrupting the quiet. I focused on becoming one with the statue.

After a while, I decided to critique what I had painted and stepped back from the canvas. I screamed, "What!"

The colors - the purples and oranges made the woman look grotesque – alarming – yet it was more than her look – it was the dark evil energy that was being emitted from her - at me! I felt this energy go through me – chilling me to the bone.

I felt fear . . . raw fear . . . shiver my body. My feet felt glued to the oak floor. I gathered strength and forced my legs to carry me out of the den. The hallway was quiet. My mind rifled questions. What is going on? Why is this happening? The deep purples and oranges made the painted woman look distorted, yet it was not so much the colors – it was more –– it was as if something, a spirit was communicating through her, and wanted to scare me – to get my attention. Is this a warning of some sort? Is something bad going to happen in the house – to me?

I talked myself into going back into the den because I began to think this whole thing was beyond belief. How could this woman, a statue, emit this energy through the painting? Back in the den, I looked into the strange woman's pupil- less eyes, and again felt this energy attack my nervous system. I bolted out of the room.

What on earth is going on? Why is this dark energy coming through this painting? I felt like I was watching a horror film only this was not a film; this was real. Nothing like this had ever happened to me before.

Back in the hallway, I attempted to pull myself together. It was hard to shake off the jitters. I decided that I had enough. I avoided the painting. As fast as I could I covered the oil palette with tin foil and wiped the brushes. I'll finish this painting in the morning, I said to myself. I turned off the light and pulled the door tight.

I walked downstairs into the kitchen and brewed a cup of Chamomile tea to calm my nerves and took this to the family room. I clicked on the TV, sipped the hot soothing liquid, and tried to watch a comedy show. Our dog, Skipper, a little cocker/poodle mix, was sleeping on the other sofa in the family room. Funny, he never came upstairs.

The next morning, I gazed through the icicle framed sliding glass doors at the blanket of dazzling snow. A snowplow was clearing the snow off our circular drive in the front of the house. Inside the house, it felt warm and bright in the morning sunlight. I assured myself that whatever that strange energy was, that it would be gone now that it was daylight.

I opened the door and walked into the bright den. The easel, canvas, still-life and the palette were right where I left them last night. I removed the tinfoil from the palette, grabbed a paint brush and was about to dip it into the paint. I glanced at the woman in the painting. I felt the same dark energy alive – engulfing me, choking me. I fled the room.

I stood in the hallway until I calmed down. I knew, without a doubt, that a spirit was coming through the figure on the canvas wanting to communicate with me – to warn me about something. I wished I knew what all this meant - why this dark energy – what is going to happen?

I was tired of standing in the hallway. I threw up my hands and said, "I'm done!" I rushed back into the den, packed all the art supplies including the statue and fabrics into the empty plastic bags, grabbed the canvas, turned it away from me, and ran downstairs. I opened the trunk of my car and put everything into it. I felt my racing heart. I leaned against the trunk and let out a long sigh. There was nothing I could do. I knew I had no other choice except to finish this project in class.

On Monday morning, I drove to the college and parked my car in the campus lot. I released the trunk and took out all the bags including the canvas. I walked as fast as I could into the art room. I sought a quiet spot at one of the long tables and set everything out on it. I set up the still-life.

Now I felt I was ready to look at the canvas. I could not believe it! I stared at the woman and felt . . . *nothing* . . . no anxiety . . . no dark energy . . . *nothing*! It was just an unfinished painting of a deep purple and orange gold woman seated on a bench surrounded by purple and orange textured cloths. I stared into her meditative eyes and knew that an entity had come through her in my den – in my house, to warn me - about something in my house. The spirit was gone from the painting. Here in the art room, it was just a painting that needed to be completed. I could not dwell on these thoughts for I had to finish the project.

I worked as fast as I could and managed to complete most of the layering and finishing touches. The bell rang. I looked at the painting. It was not my best work. It was not bad. I signed the bottom of the canvas, picked it up, and placed it against the wall amid the other paintings for Sister to critique. After that, I gathered the statue and the fabrics and added them to the rest of the pile on the table. I checked them off the sheet. I knew I would never return to pick up this eerie painting.

On the way home, I thought about this strange phenomenon that had occurred in my life. I wondered what it is was all about. I sighed and resigned myself to just go with the flow. I had opened a door within me to experience this psychic part of myself.

3
spirit communicates in mysterious ways

With the art class over, I began to prepare for our upcoming family vacation. I focused on getting the house organized, shopping for clothes for me and my daughters, getting our dog, Skipper, ready for the kennel among many other trivial but necessary tasks. We were going to Cozumel, Mexico for a week. My daughters would be out of school as it was winter break, so it was a good time for the family to leave the inclement weather. With all that was going on, I chose not to think about the strange painting and its frightening energy.

We left for Cozumel. We were there several days when Marcus told me an important business deal needed his attention, and he was flying back to Cleveland. Intuitively I didn't believe him. As frustrated as I was with him, I found myself happy that he was leaving. It would be peaceful, calmer without him. I wanted the girls to enjoy themselves. I knew I would eventually have to face the facts about my husband, his erratic behavior, and our crumbling marriage.

After we returned home, everything went back to our normal routine. My daughters were in school and my husband was at the office. I finished cleaning and straightening the downstairs. Since there was nowhere I wanted to go on this cold blistery January morning, I decided to stay home and do some chores around the house.

I went upstairs to my bedroom and sat down on the bed. I was about to remove my slippers when I felt a push on my back. I turned around to see if someone was there, however, no one was there. It pushed me again softly. Even though I could not see this entity, I felt its presence and its frenzied nervous energy communicating within me. I knew intuitively, that I was to heed this spirit's contact. I knew in my psychic awareness that it wanted me to get out of the house now!

I took a deep breath and tried to figure out what to do. I decided to call a friend. I wanted to discuss this strange happening and more importantly, I needed to get out of the house. I invited myself to lunch with her and a friend of hers whom I was not that fond of. I dressed in a hurry. I drove my car down the icy driveway into the snow-shoveled street. I pulled on my lined gloves as the car warmed up.

The women were meeting at a favorite eatery in the nearby mall. Once inside the restaurant, I spotted my friend and the other woman engrossed in conversation.

"Hi," I said trying to appear cheerful. "How is everything?"

"Great, how was your trip?"

I said, "The trip was good. It felt good to be in the sunshine – out of the bitter cold weather we have been experiencing. It was beautiful in

Cozumel."

I tried to feel comfortable at lunch. I felt awkward crashing their lunch. I could not bring myself to talk about my experience this morning. I was trying to process this strange occurrence myself. I just sat there and listened to their conversation. Inside I still felt the strange energy – creating a nervous feeling within me.

After lunch I ran a few errands, and around 2:00pm, I stopped by the jewelry store where I worked part time, to see if they needed any help. I didn't feel like going home. Howie, the owner, was at the jewelry counter amid plastic bags of jewelry.

"Do you need any help?" I asked him.

"Thanks. There is nothing to do. I'm almost finished pricing these gold chains and earrings. Susan took the day off." Susan is Howie's wife. Both are good friends as well as my employers.

The phone rang. Howie picked it up. I watched him get an odd look on his face. "It's for you."

"How could that be? I didn't know I was going to be at the store, let alone anyone else."

It was my daughter, Tracey. She was hysterically sobbing, "We had a fire in our house. Come home!" I hung up the receiver and immediately sat down on one of the cushioned chairs. I felt numb, out of sorts. I could not seem to move. I must have gone into shock. After I regained some composure, I forced myself out of the chair. Now I was shaking with emotions – worry and fear. Every nerve in my body felt wired.

"There's a fire in my house," I said as I rushed out the door and into my car. We lived about five minutes away. When I got there, I saw two fire trucks blocking the area around the house. Another big firetruck was in the middle of our driveway. Several police cars were there as well. I parked my car on the snow-filled street and took a deep breath before I walked carefully to the house. It looked untouched from the outside.

A tall policeman shouted, "Where do you think you're going?"

I shouted back, "This is my house!" I caught his sympathetic eyes as I passed him and entered the house through the wide open front double glass doors. What a mess! The frigid house smelled like burnt pots. I creased my gloved hand over my nose.

The chaotic scene felt surreal to me. There were firemen rushing around downstairs, the living room, dining room and the family room, yelling at one another as they pulled thick hoses along the wet tile floor, a water pipe had broken. Policemen were walking about. I hugged my daughters, my father, and both my brothers. I didn't think about it until later that I was surprised they were there. How did they get there so fast? Marcus was standing in the kitchen area. I walked over to hug him and stopped. His energy felt aloof – strange. He and I just stood and looked at each other. I was too fragile and off balance to say or feel anything. I felt detached. If I was myself, I probably would have felt angry, frustrated and thoroughly disgusted with my unfeeling husband.

The garage was destroyed, part of the laundry room, and part of the wall in the master bedroom as well. While we were there, a small fire started in Tracey's bedroom. It burned her cabinetry, her prized Bobbsey Twin books, her plants, and many of her cherished childhood things. Unfortunately, her bedroom was next to the master bedroom. The smoke had settled throughout the house. The carpets and wallpapers would have to be replaced because of the staining and the burnt odor.

I moved to where my father was standing in the living room.

I asked, "What happened?"

He said, "A neighbor had seen the fire coming from the garage and called the fire department. The firemen saved the house. I talked to the fire inspector. He thought the fire started in the garage from an electrical wire. It's a good thing that you weren't home when the fire started."

I shook inside for I knew what he meant. I could have suffocated from the smoke that filtered into the master bedroom which was located above the garage. I remembered Spirit pushing me to get out of the house this morning. I looked down at the dirty wet tiles under my boots and continued to shiver.

Spirit was protecting me. Flashes of the other phenomena flew through my mind from decades ago: the red dog's sudden appearance after my high school dance to protect me, the white light energy moving through my body heightening my vibration to another level, the dark energy coming through the painting to warn me about the house fire and now, physical contact . . . the soft pushes.

My father explained, "Skipper bolted out the front door, when the firemen broke into the house. Some of the neighbors are out looking for him. We have been calling for him. The girls drove around the neighborhood calling his name."

"This is terrible. I can't believe he is missing. It's January, cold, freezing. I'm worried about him." I thought about our little dog and felt tears flow down my cold cheeks. I wiped them away.

We found a motel nearby with three adjoining rooms, one for Marcus and me, one for the girls, and one for all our clothes, which we placed on dress racks! We would have to stay at the motel until our house was renovated, which would take around three months. Marcus wanted to stay at the house. I was too disconcerted to care where he slept. I felt like someone hit me in the head and then threw ice cold water over me. Everything felt surreal. I knew I needed to release all this built up tension, frustration and anger.

After the girls and I settled into the motel. I checked on the girls and found them asleep in the next room. I was glad they were asleep for this had been a very traumatic day for them. I made sure all the doors were securely locked. In the shower, I unleashed a volume of tears and sobbing - my emotions erupted.

The next morning, I called the drycleaner to meet me at the house and take everything salvageable to be cleaned. Our vacation clothes were in the garage and were destroyed in the fire.

The drycleaner arrived. I showed him the things that would be dry cleaned or washed. He took all the items and said he would deliver the clean clothes to the motel. He would hold the other items until we moved back into the house. What a mess! I was a mess. I felt raw like I was an open wound. Even though I had released some of my emotions, it wasn't enough. I still had tremendous anxiety. I fought to get through the day.

My daughters and I frantically drove around the area looking for our missing dog calling out, "Skipper."

Neighbors and strangers canvassed the area around our house, calling out his name. My neighbor, Gloria, had contacts from various animal associations. She put out a bulletin describing the little black dog with the white furry chest. The day ended and still no Skipper.

That night I lay down on the motel bed and covered myself with the thin sheet and blanket. In my psychic vision, I saw - a white blanket of untouched snow before me. I felt myself on the ground protected by thick branches of a big tree above me. It was very still. I knew that in some way I had connected with Skipper, and that he was safe under this tree. I settled down to sleep. My third eye, my psychic eye, was wide open and could see what the human eye could not.

The next morning at the house I received a call from my neighbor. She said, "Someone responded to the animal rescue hotline. There is a little dog under one of their big pine trees in their backyard about two miles away. The owners tried to get near the dog, but the dog kept growling."

"Thanks," I said, "Sounds like our Skipper!" Marcus abruptly grabbed the phone, jotted the address down, and fled the house without asking the girls or myself if we wanted to go with him. He returned with the little dog. Skipper was jumping up and down - kissing each of us. Even though I knew he was safe from my vision, it felt good to hold him. I put him in the car, drove him to the vet for a check-up, and then to his new home - the motel. He was thinner, and his wagging tail showed that he was very happy to be back with us.

It was not until later, much later, I think after the shock finally wore off, that I realized that my husband never stayed at the motel with us, and seldom ate with us in the motel dining room. Where was he all this time? What was he up to? On the other hand, he had been doing so many disturbing things over the past few years, I chose to direct my energy into remodeling the house.

Did Marcus have anything to do with the fire? I felt he was capable of just about anything, and certainly proficient at telling lies. Was he the evil that was in the house? I knew his business was having financial problems. I realized I would probably never know the answer to these questions. I decided to table these thoughts for another time. Right now, I was too fragile to confront these thoughts – or him.

We moved back into the house three months later. The house felt fresh and clean. Two moving vans brought everything from the storage unit and the motel. It took several weeks for me to put everything away. It was a lot of work. There were boxes all over the house.

Our neighbor, Gloria, stopped by to see if I needed help with anything. She brought homemade cupcakes.

"Did you hear about the tragedy in the neighborhood?"

"No," I assured her. "What happened?"

"It was awful," she said lowering her voice. "Two brothers, one aged ten and the other twelve were playing in a wheelbarrow in their driveway at their home. They both jumped into the wheelbarrow as it sped down their sloped drive onto the street and into an oncoming car. They were killed instantly."

"What a terrible loss for their family!" I felt sorry for this family that lived on a main street not far from us, even though I had never met any of them.

A few days later, I drove past the house where the tragedy had occurred. As I neared the driveway, I said a prayer for the boys and their grieving family.

As I looked at the long driveway where the children had lost their lives, I heard a female voice, a soft sweet voice say, "Charlie Stein is next." My eyes widened and scanned the empty interior of my car. My thoughts came rapidly. Did I just hear that? Who said that?

I told no one. I needed to think about this message. I knew I was meant to hear this foreboding message and accept it. What do I do with this? I just could not bring myself to tell Charlie's parents, who were friends of ours. I thought they would think me weird if this terrible thing did happen.

I think, in some way, my spiritual guide wanted me to know this was inevitable. I realized then and there that getting spiritual information, while being a *gift*, was also a *responsibility*! I also knew deep within that some things are predestined. I knew that I was to accept this prediction and do nothing.

4

synchronicity is divine timing

A short time after we were settled back into the house, Marcus and I were invited to a Bar Mitzvah; a traditional ceremony usually performed at a Jewish temple when a boy reaches thirteen. I attended the ceremony at the temple alone and then drove to the celebratory luncheon at their home. Marcus would meet me later at the luncheon.

The two-story house was in an upscale area of the city. I followed an arrow that guided me on a cement walkway to their backyard. Many adults and children were eating, laughing and mingling in the beautifully decorated area around their pool.

After congratulating the boy and talking to some of the other guests, I weaved through the crowd to a salad station and filled my plate. The spring air felt crisp as the sun warmed my skin. A slight breeze brushed against me.

I scanned the area and saw an empty chair at the glass patio table where the hosts, Ruth and Ira, and their divorced friend, Judy, were seated. There seemed to be no other seat available. I joined them. They were deep in conversation about a forthcoming trip to Israel.

"Where are you traveling to in Israel?" I asked.

Ruth was the first to answer. "We're going to Jerusalem, Tel Aviv, and Haifa through our temple. There is a meeting in a couple of weeks to fill in the details of the trip. Ira and I are excited about going to Israel. We've never been there."

Judy added, "I decided to join them. I really need a roommate to share expenses. So far I haven't had any luck in finding anyone to go with me."

Something in me rallied. I heard myself say, "I will! I will room with you!"

"Great," Judy said, "We leave in three weeks."

Marcus arrived, secured a chair and sat down next to me.

I said, "I'm going to Israel in three weeks with this group. Do you want to join us?"

"No, I can't," he said rather abruptly. His dark eyes darted away from me. He turned away from me to talk to our host, Ira.

I knew Marcus would never go to Israel for that would be the last place he wished to visit. Even though he was Jewish, he played the part that he wasn't. I knew deep within my being that I needed to take this trip alone to gather strength - to divorce my husband or not. A part of me wanted to test the waters to see what it would be like to be - *single*. Synchronicity was working in my life.

I knew that my marriage was not working yet doing something about it were two different things. The fire, its telescopic lens, played a big part in focusing on the reality of my deteriorating marriage. The fire, as destructive as it was, could have brought us together, instead it disclosed the harsh reality of my unhappy and lonely existence. I tried not to dwell on these unsettling thoughts, and that horrible word, *divorce*, for it meant change. Change for me meant moving away from my present lifestyle, my friends, my day-to-day existence, my known role as a housewife living a suburban lifestyle to a life unknown. Would I survive? This was the only me I knew.

After I booked the trip, I called my friend Beth to tell her I was going to Israel and the details. We had met during the art class and become good friends. We would sometimes go to lunch after class. I had dinner with her and her husband, Larry, at their home many times, but she had never met Marcus.

She said, "We're going to Israel around the same time as you. Larry and I are taking our teenage children with us." She read off the dates.

I said, "How amazing is this! I can't believe that we'll be in Jerusalem on the same day. It would be fun to meet up in the ancient city."

She replied, "I doubt if we'll get together as we have a tight schedule planned. I'll give you the phone number at the condo where we're staying." She read the number to me, which I jotted down in my little travel book and didn't think any more about it.

Before I knew it, I was on my way to Israel with a group of Clevelanders. Marcus drove me to the Cleveland Hopkins Airport silently and dropped me and my luggage off at the curbside baggage checking area. I hugged him. There was no response. A thought crossed my mind that he might be glad I was leaving to go on this trip. I shrugged it off.

I felt that my solo journey was the beginning of my first baby steps into a different lifestyle, a different world. I felt free, excited, yet anxious about my maiden voyage out into a brave new world – the single world. Judy had been single for several years and represented a new role model for me. At the tour meeting, I watched her interact with the single, as well as the married people in our traveling group in a confident manner. She had a pampered air about her. Her blonde hair was stylishly cut in a page boy. Her self-assured attitude appealed to me. She seemed to have it together. Her two young boys were staying with her parents while she was away.

Our group arrived late at night in Jerusalem. It had been a long plane ride from New York. Everyone was tired yet stimulated at being in this ancient city. We congregated in the small lobby until we were all checked in. The quaint hotel was located close to restaurants and shops. Our small room was comfortable and had the twin beds we requested.

The next morning Judy and I took the elevator down to the lobby and were pleasantly surprised. There was a large breakfast buffet in a room right off the lobby.

After breakfast, some of our group went into the city to meet a local artist. Judy and I decided to explore the area, have lunch and shop. We walked up and down the hilly uneven streets and in and out of several shops. We ate a light lunch. We had been warned that if we went into the residential area to make sure we covered our arms, as this was a religious custom. Women's arms were not to be exposed. We did find ourselves walking through one of the neighboring streets and covered our arms with scarfs.

When Judy and I returned to the hotel, our friends were in the lobby with a grey-haired man in his 60's. Ira said, "Come here and meet Max. He is an artist and writes an art column for the local newspaper. We invited him as our guest for dinner tonight. We want you to join us."

Judy and I shook hands with this delightful, energetic man and agreed to meet for dinner. Max oozed old world charm. I could tell he was very comfortable around tourists. He brought some of his artwork, which he had displayed next to him. I looked through his sketches and descriptive books of Israel and bought one about the Bible.

He drew my caricature, the Queen of Sheba in the book's cover and signed his name. This struck me as very funny, me, Sera Golden, the Queen of Sheba. I had read somewhere that Sheba was a biblical character, a ruler of great wealth, beauty and power. She visited King Solomon, had an affair with him, and then returned to her own land where she bore him a son. Sorry Max, I thought to myself, I'm not looking for King Solomon! I smiled at him and paid him for the book.

Ira said, "Max is going to take us for a walk around Jerusalem after dinner tonight."

This was an opportunity of a lifetime! I could not believe it. We were to have our own special guide, a native, to tour this ancient holy city at night! I immediately thought I need to call Beth and Larry and tell them about this adventure.

I said, "Max, I've two friends for you to add to the reservation." I felt that they had to join us. After all, it was synchronicity that we were here in Jerusalem, exactly on the same day. Yes, I felt strongly that they needed to do this.

I called Beth from my room. I explained about Max, dinner and his guided tour through Jerusalem.

"Sorry," Beth said, "we won't be able to make it. We're exhausted. We just walked the steps at Masada with our children, so we are all really exhausted. We are looking forward to pizza and relaxing."

I said, "I know that you'll regret it if you don't come with us. I feel this is a once in a lifetime experience! I don't want you to miss out on it. I'll not take *no* for an answer." I was adamant. I kept on until she finally consented to meet for dinner.

At 7:00 pm, our group gathered in the hotel lobby including Beth and Larry and our guide, Max. After the greetings, we followed Max's quick gait for about ten minutes to a small, out-of-the way restaurant. The owners, a wife and husband, affectionately greeted Max and welcomed us. We were seated in a private dining area in the back of the restaurant. A large mahogany table, covered in white pressed linen, was set with fine china. The food was tasty, and the waiter was attentive. Max shared that he had a home in New York City, besides his condo in Jerusalem. In his excellent English, he related many stories regarding his travels.

After dinner, Max lead us along a dirt path that took us high above the city. The stars flickered like polished diamonds on a black cloth. The moon lit our way up the rough incline. To our left, the ancient city spread out beneath us. I could see the glowing golden Dome of the Rock located on the Temple Mount in the old city.

We hiked uphill like a small caravan with Max front and center. Beth and I were right behind him. I mentally attuned myself to the ancient cities buried beneath my feet. A cool breeze enclosed me. I felt the chill and a surge of power rushed through me like an electric current, a power I had never felt before. It felt like warrior power, ancient warrior power. I felt . . . fearless - indestructible! I had not felt this intense energy anywhere else in Jerusalem or - in my life.

I remembered reading about ancient energy that archeologists sometimes encountered while they were in or near an ancient ruin. This negative energy made them ill. On the contrary, the ancient energy I was feeling was empowering. I stood taller. I knew in that instant that I had lived several lifetimes here, probably, as a warrior.

I turned and saw a glint in Beth's eyes and knew she, too, was connecting with this empowering energy, even if she didn't know what it was all about. I heard Larry, Beth's husband, murmur to Judy, "I'm worried about my teenage kids alone in the rented condo." I turned back to see him hanging onto Judy's arm. His tight face showed his despair. I could see how different our perspectives were. He didn't feel the power that Beth and I did, quite the contrary, he didn't feel safe at all.

Our little group followed Max through the

Moslem, Arab and Jewish Market. The dark abandoned shops were locked tightly. We trekked through the cobbled corridors inhaling various scents, some of spices, some of animals, some of humans, and some from who knows. Each area of the market emitted its own scent and a different energy. The corridors were vacant except for our group.

We exited the market and continued following Max at a fast pace. I felt the chilly night air and pulled my wool scarf higher around my neck. We slowed down as we approached the Wailing Wall. There were several armed soldiers guarding this area. Larry moved closer to Beth. It made me aware that we were strangers in a strange land.

We followed Max into the holy site near the Wailing Wall. This section is usually closed off to visitors by day, as this area is restricted to male rabbis for prayers, Bar Mitzvahs or other religious ceremonies. The ancient limestone creviced wall was stuffed with bits of paper, a patchwork of prayers. I found a piece of paper, and a pen and wrote my prayer, *Peace and Blessings for All*, and shoved it into a tight stone crevice, as many Jews and people of all religions had done before me. My hand felt the ancient stones, harsh and cold. I turned and watched the others leave their messages. I trembled as the night winds danced through me. I was in awe at the miraculous journey we had just taken. Max guided us back to our hotel and bade us farewell. It was past midnight. Each of us hugged and thanked him for this memorable adventure.

"Thank you," my friends said to me in unison.

Their eyes told me how much this night meant to them. I knew we would talk about this magical experience for years to come.

The Israel trip was an important journey for me. I took a solo run up and down the slopes of fear and gained inner strength and empowerment from these emotions. I could be alone or within a group and still be me. In the ancient city of Jerusalem, I connected and renewed my warrior nature and reinforced my spiritual strength. I was excited a and about the future with or without Marcus.

5
some events are predestined

At the baggage section at the Cleveland Hopkins Airport waiting for my husband, I witnessed the smiles and embraces within our group as they greeted their friends and family. I began to hope that maybe absence does make the heart grow fonder. I pulled my suitcases off the luggage rack, turned around, and saw Marcus come towards me. I hugged him as I was glad to see him after two weeks. He felt rigid, aloof. I stopped . . . and *knew* . . . our marriage was over!

"Charlie Stein is dead," he said in a matter-of-fact tone as he put my luggage in the trunk of his car."

"What!" I blurted out, not wanting to believe what I just heard. "What happened?"

As he drove the car out of the airport, he said, "Charlie was on his moped zooming along the curved drive around their lake and didn't see his sister drive up the drive. She stopped when she saw him, but he didn't stop. The moped slammed into her car. He broke his neck. He died instantly. They had the funeral several days ago and are still receiving family and friends at their home."

At first my mind could not comprehend this

terrible news coupled with jet lag from my flight from Israel to New York to Cleveland. After I regained some composure I said, "Take me to their house." We walked quietly into the somber house. The distraught couple were seated together on their sofa in their family room. Their bloodshot eyes and haggard expressions said it all.

I mumbled, "I'm so sorry." I hugged each of them and sat down on the sofa next to them. My heart was aching for them. We stayed for a while in the silence and left. I sent thoughts of love and healing to this grieving family.

On the way home, I thought about my husband - his aloofness - there was no consoling each other as we had comforted our friends. There was nothing. My head felt tight. as I tried to understand what happened to our nineteen-year marriage.

The following day I remembered the premonition of the boy's death. I knew this telepathic message was for me and I was to accept this message for there was nothing I was to do regarding this prediction except, be aware and to know there is more here than meets our physical eyes. I realized that even though we have "free will" here in this realm, there are predestined events. I was learning to accept more, even if I didn't understand it all, as I opened more and more to my spiritual self.

A few days after I was home, I got a phone call from my Uncle Nathan to turn on my television set. Marcus and his girlfriend were in Las Vegas seated in the front row at a televised boxing match. I turned the television off. It was time to confront my lying, cheating husband. I had no doubt, that he had a nice warm place to stay after the fire while the girls and I were in the motel. Was I angry? You bet! I was livid! I think all my stuffed emotions surfaced.

I tossed his clothes into a pile at the bottom of the stairs. When he returned, I said, "Get out! Go live with your girlfriend!" He hurriedly grabbed his stuff and flew out the door. I felt relieved after he left. His caustic energy was gone. I needed the anger to move me forward with my life and my freedom.

I found a tough divorce attorney and filed for divorce. Of course, my soon-to-be ex-husband continued to lie that he didn't have a girlfriend and assured everyone he met that - I was the liar. He claimed I had a boyfriend in Israel. He had lied so often, he believed himself. In his mind, he was a good honest guy!

His absurd insulations infuriated me and strengthened my desire to finalize the divorce and rid myself of him. He had changed so much from the young man I had married. I think success and playing the 'macho man' had tainted him.

My daughters were away at college. There would be plenty of time to talk to them about this decision. There was no turning back, yet getting divorced meant big change for me, and a new awareness of how I viewed myself, my family - my friends - my known existence.

I realized that I needed help to move through my anger and fear of the unknown. I called a psychologist that was recommended to me. Anna, an intelligent, sympathetic elderly woman, was to be my lifeline to heal and change. I wanted to take off the dark glasses of fear, anger and loss of identity. I needed to come to terms with the words, divorce, divorcee and failure.

In her office, after my divorce was final, I shared, "I want to move far away from here to another city. I really don't want to have to deal with my friends, especially some of the couples, who are now avoiding me."

Anna shook her curly gray hair and said unwaveringly, "You need to stay put for at least a year to deal with any issues that come up regarding your divorce. This would be a good opportunity for you to work through anger, avoidance and confrontation issues."

I remembered my rigid face that I had painted in my art class. I knew - she was right. I made the decision to face my inner dragons and stay in Cleveland for another year.

Now that I made that commitment, I asked myself, what are you going to do? An interior designer that I knew suggested that I take an interior design class from a well-known and respected interior designer. I signed up to take her interior design class since I always wanted to help people decorate their houses. I loved decorating my house. With this certification, I could apply for a job as an Interior Designer and possibly make this my career.

The interior design class of six students was held in Adelaide's small, lavish apartment in an upscale area of the city. Adelaide, her white hair piled on top her head, was in her late 70's. She commanded respect and took her class very seriously. We were to be punctual at 7:00 pm and keep up with our assignments from the workbook she provided.

Her living room was filled to the brim with tasteful, traditional furniture. The class met once a week to discuss our workbook assignment.

One of the students, Rhonda, a buyer for a department store chain in the Cleveland area would arrive after work. She was a petite beauty with thick curly black shoulder length hair, coffee colored skin, and a confident attitude. She was always impeccably dressed in the current fashion. I liked her overt personality and would meet her for dinner after class. She seemed to know someone wherever we went, mostly athletes. She was dating a well-known quarterback.

At dinner one night, she whispered, "I just heard there is a position available in the downtown store. Why don't you apply for it? It's for an Assistant Manager for our Designer department. I know the manager, Pauline, and can put in a good word for you." She wrote down her information.

"Thanks. Okay!" The words stumbled out of my mouth. "Yes, I 'll call her." Inside I felt myself tremble with fear. I hadn't worked in nineteen years. Yet, I needed a job. Marcus, true to form, had lied that he sent me an alimony check. I went to his office and collected this check and waited at the bank until it cleared. Intuitively I knew that was the last check I would receive from him. He was close to declaring bankruptcy. I would have to pay next month's house payment, car, insurance and other bills.

The following day, I forced myself to call the

manager and set up an appointment. I changed my negative thoughts from worry to excitement about this potential job, especially as it was downtown, far away from the suburb where I lived. I didn't want to work in my area of town and see people I knew daily. Some of the married women I was close with before my divorce now avoided me as if I threatened them. I didn't wish to encounter them.

On the day of the interview, I took the escalator up to the second floor of the department store. The life-like mannequins were dressed in stunning dresses and beautiful, expensive gowns.

I asked for the designer sportswear manager and was guided to a blonde middle-aged woman in a tailored blue suit. I walked over to her and introduced myself.

"Hi," She held out her warm hand. "Glad you could make it. Rhonda told me many good things about you. I'm sorry we filled that position internally this morning, however, I did want to meet you. I know the manager at our suburban store, and he might have something for you there."

No! I thought, this was where I want to work. I cannot believe this. No! I don't want to work at the suburban mall, even though it was fifteen minutes from my house. I tried to conceal the disappointment that was rising within me. This was not at all what I expected. I wanted a fresh start. I was not yet comfortable with my newly divorced self.

"Thank you. I appreciate your time." I tried to remain calm.

Before I left, she said cheerily, "We definitely want you to be a part of our company."

Destiny was taking me by the hand. Anna was right. I needed to face my dragons before I leave Cleveland. The Universe was making sure that this was a reality.

When I returned home, I called the store manager at the suburban store. I surrendered. If I land this job, then this is where I need to be. I went for the interview the following week. An hour later, I left with a job as a Personal Shopper. I was happy and nervous all at once. I called Rhonda and related the good news and suggested we celebrate with a great dinner.

Amazing! I didn't mind going to work. I could still fit into most of the current styles. Some of my friends would meet me for lunch in the mall or stop by the store to visit. Time rushed by, and before I knew it, I had been there several months. When I saw some married friends that I was no longer friends with, I simply nodded.

As a personal shopper, I contacted customers in the store and shopped with them. One day I found a customer a pair of designer jeans that she wanted to try on. I put her into a dressing room and went to talk to another client. When I returned, one of the other sales associates, an elderly woman, was ringing up my sale as hers. I could not believe it! I just stood there and stared at her.

Back in the psychotherapist's office the next day, I related the story to her. Anna said, "You need to confront this saleswoman. You need to start speaking up for yourself."

"Do I have to do this?" I said. I could feel myself getting anxious.

She suggested, "Why don't you give this more thought? Yes, I believe that you need to do this."

I was upset when I left her office. Why do I have to think about this? I hate confrontation! I cringed inside. There was nothing else to do for I knew I had no choice. I had to confront her. I didn't want this to happen again. I slept fitfully that night.

The next morning before the store opened, I reluctantly walked into work. I looked for this woman, and when I found her, I said, in a loud voice, louder than I wanted to as my nerves were speaking, "You're never to ring up my customer. I put that woman into the fitting room. That was a terrible thing to do. Why did you do this? Don't do it again!" I stared into her wide eyes. She listened silently to my lecture. As I was spoke, I saw the store manager, Jack, walk down the distant corridor, and glance in our direction. He had heard every word of my loud confrontation.

Several weeks later, there was a big change in departments. The two Designer Sportswear areas were to be grouped together under one manager. My manager had the larger Designer Sportswear area. He was promoted to the downtown location. The manager of the other area was let go. I heard that she applied for the new position and was denied. I thought she would get this job. I didn't know her that well. She was extremely thin with stringy blonde hair that fell around her tight face. She seemed to be busy whenever I was in her department.

I had just settled into my office when the store manager's assistant appeared and said, "Hey, Jack wants to see you in his office. Come with me."

Hmm. I wondered what this was all about. I tried to remain positive, yet I felt worried as I followed the assistant through the store to Jack's office.

"Please sit down," Jack said as he shut the door behind him. I slid into one of the leather chairs and waited. "I want to offer you the position as the Designer Sportswear Manager."

The words flew out, "Thank you, I accept this opportunity." We shook hands. I felt like I was on top of the world. I was so excited that it alleviated some of my anxiety about this job. I could not wait to tell Anna, the psychotherapist, and my friends about the promotion. I smiled the rest of the day.

Wow! I guess he liked the way I handled the situation with the other employee. Now I was to become her boss. Unfortunately, she didn't like this changeover and left the company.

After the initial shock, I embraced my new position and wanted to learn everything I could about the designer sportswear area.

We had a new Assistant Store Manager, Karla. She wanted to get to know all the managers, their duties, check their inventory, and started with me. She came into my office shortly after I was promoted. "Hi Sera. I would like to see your inventory list."

"Sure." I handed her the inventory sheets she was looking for. She sat down in my chair and began studying them. My phone rang. I answered it and heard a woman's muffled voice. "You're as good as dead!" I could hardly believe my ears and asked her to repeat herself. She said the exact same words!

"Who is this?" I demanded! I heard the buzz as

she hung up. I felt my face drain of color and my body weaken. I said, hardly able to get the words out of my mouth, "I had a threat on my life!"

Karla was engrossed in her task. She chose not to hear me and continued scanning the pages for several minutes until my words finally dawned on her. She stopped and stared at me. "Did you just get a threatening call?" I nodded. She shrieked, "Call Security immediately!"

As fast as I could, I dialed the extension for security, and told the security officer what happened. No sooner had I hung up the phone, a short thick man with dark framed glasses appeared and introduced himself. He was head of security. He began to drill me. "Do you have any enemies?"

"No," I assured this very direct no-nonsense man.

"Do you have any idea who this could be?"

"No, I've no idea who this could be." I felt equally agitated with his questions as with the phone call.

"Was this a male or female."

I shrugged my shoulders, "It sounded like a muffled female voice."

"We'll have one of our security guards escort you out of the store tonight."

"Thank you,'" I replied to him as he left the office. I worried about what would happen after that. Who was going to escort me after tonight? I was distressed about the whole thing. I felt on edge and could not wait until the day was over.

At the close of the day, a security officer appeared and escorted me to my car. I could not wait to get home.

The following morning, I gathered my team together and told them about the phone call. One of the sales associates, a mature woman, pulled me aside and said, "I bet the former sportswear manager called and threatened you. She is on drugs and probably doesn't have a job."

"Thank you. I'll be on the lookout for this woman. She most likely thinks I solicited her job. which I didn't." This made sense to me. It took a long time for me to stop looking over my shoulder and around me when I entered and left the building. She had set out to scare me and succeeded.

I needed to come to terms within myself that I was not going to tolerate her bad behavior and continue to be frightened. I worked on letting my negative thoughts go. I released my fears and worries by sending her forgiveness. I didn't wish to be harmed nor did I wish her harm. I stopped looking over my shoulder and started looking ahead. Time, the great healer, helped as well for the longer nothing happened, the less there was to fear.

More than a year passed. I was stronger and more confident in slaying my inner and outer dragons. I didn't fear the bizarre woman and her threating phone call. I was no longer concerned about my former married friends. I had moved past their approval or disapproval. I met with Anna, my psychotherapist, at her office and told her I was glad that I listened to her and had stayed in Cleveland for the year. However, now I knew it was time to move on.

My daughters were doing well at college. My cousin Dawn and her family had moved to Ft. Lauderdale, Florida. Her husband had recently committed suicide. I felt it would be helpful to be around her during this tough time. It was also time for me to see another side of me against another background. I put my house up for sale, and it sold within a few months. I thanked my house. We both had gone through transition. I said my goodbyes to my team and the management staff. It had been a good place for me to begin my journey to becoming self-reliant.

I decided to go to the downtown store to say goodbye to some of the saleswomen I knew. As I was crossing Euclid Avenue, a busy street, I looked and looked again - through the crowd of people coming towards me was the former sportswear manager who had threatened me on the phone. I felt no animosity towards her, nor did I fear her. I looked into her startled pale eyes and said, "Hi," as we passed within a foot of each other. She stared at me as I continued past her to the other side. I never turned around to see her reaction. Synchronicity was at work in my life! What are the odds? I guess that completed this lesson. I felt that I would never see or hear from her again – not in this lifetime – and I never did.

As I end this phase of my life, I'm thankful that I've overcome many of my fears and anxieties about being alone or living as a single woman. I've grown spiritually and accept that there is more here than my senses can perceive. I'm moving forward with my life, my lessons and my destiny.

6
karmic lessons are not easy

My cousin, Dawn, met me at the Ft. Lauderdale Airport. She was dressed in a smart casual outfit, her make-up impeccably applied. Outwardly she looked fine. Yet I could feel her shattered energy. "How are you doing?" I asked as I hugged her tightly.

"I'm trying to get on with my life and over Bill's suicide." she said with tears forming in her expressive large eyes. "I'm glad you're moving here."

"So am I." I hugged her again.

She said, "I found a brand-new second floor condo unit for you to rent that is not far from my condo in Ft. Lauderdale. The two-story building had just been completed. You'll be the only person living in the whole complex. There are two more buildings being built. How do you feel about being the only person in the building?"

"It will be fine. I've become accustomed to living alone, besides I'll have Skipper with me."

"Do you want to see it now?"

"Sure, I would like to get settled as soon as possible."

I loved the condo and it being new - fit in with

my brand-new life. I signed the paperwork for the condo and called the movers with the address.

Within a week after I settled in, I applied for a position as a sales associate in the designer sportswear area at Saks Fifth Avenue in the Galleria Mall and was accepted. This upscale shopping center was about twenty minutes from where I lived and right near the ocean. I would breathe in the moist ocean air as soon as I opened my car door at the mall. I felt blessed to be living and working in this beautiful place. My cousin and I went out to dinner quite often after work. She worked at a jewelry store in downtown Ft. Lauderdale. We liked the same foods and would split dinner as this was better on both our budgets. As the months went by, I could see she was healing from her tragedy.

I was stopped at a red light one night on my way home from work. I accidentally (yes, I know there are no accidents) hit the car in front of me. The light turned green, I thought the car in front of me was going to move, but it didn't. I immediately got out of my car to make sure the female driver was okay.

Jena, a tiny Asian woman in her late forties, assured me that she was fine. She didn't seem flustered; in fact, I thought she was calmer than me. Her bumper had a small scratch. We pulled our cars into a nearby gas station and waited for the police. While we were there, we exchanged driver's licenses, and insurance information, and found out that we both worked at the mall. A policeman arrived and took our information. We left shortly after.

Because I wanted to see how Jena was doing, I called her several days later and met her for lunch at one of the restaurants in the mall. I liked this petite woman; she had a quiet way about her. I offered to buy her lunch, but she refused.

After this lunch, we would go to happy hour at different resorts. She shared that she lived in her brother and sister-in-law's condo, had been married, divorced and had a grown son in Houston. Other than that, I knew nothing about her personal life and her family. She was a very private person.

She invited me for dinner one night at the condo. While she prepared dinner, I looked around the living room filled with sofas, chairs and a large buffet that held a collection of family photos. When I looked at the photo of her smiling, dark haired middle-aged brother, I had this strange feeling that I knew him. I thought how odd that I should have intuition towards this stranger.

Several days later, Jena called me at work. She said, "My brother Ken called to tell me that he is coming to Ft Lauderdale. I need a place to stay."

"Why do you have to move?" I could not understand why she and her brother could not stay in the condo together. It was a very spacious three-bedroom condo. My brothers were always welcome to stay with me.

"Can I please stay with you while my brother is here?" She sounded desperate. "My other friend is out-of-town for several months and has closed her place. I usually stay with her. I'll pay you."

"Yes, of course you can stay here. I've an extra bedroom with a sleeper sofa. No, you're not going to pay me. When will he be here?"

"Tomorrow!"

"Tomorrow!" I repeated for I could hardly believe my ears. Where would she go, if I was not here? I still could not fathom that she would have to vacate her brother's condo. Maybe it's a cultural thing, I thought, and let it go. She moved her belongings into the bedroom.

A few days later, I arrived home after work to her frazzled expression and asked, "What is going on?"

"Please go out to dinner with Ken and me tonight!" Was she kidding? She forgot that she had previously told me that her brother was a Don Juan type and married with three daughters.

"No," I said standing my ground, "you enjoy your dinner with your brother. I want to relax after a hectic day at work."

"You must come with us," she said in a high shrill tone. We can't have dinner alone. I heard about this restaurant. I would like to go there." She continued to go on and on until I finally agreed to go with them. He would pick us up in twenty minutes. What am I getting myself into? What a strange family? I stayed dressed in my work clothes.

Her brother knocked on my door and greeted us. He was well dressed in a dark business suit and tie. He seemed confident, successful. He gave me more than a friendly glance. Suddenly I felt very uncomfortable. Who was this man? Why did I get the feeling that he wanted to check me out? I didn't find him unattractive, however, I really had no interest in him.

Jena introduced us. Her brother held out his hand, and said, "I'm happy you decided to join us for dinner." I followed them down the open stairs of my building to his new Mercedes. I could hear the frogs croaking loudly in the sultry night air.

The valet parked his car at a popular night spot that had a gourmet restaurant on the top floor. This elegant restaurant had a long waiting list. We walked into an elevator. Dinner was quite good, and the conversation was easy.

After dinner Ken said, "Let's go into the bar area for an after-dinner drink." I was totally uncomfortable with this and really wanted to go home. Dinner was fine. Why did we need to extend this evening? On the other hand, I didn't want to ruin Jena's evening, so I went along with them. I could hear the band playing loudly as we entered the dimly lit nightclub. Ken found us a table that was vacant, that could easily accommodate eight people or more. The three of us sat down on one end of the table. He sat down next to me.

"Would you like to dance?" I really didn't want to dance with this strange man. I simply shrugged my shoulders and got up. He led me onto the large dance floor. I looked over at my friend, all alone. She looked like a miniature figurine seated at the oversize table.

He was a good dancer and his elevated shoes made him as tall as me in my low heels. I could feel his round belly bump into my thin waist. I felt uncomfortable dancing with him. Why was I part of this strange scenario? I kept asking myself.

The next day at work, Jena called and sounded frantic, "Ken wants to take us to his favorite

Chinese restaurant tonight."

"No, absolutely not. Why don't you go out with your brother, why do you need me to tag along?"

I was feeling irritated with them. The questions flooded my mind. What is going on here? Why did I feel like I was being set up? Is this some sort of karma?

"We never go out together," she replied.

"Why?" I asked.

She ignored my question. Instead she said, "Please come. I need you to come with us. I really like this restaurant and I can't go without you." So again, against my better judgment, I went with the two of them. The Chinese food was very good.

A few days later Jena said, "My brother wants to play tennis with you. "No! Absolutely No!" I blurted out. I was more than frustrated with her and him.

Jena said, "My friend used to play tennis with him all the time while he was here. She is out of town. What's wrong with your playing tennis with him? You told me you play tennis and that you liked the sport."

"Okay," I conceded again! Why was I doing this? Why was I being so condescending? Maybe, I was falling for Ken. He was very attentive and could be very charming. Maybe for the first time in a long time in my life, I felt special, adored.

Ken was a good tennis player, a good listener and a very caring person. Our tennis date led to dinner and dancing and before I knew it, I was in a sexual relationship with him. I was staying at his place, while his sister was staying at my apartment with my aging dog, Skipper.

Even though this was an uncomfortable situation I was in, I continued to stay with Ken. I didn't talk to Jena during this time. I didn't know what she thought or what she knew.

I liked Ken as a person. He was easy to talk to. He enjoyed going out to dinner, dancing, like I did. I remembered when I saw Ken's photo at the penthouse and the strange feeling the photo emitted. Was that a karmic premonition? Probably, I felt that I must have had a lifetime with him, and we were to resolve something in this lifetime. Perhaps, I was married in that lifetime, and had pursued him. The fact remained that he was a 'married man' and that was a still a big 'no - no' for me.

At dinner one night, I asked him about his sister. "You and Jena seem to have a strange relationship?"

Ken volunteered, "Jena is my half-sister. Her mother married my widowed father. She had Jena from a previous marriage, and my father had three sons."

Now I understood some of the puzzle regarding them.

As the days continued, I was staying overnight at his condo and Jena was living at my place. I honestly thought he would return home after a week, however, he was not in a hurry to return home. Our relationship was intimate on many levels. More than the sex, it was the compatibility, kindness and an easy existence, almost as if, we had been together for a long time, even though, it was just two weeks. I think I had never experienced a man so enraptured with me. It felt empowering. It was an aphrodisiac. His kind nature was so unlike my ex-husband.

Ken and I stopped back at the condo for me to grab a change of clothing. Jen was there. I thought she was at work. She didn't say a word – simply stared at us. It was very awkward for all of us.

Several days later she called at her brother's place and told Ken that she wanted to talk to me. He handed me the phone. She screamed loudly, "I can't believe you having an affair with my brother. I'm very, very angry with you. I'm moving out of your place tomorrow. I'm sending you a check for rent!" I heard the phone slam in my ear.

Wow! What I wanted to ask her and didn't get a chance to was: why did she push so hard for me to be with her playboy brother? What did she think was going to happen? On the other hand, I believe that these were scenes we were to play out - karma from another lifetime. Yes, I believe that we live many lifetimes here. We could not possibly learn everything in one lifetime.

After Jena's departure, I moved back into my apartment to take care of Skipper, my little black and white dog. I continued to see Ken, but I was not planning this to be long-term. I think he had other ideas.

One night after we had finished dinner at his place, he took my hand and said, "Why don't we start with a Louie Vuitton handbag."

These words, 'start with' stuck in my mind. At first, I was speechless. I thought he was kidding. Oh no! I realized he was serious! Red flags flew around me. I didn't need his designer handbag. Besides, I knew this was not an unconditional gift!

I could become a *kept woman*. This was exactly what I didn't want to happen. He had shown me another side that was repulsive to me. He wanted a mistress and wanted to chain her with expensive gifts. I wanted love, freedom, and mutual respect. I had grown past the security of marriage, a man to take care of me. I could not get past this blatant manipulation.

Suddenly I found my voice and my anger, "You can give the handbag to someone else. I don't need this unconditional gift. If I want an expensive handbag, I'll buy it myself!"

Then he became nasty and said, "Other women like my gifts and like me. I could call up another woman right now who would be very happy to get this gift."

His comment infuriated me. I hurried out the door. "Please call her!" I shouted as I slammed the door behind me. I ran to my car. He didn't follow me, although he did try calling me. I ignored his phone messages.

The more I thought about it, being with a married man was never going to work out well for either of us - especially me. No, this affair was never to be anything but a brief sojourn. Another karmic lesson, as well as, a big lustful mistake.

7
everything is a lesson here

Like their nomadic mother, my twin daughters had relocated to Phoenix, Arizona. Their father had stopped paying their tuition a year or so ago. They had stayed in Cleveland and worked various jobs there. They had visited me in Ft. Lauderdale to see if they wanted to live there and decided against this. They felt Phoenix was their destiny. The desert seemed more like home to them. Time had flown. I could not believe that I lived in Ft. Lauderdale for three years.

I flew into Phoenix for a short visit. I wanted to celebrate their 20th birthday with them and see how they were doing. While I was there, Skipper, now 17 ½ years old became seriously ill. He was being boarded at a reputable kennel in Ft. Lauderdale. The kennel owner called me with the bad news; she had taken him to her vet.

I called the vet, a very compassionate man, who said, "Your dog is in a lot of pain. His kidneys aren't working; he can't move. If he was my dog, I would put him down." I made that horrible decision over the phone. I cried and cried over his loss. I was sorry I could not be there to say goodbye to my old friend.

My daughters were living in a one-bedroom apartment with two queen-size beds crowded into the bedroom. They owned one falling apart car. One daughter worked nights at a nearby hotel, while the other worked days at a department store that was miles away. Seeing their stressed faces, I knew it was time to be around them for a while to help them financially and emotionally; maybe we were to help each other. I felt that it was time to move out of Ft. Lauderdale.

"So how do you feel," I asked them, "if I moved to Phoenix and you lived with me."

I looked into their brown eyes and thought I saw them soften.

I said, "I know this is not an easy choice for you as you like your independence, however, I know everything will work out. Remember it's not forever."

They thought about this for a moment, looked at each other and agreed. I left Phoenix with a to-do-list to set the move in action.

My cousin picked me up from the Ft. Lauderdale Airport. We talked about my move to Phoenix and her relationship with a very nice man from Canada that she had recently met. Their relationship had progressed, and she was ready to marry him and move there. Funny how things work out; we would be living in totally different parts of the globe. We hugged knowing that we would see each other again. We would make that happen.

Once in Phoenix, I purchased a newly built two-bedroom townhouse, which was perfect for the girls and me, as it was available immediately. All I had to do was pick out paint colors and select tiles for the kitchen and bathrooms. The girls could store their furniture in the two-car garage.

Phoenix - her blazing sun, brown desert and cacti scenery test its inhabitants. Some will move back to the lush greenery they suddenly crave, despite the bitter snowy winter that they could not wait to flee. I embraced the desert, seeing its subtle beauty in its blooming self-reliant cacti, statuesque mountains, magnificent sunsets, sunrises and of course, its mystical energies. I felt excited, open, ready to explore more sides of myself. It felt good to reconnect with my daughters.

After we settled in, the girls found employment nearby. Looking to meet like souls, I ventured out to a singles' function. There I met Suzie from New York and Elaine from Kansas City. We were drawn to each other like spiritual fireflies.

Suzie, divorced, had recently moved to Phoenix with her teenage daughter. Suzie had a golden hair, thick build, and a passionate personality.

Elaine, also divorced, had lived in Phoenix a few years. Her daughter was a high school senior. Elaine had dark hair and dark eyes, and she was sensuous and far worldlier than me. Our common modality, besides being drawn to our spiritual nature, we were single women with grown daughters living with us.

I shared with my new friends that I wanted to learn more about my spiritual side. They were on this quest as well, yet their priority was their quest to meet guys. Even though Suzie had a sugar daddy in New York, she was ready to date other men. Elaine, married five times, was actively looking for number six. I, on the other hand, wanted to date, yet was not as bold as they were. What a group we were!

One night, Elaine invited us over to her house for a meditative spiritual workshop. After the meditation was over, we congregated in her small kitchen. I saw a flyer promoting a self-discovery training lying on her kitchen table.

The flyer intrigued me. As I read it, I said to Elaine, "This looks interesting!"

Elaine replied, "This was the best thing I ever did for myself. I loved Path to Self-Discovery."

"This training looks like something I need to do." I handed the flyer to Suzie. "Here, look at this, I definitely want to sign up for this training. It's hard to believe that it's free. I think this would be a good thing to do."

After glancing at the flyer, she nodded, "Yes, it sounds like something I want to do as well. I'll go with you."

"Okay." I wrote down the phone number that was on the flyer. "I'll call them tomorrow."

Several weeks flew by. Suzie and I met outside an empty store that would hold the training. Once inside, we sat together in the large meeting room and listened to the facilitator state the rules and regulations. We had to sign an agreement that we would complete the training. I questioned what I was doing here. Was this training for me? Did I want to share myself with these strangers? As I viewed these worrisome thoughts floating through my mind, I knew that this was exactly where I needed to be. It was time to work on my negative stuff. I wanted to be open and share myself with others and get rid of the negative thoughts that tell me I can't do this, or I'm not good enough.

The forty students in the class were very supportive of each other and had survived being in this mini observatory for four weeks. I was removing negative programming from my past through self-observation.

We played many interactive games. One game we played concerned life and death. The facilitator divided us into two groups. Half the group were seated on chairs portraying a sinking ship, and the other half were to determine who was to live or die.

A female walked around the chairs until she came to me, she said, "Do you want to live?" I bowed my head so that she would not choose me to live. Wow! What a revelation! I need to stop being a victim, give up my vital force to others. I need to live! I want to live.

On the other hand, if I was chosen as one of the survivors I would have to deal with the guilt that I was still alive, and the rest of my group were dead! I knew either way – whatever choice I made must be for the right reasons. This session certainly made me think about my values.

After this session, I felt grateful for life – my life. I learned the only safe place to be is the present moment, the Now. I was learning more and more about myself and the outdated tapes I had going on in my mind.

Happy with the first training, Suzie and I

signed up for the second one. I hoped to be more vulnerable, more open in the next session. I heard this training was more intense. I really wanted to release negative blocks, known or hidden, that were holding me back. This second training would start at the beginning of the month.

In the meantime, I donated my time at a charity law agency. From the time that I arrived at the office to the time I left each day I was busy. I learned many office skills including how to use the computer. I interviewed some of the clients and wrote a summary to help the attorneys.

Teresa, a rather striking Italian woman, a woman that you would look at twice, was the director of this program. She was not tall, however, she seemed taller than she was, probably as she wore high heels. When she was in the office, she always made of point of talking to me.

As I walked into the suite of offices, I caught the tail end of Teresa's voice shouting louder and louder as she tried to make her point to someone on the phone. After the conversation ended, she softened her tone and said, "Come into my office."

What does she want? I hope she's not going to yell at me! I'm only a volunteer. I mulled this over as I solemnly walked into her office.

I sat down in a black leather chair. She shut the door. Her large desk took up most of the small room and was completely filled with files and stacks of paper. She looked so tiny behind it. Her dark eyes were almost hidden by her thick blonde bangs. I continued to gaze everywhere but at her because I felt very uncomfortable.

"I've been watching you and you look like

someone I'd like to know." She added, "Sorry you had to experience my ranting." She must have noticed the startled look on my face.

"Thank you," I managed to squeak this out.

She casually asked, "Would you like to go out to dinner sometime?"

This was getting even more uncomfortable. Was she kidding? I just witnessed her unsettling tirade as she rifled bullet-like threats at her target.

"No," I replied too quickly. My words popped out of my mouth and hung in the air. I think I was shocked that she wanted me to go to dinner with her. Then immediately, I regretted what I said, and as I stood up, and was about to walk out the door, I turned to her and said gently, "Thank You. I'll think about this."

I truly believe there is good in everyone. The more I thought about Teresa, and her invitation, I decided that I really needed to meet with her. I remembered that she was helpful to me when I arrived at the agency and remained so. I decided not to let one negative outburst define her. Intuitively I knew there was more to her than her outward persona dictated.

When I returned to volunteer the next week, I knocked on her door and said, "I would be happy to go to dinner with you."

She smiled warmly and replied, "How about going for Mexican food tonight after work? There is an authentic Mexican restaurant I'm fond of that is in Old Town Scottsdale."

"Sure, I would love to go there," I said and returned to my desk. I was busy with phone calls and entering data into the computer.

I watched her lock up, then I followed her to the restaurant. Once we were seated in a booth, Teresa shared, "I'm attending ASU to get my master's degree. I'm separated from my husband of twenty-two years. We have two grown daughters. I know you're divorced and seem comfortable with being single."

"Yes, I certainly can relate to what you're going through." I thought now it's my turn to help someone through their transition.

Our margaritas arrived. After taking a sip, she said, "Again I'm sorry that you had to witness my melt-down. My frustration is with a colleague. She is constantly undermining me behind my back. She even had a conversation with my boss. He is on my side. I really need this job."

"Thanks for sharing this with me."

Now that I understood the reason for Teresa's outburst, I began to like this hard-boiled executive and heavy-duty scholar. I was glad that I was able to get past my first impression of her.

After this initial dinner, we met for dinner quite frequently. At dinner one night, I mentioned to Teresa that it was time for me to find a paying job. My daughters had full-time jobs and had moved into their own apartment.

Several weeks later Teresa said, "I heard of a job opportunity that would be perfect for you. It's for an admin position at a large real estate company in their law department in downtown Phoenix."

I said, "Thanks! I'll contact their HR department and set up an interview." I was excited and nervous at the prospect of interviewing for this position.

Due to the positive feedback from everyone connected with the charity program, I was hired at the real estate company within two hours. I left there feeling excited at this job opportunity.

I called Teresa with the good news. "Do you want to go to the Mexican Restaurant in Old Town and celebrate?"

She said, "Sure, that sounds like fun."

After dinner she hugged me and said, "I'm so glad you got the job. l will miss you. Let's keep in touch."

I answered, "Absolutely."

I thought what serendipity to have met Teresa and for her to suggest this job. Then how quickly I got it. One thing seems to lead to the other as we learn and experience in this physical dimension. I wondered what lies ahead for me in my new job. I think there are no accidents. Everything is a lesson.

8
open to the healer within

A month later, the second session of Path to Self-Discovery began. Suzie and I met up at the vacant store. I felt more at ease this time. I felt more confident within myself as well. I really wanted to work on myself and release more of my negative blocks and outdated belief system.

Our female facilitator had us find a partner of the opposite sex for a structured game we were to play. We were to act out characters from television shows past and present.

Rick and I quickly gravitated to each other. He was six years younger than me, a graphic designer who worked out of his home. I was attracted to him: his dark blue eyes, and slim build.

The instructor gave us a card with dialogue on it. Rick and I were to play well-known TV celebrities of the 1950's, Ralph (Jackie Gleason) and Alice (Audrey Meadows) Kramden from their television sitcom, The Honeymooners.

As I read my part of the script before the group, I saw how, like Alice, I could have a deadpan expressionless face like I had drawn in my portrait. I didn't want to be like Alice. I wanted to be me. I wanted to be more open, expressive and not avoid confrontation. This dialogue showed me that I still had work to do on myself. Rick, on the other hand, was intimidated by strong women and he wanted release from that feeling.

Rick had a sympathetic ear to all my emotional baggage. I listened to him as well. He had never married, been in short relationships, and longed for a long-lasting relationship. I shared that I left a nineteen-year marriage and was not ready for a long commitment. We evolved as friends and then lovers. He had a deep spiritual side that I resonated with. He had taken yoga, read similar books as I did on empowerment and self-awareness.

One day during break, he asked, "Do you want to come to my place after class for a glass of wine and a spaghetti dinner?"

"Sure, I'll bring the wine."

After his home cooked dinner, we moved into his bedroom. He was a caring sexual partner. After this romantic evening, I spent Saturday nights after our training at his apartment. During the work week, we saw each other at the trainings.

Several weeks later at Rick's apartment, he asked, "Do you want to watch a movie, "Resurrection," that I taped. It's fiction about a woman who experiences the afterlife after a car accident which kills her husband. She discovers she has a special gift while she is recovering. She could heal people by touching them or through clairvoyance."

After the movie was over, I said to Rick, "What an interesting movie. I wonder if it's based on truth. I think anyone can heal themselves if they follow their breath and inner guidance. Some facilitators use different techniques such as: tai chi, qigong, yoga, and hands-on-healing. The healing comes from the healer within not from the facilitator."

Rick said, "I've heard that."

I said, "I've experimented with hands-on-healing and use it to remove pain and sometimes hasten healing. First, I say, *From the Lord God of my Being to the Father within, please heal this child perfectly now*. Then I breathe into the painful area, as I move my hands over it. The person being healed needs to breath into this area as well. I become a channel for Divine healing energy. The breath is the healer - not me."

"Can I do this?" Rick asked.

"Yes, I believe that you or anyone could do healing. If I can do this - so could you."

He said, "I'll try this technique. When did you realize you could do this?"

"Years ago, when I was still married, a neighbor had surgery on her leg. Several weeks after her surgery, I sat next to her on her sofa. I felt a sharp pain in my left leg. I asked her if it was her left leg that was hurting, and she nodded yes."

"Because of this experience, I began to read books on healing. I wondered if I could use my hands as well as my mind to remove the pain from my right arm from a tennis injury. So, I experimented. I put my left hand on my right shoulder and swept my hand down my arm and felt the energy flow as I pulled each of my fingers. I kept doing this daily several times a day until I the pain was gone. I practiced this technique, like riding a bicycle, the more I did it, the better I became at it. My healing channel was open. The pain went away and never returned. Can I heal like the woman in the movie? I think 'not' for she had a special gift."

Rick said, "Too bad we don't learn some of these techniques at the trainings."

The trainings were making me more aware of myself. I was observing myself: how I act, how I think. I was evolving slowly from the caterpillar to the butterfly. Yet, I knew I still had a long way to go – to get my wings.

At the next training session, I asked Rick, "How about getting a quick lunch. I know a great place that is close by. My treat since you're always making dinner."

"Sure, we have an hour before the training starts up again."

After lunch, Rich said, "Thanks. I liked that place, food was fresh and tasty."

We walked to the car. I said, "I want to get money out of the ATM. It shouldn't take long."

He cautioned, "Remember we only have ten minutes to get back to the class. If we're late, we'll have to apologize to everyone! I don't want to be late."

I replied, "Me neither." I thought he is such a worrier. "I'm just getting cash. It won't take long. There is no line."

His words struck a sour note. He was rushing me. I abruptly shoved my debit card into the ATM, and it spit it out. I shoved it back into the machine several times, each time with even more agitation, and again, it spat out my card without money. I was getting more and more frustrated. I turned, and looked at the growing line behind me, and stubbornly shoved the card into the slot trying to force it to give me my money!

Rick was not happy. "Let's go. We're going to be late." He was annoying me just as much as the machine.

I could not believe that the machine would not take my card. I was angry that this simple task was turning into such a disaster. Why is this happening? I stopped. Then I got it! I took a slow deep breath. I gently put the card into the slot, gently pushed the buttons and lo and behold, I received my money. Another lesson to my growing list, and this was a big one! I need to be aware of how I treat humans, animals, even machines. We are all connected! We are all energy! By being aware of my anger, and turning it into calm energy, I was able to get my money easily.

"We're late. I can't believe we're late. You made us late." Rick kept repeating as he drove us back to the training. I didn't answer him. We were both upset. He parked his car and we ran into the building. Out of breath, we were told to wait behind a black drape. Someone pulled the drape open to our fellow participants and staff who were seated in front of the curtain. We were to apologize to them for being late. I felt like I was in a fishbowl.

Rick spoke first, "Sera held us up by trying to get money out of the ATM. I wanted leave to get here on time."

My turn was next. I averted all the eyes and spoke shakily. "I'm sorry. I take full responsibility for my part in being late. I vow to be on time. This will never happen again."

I was upset that Rick didn't support me nor did he apologize to the group. I knew I was responsible for us being late, yet we were both in this together, or were we? I mentioned this later, however he insisted it was totally my fault. He said, "Let's not continue to talk about this." I let it go unresolved. However, the relationship weakened at this point.

Before I knew it, there were only a few more training sessions left. Hard to believe, the weeks had flown by so quickly. After an exceptionally long and challenging training class, I stayed over at Rick's apartment even though we had slowly stopped spending time together. We were both exhausted because the training had lasted longer than usual. The trainings mirrored many of my shortcomings. Through self-observation, I was able to confront and work on many of my old issues such as avoidance and lack of self-esteem.

Rick fell asleep quickly. I could hear his light breathing. As tired as I was, I simply could not fall asleep. I propped myself up against the headboard, not knowing what to do.

I felt chilled and pulled the light cotton blanket up to my chin to warm myself. I looked across the dark room to the dimly lit doorway. I could not see anything; yet I felt each presence, as one by one, they entered the room and slowly, very slowly continued around the double bed. I sensed the swishing of their robes and guessed there were eight of them. I intuitively knew they were highly evolved souls. Wanting to wake Rick. I poked his shoulder hard, then his arm. He didn't wake up.

They continued to communicate with me

telepathically; it felt like this was a celebration. I didn't hear them, however, I knew I was receiving valuable information.

The "high ones" were with me for quite a while. Then I sensed each one turn and slowly, very slowly, follow the other out of the room. Again, I sensed in my inner knowing, the shuffling of their robes. As each entity left through the doorway, I felt warmer. I moved the blanket away from my body. When they were gone, I continued to sit on the bed and stare across the dark bedroom at the empty doorway. The room felt quiet, vacant.

Rick woke up. "What is going on, why are you up?" I explained what had happened.

He said, "Why didn't you wake me?"

"I tried. You were in a deep sleep. I think you were supposed to remain asleep during this encounter. It felt like a celebration for completing the training."

Rick said, "Who were they?"

I answered, "High beings. I felt I knew them, however I was not physically able to see or hear them. I sensed them intuitively. I knew we were communicating on a higher level than my physical reality. I felt so honored that they had entered our dimension to be here. It was an amazing gift."

Rick fell quickly back to sleep. I continued to sit there just staring at the door opening.

Path to Self-Discovery Training was ending, and so was our short relationship. Rick and I both knew that we would not see each other after the last day of the training. The training was the only thing that kept us together.

Sunday was our last session. We gathered at

one o'clock and ended around four o'clock. The staff slid the sliding doors open, and we were pleasantly surprised with cake and ice cream honoring our completion. Friends and family flooded our meeting room with well wishes and flowers. I hugged Rick briefly and off we went in different directions to find our friends, fellow classmates, and new beginnings.

Elaine had invited Suzie and me to her apartment for a graduation dinner and sleep-over. When we arrived at Elaine's apartment, we were surprised and delighted to see a familiar face, Sarah, a gifted psychic and medium, open the door for us.

She hugged each of us as we walked into the living room. "Congratulations! You made it!"

I had met Sarah, a tall, 60-ish, dark-haired woman on several occasions. I noticed she was aging like a rare vibrant wine. She lost her son five years ago. She survived her grief through daily prayer and meditation; she healed and connected to her spiritual side and to her guides. She was able to clairvoyantly connect with her son and others who had passed over. Her aura was filled with light and love.

Sarah said, "This is Todd. He is a friend of mine, and a psychic. He is visiting from California." He looked like he was in his 20's, clean cut, casually dressed in a white tee shirt and jeans. He had a warm energy about him.

Sarah said, "Elaine has gifted you both with readings."

"How fun! Leave it to Elaine to surprise us with these readings. What perfect timing!"

I was excited with the prospect of hearing what the future held for me from this reading. I felt like an empty shell, open and vulnerable. My belief system was totally torn away. My mind felt like it had been cleared and wiped as clean as an empty chalkboard. It was a strange disorientated feeling. I was not sure if it was from the training session or the high ones or both.

Sarah said, "Who wants a reading?"

I felt drawn to Sarah and walked towards her. Suzie chose Todd for her reading, and they went off into the living room. I followed Sarah into the tight kitchen. She pulled a napkin off the counter and found a pen in a kitchen drawer.

We sat at the kitchen table. Her serene face stared into mine. Then she was silent, closed her eyes as she communicated with her guide. About five minutes later, she began to write on the napkin. She was still in an altered state. After she came back from the trance, she read the message to me. The message seemed to be channeled through her from an ancient soul.

"You desire freedom yet impose restrictions and limitations. Fly free to and fro. Movement shall be swift and sudden. You must complete this next cycle of learning."

"Four months shall lift the clouds, the sun shall break thru and shine, for you are a star of this new age and can emerge to shine thru all this lifetime."

"Set your children free to free yourself. Release the guilt associated with Love and the physical sharing shall bring great joy and deep profound Love thru eternity."

She handed me the white dinner napkin with

its Christmas themed border of red bows and green holly trim. I wrote the date 1/ 86 on top of the paper napkin. I knew I would keep this message and read it again and again.

9

step out of your comfort zone

I attended a Unity Church on Sunday for their early service seeking spiritual camaraderie. They had planned their first art fair and needed artists to participate. I decided to challenge myself and signed up as a contributing artist. The fair was to be held the following Sunday in the afternoon after services were over.

At home I looked through my paintings to decide which ones I wanted to exhibit at the art fair. I even searched through my wardrobe to decide what I wanted to wear to the event. Should I be casual or arty? I decided to wear an olive-green outfit, a bright scarf, and of course, fun Indian jewelry. I was nervous and excited about participating in my first ever art show.

On Sunday, I arrived early at the church, found a comfortable place on the lawn to set up my easel. I placed a painting of my dog Skipper on the easel and placed an abstract painting of a cactus on the ground. Standing in the warm March sun, I waited. The courtyard was brimming with artists, jewelry designers and sculptors.

While I was standing there, I remembered a story that I read about a monk. He lived alone in a hut in a small village. A young woman from this village had a brief affair with a traveler. She realized she was pregnant after he left. When her parents found out about her pregnancy, they were devastated. How could this have happened to their daughter? They were humiliated and disgraced. The girl eased their agonies by telling them it was the monk's baby.

Upon hearing this, they rushed over to the monk's hut and said, "What have you to say for yourself? You impregnated our daughter. Now she will live with you."

He looked at them and softly replied, "Ah so."

The girl moved in with the monk. He treated the girl kindly. After several months of living with this gentle monk, she could not tolerate the punishment that she had subjected him because he was treated badly and avoided by the community. She returned to her family and told them the truth. They went to the monk, apologized for their terrible accusations and begged his forgiveness.

The monk looked at them and softly replied, "Ah so."

To me this story meant to accept whatever happens – to get out of ego mind. I didn't want to get caught up in other people's judgments about my paintings whether they liked the paintings or hated them.

A smartly dressed woman walked by and stopped. She liked my work. Ah so, I thought to myself for I didn't engage my ego in whether the painting was good or bad. Another man with his wife stopped, and after studying the paintings, he compared them to his cousin's work. I could tell he disliked his cousin's art.

Ah so, I thought to myself. Again, I didn't succumb to ego. This simple lesson helped me feel that I belonged at the art show and kept me in a positive mood.

A gangly tall man, in his late forties, with blonde spiked hair strolled up to me and said, "I really like your paintings. "Do you have more to show me?"

"Yes, of course." I handed him my personal card.

"Thanks, my name is Jerod. I'll call you." I watched his rather thin frame in his ill-fitting suit move through the art show. I knew he was interested in me not my paintings. I was not particularly attracted to him, yet there was something there. Okay, I thought to myself, you need to be more open – see what happens.

I said to my neighboring artist at the close of the show, "I haven't sold any paintings; however, I think I've a date."

"You did better than me," she retorted.

Jerod called several days later. We went out to dinner and comfortably discussed metaphysical subjects. He was divorced and had a married son in Wisconsin. He was a realtor and an independent builder. He had built, bought and sold many homes in Arizona. I always had a desire to buy and sell homes, fix them up, make them better than they were before and suggested that maybe we could combine our talents someday.

We spent time together after work and during the weekends. We went out for coffee or out to dinner. I was falling in love. He was very much into me. He was very affectionate. I liked that part of him. I liked that we were both working on ourselves. We spent as much time as we could together and before I knew it, we were a couple.

I kept in contact with my friends, Elaine and Suzie, however, we drifted apart. My twin daughters were engrossed in their careers. Eventually they pursued their dream jobs, and each relocated to a different city: Tracey to Chicago, Illinois and Abby to Rochester, New York. This was hard for them as they had never been separated before. We decided to meet up on their birthday and my birthday.

One day Jerod said, "There's a training called "Positive Mindfulness" that sounds interesting for they use meditation techniques to positively reprogram the mind. Do you want to go with me?" He handed me a colorful brochure. "It's scheduled for next Saturday and Sunday."

After I glanced through the brochure, I replied, "Yes, this sounds very interesting. I'd love to go to this."

"Good, I'll make the arrangements for us to attend."

On Saturday morning, we walked into the large hotel in downtown Phoenix. Big printed black letters, Creative Mindfulness, on several signs directed us down a long hallway to a large training room. We checked in and spotted two chairs together in the middle of the second row. I glanced around the meeting room. There were around forty people, all different ages, different cultures, some in business attire; some casually dressed like us.

A personable golden-haired man in his late twenties stood in the front of the room and said, "My name is Chad. Welcome to Creative Mindfulness. I'm your facilitator. You'll process this information individually. I'll take you to an inner door in your awareness, however, you'll open and walk through it. You'll experience these meditations within your own comfort level."

"Now, I would like you to settle into your chairs and relax as I take you into a short meditation. I want you to become quiet and connect with your breath. Count seven breaths in and seven breaths out through your nose, and when you're relaxed, let yourself breathe normally. We'll continue this breathing exercise for five minutes."

Intent on listening to my breath, I barely heard him say, "Now that you're relaxed, I'm going to count from ten to one. Let us begin 10, 9, 8" . . . and when he got to 5, he said, "I want you to tell yourself that if you need to come out of this for any reason, you'll come to full awakening." He continued, "4, 3, you're going deeper. At the count of 1, you'll be at center." He continued to 1 and said, "You're at center."

"I want you to picture in your mind an empty room. This is your special room. You can make it as technically advanced as you want or not technical at all. I want you to take your time, design your room: choose a desk, chair, computers, books, headsets etc. or you could fill the space with a fireplace, cozy chair and chocolate chip cookies and milk. Fill in as much detail as possible. This is your special place."

What an interesting project. I created my room in a soft cream color with large windows, a big glass and chrome desk. A powerful computer sat on the desk. I sat on a comfortable bright patterned swivel chair with a high back. Behind me, a built-in rosewood cabinet lined the back wall, above it an interactive huge computer screen. All kinds of high-tech equipment were on the cabinet that could bring information from around the globe and other dimensions. A hand carved wood door was ten feet high as the ceilings in the room were high. Soft harp music could be heard in the background. Everything in the room could disappear in an instant when instructed and become a meditation room with comfortable floor pillows.

When sufficient time had passed, Chad said, "Now we are going to come out of this by counting from one to ten." He began the count, "1, 2, 3," and then added the affirmation, "I'm feeling healthier, more energetic than before, 4, 5, 6." He continued, "7, when I reach 10, you'll open your eyes and come to full awakening." At ten, I opened my eyes to the meeting room and its bright fluorescent lights, and I did feel more energetic.

Chad took his time and looked around the room to make sure everyone's eyes were open. "Remember this is your room, design it, create it anyway that suits you. If you want to meet Einstein in your room, invite him, or if you want to meet the Dalai Lama there, feel free to do this."

I thought, that is a great idea – maybe next time.

He continued, "I want you to instruct yourself

as you begin to count from ten to one, that you can come to full awareness at any time during your meditation."

Out in the Phoenix brilliant sunshine, I said to Jerod, "I really enjoyed this class. It was fun. I'll go into my special room, my well-equipped office with advanced technology gadgets and see what happens. What type of room did you create?"

"I created a meditation room – with dim lighting and one comfortable chair. I'll go there when I want to relax, feel peaceful and centered."

I said, "I like that idea – maybe put in an extra chair, and I'll meditate with you." He grinned and pulled me towards him.

The following day, we again followed the signs to the meeting room. Chad warmly greeted us at the doorway. We walked into a filled room and found chairs together at the back of the room.

From the podium, Chad said, "Welcome back. I want you to relax, settle into your chairs. Let us begin with your breath." We did the breathing exercise.

I took a deep breath in, and counted to seven, and then breathed out through my nostrils to the same count. I felt and heard my breath, like a soft breeze. I relaxed and then began to breathe normally.

Chad said, "We're going to center by counting from ten to one." He started the countdown beginning with ten. "You're going deeper than before. If you need to come out of this for any reason, you'll return to full awareness."

At the count of one, I faintly heard his voice, "You're now at center. I want you to meet your guide. Look around, you're out in nature, standing on green grass surrounded by beautiful trees and flowers. You hear birds chirping. You see a figure coming towards you. It could be male or female. Introduce yourself, ask your guide his or her name, and as many questions as you would like."

Now in a state of deep relaxation, I saw the green hill, and coming towards me was a tall beautiful woman with long blonde hair. Her etheric body shimmered. I introduced myself and asked her name.

Somewhere in my mind, I heard, "My name is Samantha, and I've been your guide through many lifetimes. You'll write and teach spiritual truths in this lifetime. You'll continue your spiritual quest to complete your soul's purpose here on Earth and share what you have learned. Observe yourself, discover what you want to keep, and what you want to change as you connect to your Higher Self, that higher aspect of yourself that can be attained and held in the physical body. It's the part of you that knows, sees and understands at the highest level possible."

In the background, I heard the instructor's distinctive voice, "It's time to leave. I want you to thank your guide."

I mentally said, "Thank you, Samantha."

Chad started the count, "1, 2, 3. At the count of 10, you'll come back to full awakening and will open your eyes."

I heard him say the affirmation, "I am feeling happier; I am healthier; I am more energetic." I felt more connected, happier.

". . . 8, 9, 10. You 're back to the present, open

your eyes."

I turned and looked at Jerod. "I feel so grateful to have contacted my guide, Samantha. I would never have thought to ask, what is your name or actually have a conversation with her."

He said, "I agree. I didn't know I had a guide, Timothy, or that I could communicate with him."

Chad said, "Can I have your attention. Since this is the last session, I want you to remind yourself whenever possible that you're feeling happier and energetic. If you're experiencing a medical challenge, say in your mind: I am healed, I am in perfect health. The mind can work miracles. Thank you everyone. I hope you have enjoyed the classes. If you have any questions, please see me after class."

Everyone applauded. It was a life-changing experience; one I would never forget. Some people lined up with questions to ask Chad or to sign up for future sessions.

"I'm glad we took these classes. Thank you." I slipped my arm under Jerod's arm as we left the room. I looked up at him. "I do feel happier and more energetic."

He smiled and said, "Me, too."

10
we are magnets - like attracts like

Now that I had a full-time job and a full-time boyfriend, the days seem to disappear. I was in love with Jerod and with life. There was much to learn and do at my new job. I was thankful for the administrative and office skills I learned at the law agency.

Soon after I started my job, I became friends with another administrative assistant, Jackie, an athletic looking blonde from Mississippi. We both liked to walk outdoors during lunch. We would eat quickly; then pull on our socks and tennis shoes and rush out into the fresh air. We usually walked to the downtown area and back.

On our lunch walk one day, I shared, "I had a frustrating morning with too many unpleasant phone calls. I feel out of sorts, way off my center. I can't believe that I let their negative energy penetrate my inner space. I know better. Yet, I can't seem to shake off this anger."

Jackie listened to my rantings. The sky was an azure shade of blue. The Phoenix sun was shining, making everything brighter, and a warm breeze was trying to get my attention. However, I didn't care as I was too absorbed in negativity.

Jackie said, "Let's go into this card shop." We walked into the little store packed full of greeting cards and novelties. I read some of the funny and inspirational cards: nothing helped my somber mood. Jackie bought several cards.

Outside, the busy sidewalk was filled with the lunch hour crowd. What? I stopped walking because I felt an intense energy like a rabid animal rushing at me - to harm me! I psychically knew it was a male. Something shifted within me. I immediately closed my eyes, took a deep breath, and turned my thoughts to love, peace and released my breath softly through my nose. I felt the dark energy move toward me, ready to strike me, almost touching me. Then I felt him veer away. I dared not move nor open my eyes until I felt his harmful energy was gone.

Jackie gasped, "Oh, Sera, I can't believe it! That nasty man was intent on knocking you to the ground!"

"I know I felt his violent energy," I said as we walked back to work. "I sensed his dark negative aura like sharp knives coming towards me and was aware right at that instant that it was *my negative energy, my negative thoughts,* drawing him to me.

She asked, "What is an aura?"

I answered, "Auras are energy fields that surround the body. Some people can see, feel and even photograph them. I've seen colors around people, however, I rarely feel this kind of dark aura. This was a powerful lesson! We are magnets - like attracts like. My negativity attracted his negativity. Now I see why it's so important to stop negative thoughts, angry thoughts. I need to monitor my thoughts and my emotions! I cannot allow negativity, either mine or another person's, to enter my awareness. It's too dangerous!"

She said, "I agree. I'm still shook up about that man. I need to watch my thoughts as well."

I stopped to read a notice on the bulletin board about a job opportunity for an administrative assistant position in another department in the building. The position interested me because it paid more money. I applied for the position with HR. I would have to take a typing test.

A few days later, a woman from HR called and instructed me to meet her on the fourth floor. I left immediately and headed to the elevator. She was waiting for me when I got off the elevator. I followed her to a tiny office with a large glass window.

She said, "Start when you're ready. Follow the directions on the computer. When you're finished, you can go back to your department." She left the room and closed the door.

I sat on a wood desk chair in front of an oak desk and glanced out the big glass window at the carpeted foyer. I completed the practice sessions on the computer and started the timed test. Suddenly I felt this frantic energy in and around me, as I was typing. I opened my eyes wide. I could not believe what I was seeing . . . on the desktop, the black Rolodex's white index cards were spinning faster and faster - a small Ferris wheel out of control.

Was this my nervous energy or another energy in the room or both? What was going on? I guess I was not supposed to get this job for my typing became sporadic; I lost my place and had to stumble back and forth through the text to find it. I could only imagine how low my typing score showed on the computer printout.

"What was that all about?" I thought to myself. No one saw this phenomenon - except me. I knew I would not get the position. I returned to my desk and forgot about this incident until later.

I focused my attention on my work and thought about the fun trip Jerod and I were planning to Hawaii. We decided to make this trip at the beginning of the year to celebrate our one-year anniversary and were busy researching all our options.

A florist arrived with a beautiful floral arrangement. Leave it to Jerod. Our Hawaii trip inspired him to surprise me even though our trip was far away. Sitting at my open desk, I was admiring the bold orange and blue Bird of Paradise flowers, when out of the corner of my eye, I caught a glimpse of Kate, her greying hair flying in the air as she walked down the hallway. She had the office across from my desk.

Next thing I knew her blazing blue eyes were near mine. I could smell her chewing gum breath. She glared at the beautiful flowers, then at me, and slammed her fist on my desk, and shouted, "I hate you!"

She had incurable cancer and hated everyone and everything. I overheard her screaming and ranting at her son and daughter-in-law when I passed them on the back stairs as I left work one day. I know from all my studies that you either come from *love or fear*. She was stuck in the latter. After her nasty behavior towards me, she flew into her office and shut her door.

It took me a few minutes of wondering what that was all about, for me to realize that she was not happy, that I was happy, and had received this beautiful flora arrangement.

What can I say? I was unnerved and annoyed the rest of the day. I kept worrying that she was going to come out and scream at me again or attack me. Thank goodness, I didn't see her for the rest of the day.

On the way home, I felt I had to confront Kate and her nastiness, even though I still dislike confrontation. I just didn't want another threatening outburst.

The next morning, I watched Kate pass my desk and go into her office. She looked straight ahead. I found courage and walked into her office and closed the door behind me. She had just taken off her coat.

Aware of my agitated state, I said, "I'm sorry you have cancer. I know you're afraid of dying, however, you have no right to treat me or anyone like you did. That was a mean thing to do!" I stared sternly into her open eyes, hardly believing I had the gumption to say these words. I added, "Don't you ever do that again!" I turned quickly and left the office.

Once at my desk, I felt myself shaking. I honestly didn't want to hurt her, yet she needed to know how I felt. It was hard for me to settle back to work. I kept a watchful eye at her door.

She must have left the building when I went to

lunch, because her door was wide open, and her office was empty.

Ready to start my workday the following morning, I began going through the correspondence on my desk. I was still nervous about Kate, however I kept putting those thoughts out of my mind.

Helene, the chief attorney of our legal department, called and asked me to come to her office. What is this all about? I wondered. She and I were bagel buddies. I would arrive at work, early morning around 8 o'clock, and call out, "Helene, what kind of bagel do you want?" We were the only ones on the floor at that early hour. Then I would get delicious fresh bagels with cream cheese from the downtown deli. It was an early morning perk for both of us.

Her door was open. I entered her spacious office, peered over the mountains of stacked papers on her desk, into her clear spectacles. I sat down in one of her leather chairs in front of her desk and waited. She looked at me, and then got up and closed the office door. She sat next to me.

"Kate told me what happened," she said in a concerned voice. "She is grateful to you for what you said to her. We discussed her actions and she is very sorry. She wanted me to tell you this."

Tears spilled down my face, I tried hard to stop them. Helene handed me a Kleenex box. I was taught to fight my own battles, and here, was Helene defending me. I never would have gone to her or anyone to tell them about Kate. I finally composed myself, Kleenex in hand, and left the office.

After my meeting with Helene, I would see Kate

as she went in and out of her office. When our eyes met, she smiled at me. Of course, I smiled back. One of the other administrative assistants told me that Kate had apologized to her family for anything she said that may have offended them. They were now rallying around her with love and support.

Kate was not doing well. I noticed how thin and frail she looked. As I watched her slowly go past my desk, my telephone rang. It was Helene. She asked me to come to her office. I hung up the phone and wondered what this is about? When I walked into Helene's office, I saw Georgette, the manager of our department standing next to her. Georgette is a highly intelligent woman with a very responsible job. I could not help but wonder what she was doing there. We seldom saw her as she was so busy. Helene shut the door.

Georgette said, "We need your help. Kate is failing. She needs to keep her job and her insurance. We want you to take over her responsibilities."

Without hesitation, I said, "Yes, of course I'll do it. Is Kate good with this?"

"Yes, she suggested it," Helene assured me.

Wow, I 'm to help this dying woman. I thought, this was the reason I didn't get the other administrative job. That frenzied feeling I felt as I was typing was my Spirit Guide. I remembered the same feeling I felt when I was gently pushed to get out of my house – before the fire. Also, if I took that other position, I would be in another part of the building and not have this opportunity to help Kate with her transition. I remembered the distracting twirling Rolodex. No maybes about it, this was karmic.

In the mornings, I would do my job, and then go into Kate's office after she arrived and help her. Her job was not that difficult. We had lunch together during which she shared her life with me. I found sides of her that were wonderful, and I enjoyed our time together. We would laugh at silly things. I saw as the weeks went by that she was having trouble walking. I supported her weak body, as we walked across the busy street, to a little restaurant we both liked.

Shortly after I arrived at work one morning, Helene gathered the department together to tell us that Kate was in the hospital and not doing well.

The following day after work, I drove to the hospital. I smelled the strong hospital disinfectant as I made my way down the long vacant corridor to Kate's room. She looked so small, so fragile, so peaceful. She smiled at me through her parched lips. It was an easy visit filled with laughter and love. When it was time to go, I kissed her paper-thin cheek, knowing that I would never see her again, not in this lifetime. Yes, I would miss her.

I felt spiritually that I was placed across from her office to interact with her, to acknowledge her fears so she could heal her relationships before she left this plane. Perhaps she helped me in another lifetime, and this was . . . *karmic pay back.*

11

our mothers are our greatest teachers

My dream of buying and selling homes was realized when we purchased a home in Fountain Hills to renovate. Jerod opted to move into the property, and upon hearing him say this, I decided, just like that, to move in as well. I sold my townhouse.

After the move, I found the daily drive from Fountain Hills to downtown Phoenix getting longer and longer. I felt it was time to leave my job and devote myself to our business of home renovation. Jerod wanted me to preview properties with him for his real estate business.

Saying goodbye is never easy. I would miss my co-workers and my employer. On the last morning, I bought bagels for Helene and me.

We sat in her office and chewed on the bagels. "Sera, we'll probably lose weight because our bagel days are over."

I chuckled and said, "You're probably right!"

Not having the long commute anymore or a steady job, I turned my attention to helping Jerod with the remodeling of the house we were living.

in. We were fixing up the whole house: remodeling the bathrooms, updating the kitchen, putting in new flooring, new paint and a deck. Jerod was doing most of the physical work, although I did assist him when I could. Between fixing up the Fountain Hills house and helping Jerod with real estate, there was much to do.

Since we were so close to Arizona State University, I signed up for an art class. Most of the students in the class were right out of high school pursuing a career in the Arts.

One of our assignments was to create a self-portrait in pointillism, a technique in painting where small dots are applied to form images. We used Cyan blue, Magenta red, Yellow, and Key black marking pens.

After I arrived at class. I realized I had completely forgot to bring a photo of myself for the pointillism project. Most of the students had brought in a photo and had started working on their painting.

The female instructor said, "For those students that didn't bring a photo, I brought my camera. Follow me." Along with several other students, I followed her outside into the cool morning. When it was my turn to be photographed, thinking quickly, I grabbed a scarf from my handbag, wrapped it around my head, and tied it under my chin. I stuck my head amid the thick branches of a bushy tree outside the building and looked at the instructor's camera. I heard the clink as she snapped my photo and the whiz as the photo emerged from the Polaroid camera. She handed me the printed color photo.

Inside the classroom, I picked up a thin piece of black chalk and set about drawing images onto the canvas, so I would have a guideline before I started dotting with the four marking pens. Pointillism is unforgiving; if you make a mistake, it's not easy to correct.

After looking intensely at the photo for a while, staring into my own eyes, I found this was way too subjective. I could not detach myself. I turned the photo upside down and sketched the shapes onto the canvas.

We had several weeks to complete this detailed painting. I filled in the whole canvas with different shapes because I felt that life was present everywhere seen and unseen.

When I stood back to critique the finished painting, I realized that it was a glimpse of my life - my future life. I saw my daughter in a wedding dress with a man and two children, a girl and a boy. She would marry ten years later and have a daughter and a son. I saw my other daughter in a wedding dress with a man with a helmet that bicyclists use, but, that has not yet happened. My parents were in the painting as well. There was an angel with her wings spread at my left side and a tall etheric woman, probably my guide, Samantha, whispering into my left ear. A small animal with his left paw extended sat on my right shoulder. His expressive eyes stared straight ahead.

Much later, my daughter, Tracey, wanting to get another Himalayan cat after her cat died, located a breeder in Macon, Georgia. I was staying with her in her townhouse in Atlanta, Georgia at the time. The night before our trip, I saw in my inner vision a cat's two iridescent blue eyes staring at me.

After we arrived in Macon, the breeder took us to a trailer which held many kittens, mostly tabbies. She went in the back and brought out a seal point Himalayan kitten that immediately came running to me. His iridescent blue eyes were the same eyes I saw in my vision the previous night. My daughter was drawn to a tabby colored cat.

When we were ready to leave, I asked, "So which kitten are you getting?"

She said to the breeder, much to my surprise, "We'll take the Himalayan."

On the way back to Atlanta, I named him, "Beau," short for Beauregard, as he was a southern kitten. The kitten slept comfortably on my lap all the way back to Atlanta.

Years after we picked up the kitten, I asked my daughter, "Why didn't you take the tabby kitten you were playing with the day we got Beau."

She replied, "I almost did. I knew Beau belonged with you. That is why I bought him."

"Come and look at this painting," I said.

Tracey followed me into the bedroom. The pointillism painting was framed and hung above my dresser. I pointed to the animal in the painting. "Do you think that animal is Beau?"

She stared at the painting and said, "Yes, I can see the resemblance."

The Fountain Hills house took almost a year to

complete because of the amount of work that had to be done. We sold that house and purchased another house in the Tempe Lakes area to remodel. This two-story house oozed charm, yet it needed a face lift. The backyard had a view of the lake.

Once Jared and I were settled in, I called Teresa, the director from the volunteer agency. She lived in the Tempe Lakes community within walking distance to our house. She had finally left her stressful job and was actively working on her degree and her marriage.

After her morning walk, she would stop at our house, sit on one of the patio chairs and contently gaze at the peaceful lake. Her house was not on the lake.

One morning I asked, "How about doing something creative together? Maybe we could write a book?"

She said, "What kind of book?"

"How about a book about women? We could interview successful women and find out how they became successful."

Teresa said, "I would like to learn more about these women. What made them the way they are; what they had learned?"

"Yes," I agreed, "I would like to meet women, who would be willing to share their life lessons with us. Maybe it isn't necessary that they be successful businesswomen. They could be successful in life. Perhaps they could share something that they learned that could help other women. Where do we find these women - ordinary, yet extraordinary women?"

Teresa was silent for a moment. "I know someone we can start with, a woman that I occasionally meet with during my morning walk. Her name is Olivia. I'll ask her if she wants to be interviewed for our project."

A few mornings later, Teresa called, "Olivia and I'll stop by after our walk. She has consented to be interviewed."

"Great." I took blueberry muffins out to the patio table, with mugs and a thermos of hot coffee. I scattered notepads and pens around the glass tabletop. I was excited about our first interview.

Olivia

"Hi Olivia," I said as I shook her hand. "Let's sit at the patio table." Olivia was Teresa's height, about 5'1", in her middle 60's; silver threads were woven through her dark short hair. Her energy was low and solemn.

After coffee I asked, "What would you like to share?"

"My wonderful friend, my husband, died unexpectedly a month ago. We were professors at ASU. We had just retired and were looking forward to our time together. We were inseparable. We loved to travel and have been around the world twice. I miss him terribly." The tears flooded her cheeks.

"My husband and I became Buddhists. I learned life is a struggle and we are caught in the endless cycle of birth and rebirth until enlightenment is reached. We practiced meditation and mindfulness, being in the moment.

I believe in an afterlife and that my husband and I'll be united again. Right now, I'm going through grief. I think I'm still in a state of shock, in denial. Life hands out hard lessons."

After Olivia left, I felt tears well in my eyes. I prayed for her grief to subside, for her to heal.

Teresa returned a few days later to work on our project. She drank water from her water bottle and gazed at the placid lake. The brilliant morning sun was glowing, creating brilliant sparkles around us. The ducks were quacking at each other.

I said, "I think we need to prepare for these interviews. Why don't we make a list of questions we want to ask these women?"

Teresa replied, "I agree. Why don't we take a few minutes to think about this and then jot down our thoughts?"

"That is a great idea," I said. We wrote for a while.

She glanced at her sheet and said, "I would like to know more about these women – what did they learn, and would they share their life lessons with other women?"

I looked at my list of questions and said, "Okay, I want to know what their mothers were like and how did they influence them?"

I asked, "What was your mother like?"

After quite a long pause, Teresa replied abruptly, "Nothing to say." I looked into her tight face. I didn't pursue this further.

She said, "What was your mother like?"

I took a deep breath, "Okay I'll share this with you. I remember my mother, Rose, a beautiful, kind woman with a dark secret. My sensitive mother was manic depressive. I was not aware that she had this condition, until she was in her early 50's, when I witnessed her mood swings as either very high or very low."

Teresa leaned towards me.

I continued, "When she was very low, my mother thought about taking her life. She wound up in psychiatric hospitals throughout the city. Then the only way the psychiatrists knew to snap her out of this melancholy was through shock treatments. She attributed her disorder to diet drugs that had a speed effect on her. I think these drugs contributed to the underlying problems that were always there for her."

I took a sip of coffee and said, "I resonated with her. I could feel her deep pain, her deep sorrow. I felt her darkness like heavy bricks squashing my inner light. Was I like my mother? Did I have this illness? I worried as I fell into my own depression. I could not seem to get out of this funky state. "

Teresa poured more coffee into her mug and sat back in her chair. "How did you deal with this?"

"I called my mother's psychiatrist to ask about her. The psychiatrist explained her condition, and then asked, 'What is wrong with you?' He heard the dreariness in my voice."

"I said, 'Nothing.' When I hung up the receiver, I realized that there was nothing wrong with me. It was my mother who needed help. I was not my mother, nor did I want to mimic her behavior. I knew I needed to release this weird negative energy, yet it clung to me like a thick cloud. My sleepless nights were draining me."

Teresa refilled her coffee and poured some

into my cup. A slight lake breeze whirled around us. It felt cool and crisp.

I said, "During this time, my husband, Marcus, and I had planned a weekend trip from our home in Cleveland to a resort in Pennsylvania with our daughters. I was hoping this change would get me out of my fuzzy feeling. We had loaded the car, and several hours later we arrived at the beautiful rustic resort. We went to the pool area and spent the day in the warm sun. We ate a quiet dinner in the lodge."

"That day and the next day drifted in my disconnected state: we hung out at the pool, ate our meals, and walked around the resort. Marcus played golf during the day."

Teresa took another sip of coffee. The ducks were quacking on the lake.

I continued, "The next morning, we checked out of the hotel. Marcus could hardly walk from playing golf. His back had gone out. A man sympathized with him and gave him a muscle relaxant. He took the pill and had become very groggy. He managed to get himself into the back seat of our car and fell asleep. I had to drive back to Cleveland, I, at the time, was still in my funky depressed state. I didn't want to drive for two hours on the Pennsylvania freeway, yet I knew I had no other choice."

"With much trepidation, I inched the car onto the freeway. I squeezed the steering wheel so hard, my palms were beet red. I drove 35 mph even though the speed limit was 55 mph. The truck drivers honked at me as they passed me. That made me even more nervous. Other drivers glared and yelled at me as they sped around my car."

I took a sip of coffee and said, "An hour or more later, I saw a restaurant sign and pulled off the freeway into the truck stop. It felt as if I still had the steering wheel in my cramped hands."

Teresa said, "That was a terrible experience."

"It was a relief to be off the freeway. I woke Marcus, who, thank goodness, felt much better. He drove the rest of the way home."

"We walked into the bright restaurant for a casual lunch. As I ate, I realized that the dark feeling was gone. I could hardly believe it! One fear destroyed the other. I was tired, yet I felt normal. I felt like myself again."

"Well, that's good," said Teresa.

"That night I slept like a log. I knew that as much as I loved my mother, I could not join her in her despair without destroying myself. I had to detach from her. My mother became another person's mother until I could deal with her. I became kinder and more loving to her through this dissociation. Eventually I accepted her as my mother and loved her as she was - not as I wished her to be. From her, I learned compassion, acceptance, and self-preservation. She was my spiritual teacher in this lifetime."

"Next time we meet, I want to interview you." I said this very quickly as I knew this would not be easy for Teresa to do because she was very secretive about her personal life.

She retorted, "You asked me before. I don't know if I want to be interviewed!"

Maybe it was a good thing that I could not see her eyes through her thick blonde bangs.

"Think about it," I said gently. "It would be

good to share, be open to help others. After all, we are asking these women to do the same."

She shrugged her shoulders, turned abruptly, and before she walked out the front door she looked back and said, "I'll give this some thought."

At our next visit sitting outside at the patio table, I asked, "Where can we find women to interview, women that are open and will share their life story with us?"

Teresa

"Okay," Teresa said out of the blue, "You can interview me." The sun brightened her delicate features and white gold hair. I stared at her for a second, startled that she had agreed to be interviewed.

I asked her before she changed her mind, "What do you want to share? What was your mother like?"

"Who knows; she was into herself. She would never have gotten the best mother award. She lacked responsibility, yet she was successful in her career. She went to college when women didn't do this. She was bad tempered and showed little affection towards me. My mother walked out on me."

A few ducks squawked on the lake; a breeze stirred the napkins on the glass tabletop.

"How do you feel about that?"

"I think I'm guarded," she replied without hesitation, "afraid he is going to leave me." I knew *he* was her husband.

"What advice would you give to others?"

"Assert your rights, as a female. I feel there is a tendency for others to abuse our rights because we are still second-class citizens. We need to stand up for ourselves. I feel we lack credibility. I do what I want to do! I don't like anyone telling me what I can or can't do! I know what's best for me."

She immediately left without saying another word. I intuitively knew that there was more Teresa was not choosing to talk about regarding her mother. However, I also knew that was all she was going to share. This was a very big step for her to share this much with me – or anyone.

12
there is a power that draws us together

S everal days later Teresa met up with Olivia, the retired professor, on her walk around The Lakes. Olivia suggested we interview Donna, a Native American, a lobbyist, political activist, historian and storyteller. She gave her Donna's phone number. And so, we moved forward on our quest to interview ordinary, yet extraordinary women. Synchronicity was working for us.

I picked Teresa up at her house and started on our way to Donna's house. I said, "I've been thinking about our interviews. I think we should continue to ask what their mothers were like or just ask what they wish to share. Our interviews will probably last an hour or so.

Donna

Teresa said, "I like this idea. I would like to know what they have learned. We're not writing their biographies, just an important snippet of their wisdom. They can relate any area of their life they think is significant. I can't wait to meet Donna.

Olivia thinks she is a remarkable woman."

A tall Native American woman opened the door and greeted us. We followed her into the small cozy living room. She moved wearily and sunk her ample form into a big oversized chair next to the door. She sighed deeply and folded her hands.

Her large dark eyes held deep anguish as she said, "I just arrived home from Washington D. C. where I was a spokesperson against the bill that would close the Phoenix Indian School. This school has provided high school education and vocational training for over twenty Indian tribes. The bill was ratified. The school will be closed."

"At times like this to regain my strength, I remember my deceased mother, Martha."

She closed her eyes and began to chant. The soft chanting continued for some time. I watched Teresa slide onto the floor and sit cross legged on the carpet. I did the same. I felt my eyelids grow heavy, so I shut them. The chanting took me out of the living room to an ancient campfire. I saw the flickering flames of the fire dancing before me.

Donna spoke in a low guttural tone, "When my mother was a child, her parents died of influenza. With no one to care for her, she was placed in an orphanage in Oklahoma. She was expected to follow their strict religious discipline and relinquish her Indian culture and religious beliefs. Release your story telling, she was threatened, and don't talk about the animals speaking to you. Mother renounced her Indian beliefs and learned English to survive."

"She was uprooted once again when her uncle

came for her. Intuitively she knew that this move would not be good for her. Her suspicion became a reality when she found out that her uncle abused his wife and was *very* abusive to his children. If the children were not quick enough in their chores, they would be beaten. She became a child slave."

"On a bitter cold night, beaten with a bat, mother was thrown outside. Bleeding, hungry, her clothes torn, she lay crying, begging for an answer. 'Why must I suffer?' she asked the stars, as she shivered in her thin dress. 'I'm only a child!' she cried to the cold wind. Two large furry dogs came, and snuggled down beside her, comforted and warmed her throughout the cold night. She fell asleep."

"At dawn she awoke and trudged toward school. Traveling a short distance, she saw steam coming from a tin can on the snow-filled ground ahead of her. Could it be? Yes, she smelled the wonderful aroma of meat and beans. She raced toward the can, and as she lifted it, she felt the heat. She took a scoop of food with her fingers. She thought she heard a rustle and looked behind her. She caught a glimpse of the foreigner, a white man. He was one of the few visitors that would visit the family and talk with her in English. This kindness immediately warmed and empowered her spirit towards other races, all people."

Donna's voice grew louder as she brought our awareness back to her living room. "My mother's benevolent philosophy began from his kindness, and the knowledge that no one is ever alone - that there is a powerful energy – that draws all people together. Don't ever feel that you're alone in this world; there is a spiritual strength, and that strength comes from you. There are different spiritual levels. Some advance, others don't and can be harmful and destructive. If you give your energy to these negative people, it robs you of human kindness."

"Thank you," Teresa stood up and gathered her things.

"We appreciate your sharing your mother's story with us," I said as I picked up my handbag and my written notes.

After we left, we felt energized; we decided to stop somewhere and savor this incredible experience. We went to a local coffee shop to hold onto this moment for as long as we could.

Now that we interviewed Donna, I was excited to interview other extraordinary women, I decided to call Helene, my former boss. I asked her if I could interview her for the book. She consented to meet me for a quick lunch at a restaurant in downtown Phoenix close to her office. Teresa could not make the interview because she needed to study for a test.

Helene

It was great to see Helene again. She looked like the successful attorney she was, with her frizzy short blonde hair, her tailored suit and her thin rimless glasses. We sat at a table in the small restaurant and ordered lunch.

I teased, "I probably should have stopped and brought you a bagel."

She smiled and said, "I do miss our morning

treat."

Fumbling in my handbag, I found my pen and note pad and asked, "What was your mother like?"

"My beautiful mother," she answered, "loved my sister. She had no interest in me. I admired my father as he encouraged me to be whatever I wanted to be. I was a competitive swimmer. I attended Kent State during the riots. Those were dark days."

"Yes. I remember seeing the riots on TV. Horrible!"

Helene said, "My role model was an English instructor who ignited a *fire* in me for grammar and literature. I read Hermann Hesse's *Demian*, which touched my soul. Always competitive, I dared myself to pursue a career in law. True success is being okay with yourself."

Helene fingered her Minnie Mouse gold charm on her necklace. "I wear this, so I'll remember not to take myself too seriously." She glanced at her watch, "Sorry, I've a meeting. Great seeing you."

I said, "Thanks for taking time out of your busy schedule to meet with me." I hugged her tightly.

Before I drove away, I remembered her tactfulness as she handled the delicate situation between Kate and me. She is a very wise woman and a strong leader.

Dr. Tamara

At my office visit, I asked my gynecologist, Dr. Tamara, for an interview. She agreed, checked her schedule and agreed to meet next Tuesday.

On Tuesday, I drove to Dr. Tamara's. A nurse guided me to her well-designed office. She was ready and motioned for me to sit in one of the two upholstered chairs in front of her desk. I looked at the tall Romanian woman and noticed her dark hair had strands of grey. Her intelligent hazel eyes greeted me warmly.

"Thank you for this interview," I said. "What would you like to share to help other women?"

She said, "I was forty years old and knew nothing was ever going to be the same! I chose to leave my medical practice, my comfortable home in Bucharest, with family, my husband and our eleven-year-old daughter and move to New York City. I wanted to be an American doctor."

"So many obstacles to conquer, I wasn't young, I knew three words of English - hello, goodbye and beautiful, and more importantly, *I was a woman*. Few women were being considered for residencies at the time."

"I forwarded eighty letters to different hospitals - eighty! I was rejected eighty times. I wanted to forget it - give it up - return home. I had to fight this inner negative dialogue with every ounce of determination in me."

"Eventually I was accepted for a residency at Queens Hospital in New York City; however, it was by sheer default. The chosen candidate reneged at the last minute. The hospital administrators needed to fill this vacancy immediately, and I was available. I paid my dues by working long, hard hours. Many times, I thought I wasn't going to make it. I focused on my goal: to become an American doctor."

Dr. Tamara's intelligent eyes locked mine as she said, "If you begin a plan that you truly want to make happen, you can, and if you're willing to pay the price, success can be yours. I thank my parents for guiding me in the right direction. With them my becoming a doctor was a given. It was never 'if,' it was - when you become a doctor."

"Thank you for sharing your journey." I left her office knowing that no matter how difficult it may be, I, too will continue to interview the women and complete this book. This was my plan.

13

things fall in place if they are meant to

Meanwhile, Jerod and I were not on the same page with anything. This had been going on for over three months. He was away quite a bit because of his multi-level business he was currently enraptured with. I felt alone, abandoned.

When we were together, he was sullen and uncommunicative. He always had this tendency to withdraw into a shell like a turtle and not communicate. He told me that this stemmed from issues with his domineering mother. I was at the point that I could not go through another dinner of painful silence. I felt his lack of communication and caring tear at our three-year relationship.

Jerod inherited land during our renovation of the Lake house that he used to purchase a stately five-bedroom brick house in Mesa, Arizona. He rented the Mesa house to a family with six children. From the onset, I intuitively felt uneasy around the father. I urged him not to lease to him.

He ignored my pleadings and let them move into the property without the security deposit or the last month's rent. The father paid part of the first month's rent and insisted that the rest was on the way. However, he never paid Jerod any of the money he owned him.

Jerod had to evict them, which took several months. They were living there *free*. When the father received the subpoena, he became livid and threatened not only Jerod, but his own family as well. How sad! He was unstable and eventually placed in a mental facility.

After the family moved out, Jerod wanted us to move into the vacant five-bedroom Mesa house. Maybe this was someone's dream home, but it was not mine.

I said adamantly, "I don't think we should move into this Mesa house. Every time, I enter it, I feel this dark, oppressive energy encircle me – probably residue left from this man and his unfortunate family that lived in the house."

Jerod replied, "Once we're in the house, I'm sure you'll be okay. I don't feel this dark energy."

"No, I don't think I'll be okay. Trust me, the dark energy is there. This move will not be good for our relationship."

He chose not to answer me. We sold the Lakes house we both loved. We moved into the Mesa house as two strangers. I could feel the negative energy in every room. I smudged the house with incense; yet, the negativity clung like thick soot.

Teresa called a few days after the move. "A group of women from Tempe Lakes are going on a fun bus trip to Sedona in northern Arizona on Sunday. I just signed up to go with them. If you want to go, I can add you to my reservation."

"Yes, count me in," I said, eager at the chance to leave my present situation, even for one day. "You know if I can get a job in Sedona, I'll move there. Jerod and I both know our relationship is over. I need to move on – out of our relationship and this dark house. I've been to Sedona once and loved it. I remember the beautiful red rock formations, the cool fresh air, and small-town atmosphere. I felt drawn there. Maybe this is my destiny, where I need to be."

Teresa replied, "You have been unhappy for a while now. Maybe change would be good for you."

On Sunday, at 7:00 am, we stood In line with the other Lakes women and their friends to board the bus to Sedona.

About an hour out, the bus driver stopped at a small truck stop. We walked off the bus into the bright sunshine. I felt open to adventure, newness. I felt freer than I had in a long, long time.

We arrived in Sedona an hour later. The bus pulled into the parking lot at Tlaquepaque, a Mexican inspired shopping center, just as the shops were opening. As we exited the bus, we were handed a store directory. I glanced through it and pointed to two shops that I wanted to check out. One was a gift shop, and the other was an upscale dress shop. We walked towards the gift shop.

"I'm going to ask if they are accepting applications. My resume is in my handbag just in case." I quivered inside as I said this.

As we walked along the beautiful flowered pathway I said, "It says in the directory that the builder brought over original Mexican artifacts, wood, and tiles from a small village in Cuernavaca, Mexico to build this mall."

We found the gift shop and entered through

the open doorway. I immediately embraced the creative ambience: the handcrafted wood and glass cases filled with original jewelry, all kinds of leather bags, belts and unusual handmade items were on display. I walked to the center case and peered through the glass at beautiful diamond and gemstone rings, silver and gold bracelets and earrings. Another collection of designer jewelry had been carefully placed on top of coins in a small one-of-a-kind showcase.

"Welcome." An earthy woman with short blonde hair and big blue eyes smiled at me. She wore a white embroidered blouse, a long casual black skirt and cowboy boots. She had a glow about her. She was pinning unusual gemstone earrings on colorful cards onto a display wall.

"Thank you. I really like your shop." I took a deep breath, "Are you accepting applications?"

She looked at me and replied, "Yes, we are. My name is Elizabeth. I'm the manager." She walked behind the large counter and found an application and handed it to me.

I took the application and said, "I've a resume," and gave it to her. "I presently live in Mesa, Arizona, however, I definitely plan on moving here." I heard the words fly out of my mouth to confirm the fact that I was moving to Sedona.

"I'll see that the owner gets both the application and your resume," she assured me.

"Thank you," I replied excitedly. "I look forward to hearing from her."

After we left the store, I said to Teresa, "I've such good vibes about that place. I hope they call me."

We went into the upscale dress shop which was a few shops away. I really liked their clothing. They were *not* hiring. My fate was in the hands of the owner of the gift shop.

After lunch, we walked up and down tiled steps and narrow corridors and found hidden galleries, and more unique shops. We sat down on a carved wooden bench to rest.

"You're brave to even think about moving to Sedona. You don't know a soul here."

I answered, "I hope I get the job. You can come visit me, and we could continue to work on the book."

"That would be fun. I'll come for a visit. You can continue with the book. I've too many things going on. Good luck with it."

I replied, "Thanks. Are you sure?"

"Positive."

I could see that some of the ladies were heading back to the parking lot. "I think it's time to get back to the bus."

The next morning, I received a call from Karen, the owner of the gift shop. She wanted to meet me in person and set up an appointment on Tuesday at noon at her shop in Sedona. I accepted and then suddenly – I felt overwhelmed because everything was happening so quickly.

What was I doing? I held myself tightly. I was leaving our declining relationship. That's what I was doing! Now I need to tell Jerod. I sighed deeply. I knew it was over. I just could not deal with his silent treatment anymore. It was too hard not to be able to discuss things, to have his thick wall shut me out. His avoidance was too powerful for me to combat.

After I calmed myself down, I walked into the other room and said, "That phone call was from the owner of a shop in Sedona. I applied for a job while I was there yesterday, and she wants to meet me tomorrow. Will you watch Teddy?" Teddy was our three-year-old cocker poodle mix dog. "I need to leave early and will be back late afternoon."

He looked at me for a long time and said, "Okay." He sulked for the rest of the day.

I awoke early and drove the two and a half hours into Sedona. I sighed deeply as the red, orange, and purple majestic mountains came into view. I parked in the parking lot at Tlaquepaque and went to a restaurant on the premises. I sipped coffee until it was time to meet Karen.

The owner of the store was standing at the jewelry counter and when she saw me, she walked forward to greet me. She looked to be in her 50's, with reddish spiked hair, designer glasses and an intimidating gaze. She extended her strong hand to me. We walked outside and sat on one of the stone benches in the little courtyard adjacent to the shop.

"I usually don't like to hire anyone that doesn't live in the area," she said firmly.

I assured her, "I'm definitely moving to Sedona whether I get this job or not," surprised again by my own words.

We talked for a while and then she said, "Thank you, I've several others to interview before I make my decision. I'll get back to you."

I thanked her and walked back to my car. What will be, will be. I turned it over to the higher powers.

The next afternoon the phone rang, and it was Karen, "I want to offer you the job! Can you start next Tuesday?" I went to answer and instead sobbed into the phone. I realized at that moment: my relationship was over. "You need to think about this," she cautioned. "Call me back tomorrow." I hung up the phone and continued to weep. Then I stopped. I could not stay with Jerod; it was time to go on. What was more painful: the leaving or the staying? At least with the leaving, we could both heal and go on with our lives.

Jerod came into the room and asked, "What is going on?"

"I was offered the job in Sedona. I'm to start work next Tuesday. I hope that regardless, of what happens in our lives that we'll remain friends. Remember that psychic told me that we were powerful leaders and friends in an Aztec lifetime." His tall frame turned slowly and left the room.

Early the next morning, I called Karen and said, "I'm fine. I just ended a relationship. I definitely want the job!"

She said, "Okay, I understand. I'll see you next week."

Jerod consented to take care of Teddy, while I went back to Sedona to look for a place to live. I could not believe how quickly things fall into place if they are meant to.

When I arrived in Sedona, I looked at my watch. It was 9:15 am. I drove past the shopping mall and saw a big wooden sign, *The Flowers Café*. I parked and walked up the wood steps to the patio. I bought a local newspaper and browsed through the rental ads. Nothing there. I didn't know where to start to find a place to live. I silently asked my inner guide, Samantha, for direction. After breakfast, I drove a short distance. I felt drawn to a real estate office and parked my car.

"Hello." A well-dressed middle-aged woman called out as she came out of her office. "How can I help you?"

"I'm looking for a newer condo to rent not far from Tlaquepaque ASAP – with two bedrooms, one or two bathrooms. I was just hired to work in the gift store there. I presently live in Mesa, just south of Phoenix. I hope you can help me." I suddenly felt alone and lost. Doubt was cracking its heavy whip inside my head loudly.

She smiled broadly, "My name is Jane. Yes, I think there are several properties that you would like. I need to check on their availability."

"Please wait here," she motioned to one of the upholstered chairs, "while I look up some listings on my computer and make some calls."

Seated in the comfortable chair, I kept the inner worrisome dialogue going, was I wasting my time; would this be in vain? I didn't want to spend the night in Sedona and days viewing places. Then I stopped. I wondered what symbol I should use to divert this negativity. I imagined a colorful rainbow. Not only did it stop the bothersome chatter, it created a peaceful beautiful place inside me.

Jane returned to the foyer. "Come with me. There are a few condos I want to show you."

While she drove she said, "I found several places that are newer that I think you might like.

But, there is nothing in your price range that is newer and close to town. Besides, I know you'll enjoy the beautiful scenic drive to and from work. The area I want to show you is called The Village of Oak Creek, which is not near Oak Creek Canyon. People often get confused with the similar names. You drove past The Village of Oak Creek on your way into town."

Glancing out the window, I studied the beautiful shapes of the red rocks. Some of rock formations looked human, some like animals. I thought they are reminding me about something, although I was not sure what it was. I thought about my desire to be a writer. I would love to have something I wrote published. Would magical Sedona grant me this wish?

Jane turned off the highway into a complex of about thirty condos. They looked charming: newly built single-level condos with red tiled roofs surrounded by desert landscaping. I could feel my heart skip a beat. She pulled into a guest parking space. We walked the short distance to a condo. As she knocked on the front door, she whispered to me, "The tenant is here."

A friendly dark-haired woman answered the door. "Please come in, my name is Alice. Thank you for calling to let me know you were showing the condo. I'm just finishing my travel magazine to take to the printer. Please look around. Don't mind the boxes because I'm moving." Her desk was covered with all sorts of printed material. I walked around the condo. It didn't feel right for me.

"Why are you leaving," I asked, for I felt a strong kinship with this stranger.

"Oh, I own this travel magazine, and I'm not making enough money to continue to keep it."

The words flew out, "Alice, stay, I feel it will work out for you. Your place doesn't feel right for me. I just feel it's right for you."

She seemed to contemplate my words.

"Jane, I really like this complex. Are there any other places available for rent?"

"Yes. As a matter of fact, there is one right across the way. The builder's wife bought it for an investment. I can show it to you."

As Jane and I walked out the door, I said to the tenant, "Think about staying as I would love to be your neighbor." There was something I liked about this spunky woman.

We walked the short distance across the concrete driveway to the other unit. Jane entered her code on the lockbox. We walked into the vacant condo and immediately I felt a sigh of relief. I just knew – it was perfect! I breathed in the condo's serene energy.

I walked through the two bedrooms and two bathrooms, all were a good size. It was immaculate.

I stopped and said, "I didn't see a washer or dryer anywhere."

"No. There is a laundromat in town."

Oh well. I thought to myself, I need to make this work.

Sliding the patio glass door open, I was surprised how close the patio was to the red rock mountain's base. I stood outside for a moment and breathed in the fresh air.

When I walked back into the living room, I said

to Jane, "This is it! I really like this place."

We were walking out the door, when I asked, "What mountain is next to the condo?"

"Courthouse Butte."

We drove back to her office. I signed the paperwork and gave her a check for first month's rent and a small pet deposit.

"Do you need a mover? I know a good reliable one," she asked as she handed me the condo keys.

"Yes, I do. That would be great."

I called the movers from her office, and yes, they could pick up my furniture and other belongings from Mesa on Friday. It was a relief because it was such short notice.

"Jane, I'm so grateful to have found you; thank you for all your help! I guess Sedona wants my energy here." I left her office feeling very optimistic. Once outside, I stopped and silently thanked Sedona, my new home.

On the long drive back to Mesa, I thought how lucky that everything had fallen into place. I was excited at the thought of living in Sedona. I felt drawn to this sacred place – to her red healing womb, energy vortexes, Native American ruins and like-minded New Age community. I've heard some people nickname the New Age Sedona community as – 'woo-woo.' I guess I'm a 'woo–woo' as well.

Jerod took the news stoically when he heard I would leave on Friday. He avoided my eyes, his posture bent as he said, "I'm going away until after you move out. You have my cell phone number in case you need me."

As much as I knew the relationship had ended,

needed to end, I didn't want him to suffer. I wanted our friendship to continue. He went into the other room and gathered his clothes into a suitcase.

"Keep Teddy because I don't know where I'm going."

I hugged Jerod briefly. "Okay, keep in touch," I said before he hurried out the door.

I looked at Teddy. I wondered if he knew. I know he loves us both. I picked him up and held him tightly. "Don't worry," I said, "you're going with me." He tilted his little furry white head.

14

negativity creates negativity

After Jerod left, I began to pack and fill boxes. I placed items I thought I would need right away into my car. The gloomy house felt as negative as usual. It became dark before I remembered the patio furniture outside and decided to bring the small patio table and two chairs inside the house. I thought I probably need to clean them off before I brought them inside.

The air was stifling, a typical summer night in the Arizona desert. It was hard to see in the dark. The outside yellow light bulb shed very little light. I set the cleaning supplies on the patio table and picked up the patio chair – "OW! – something bit my middle left finger. I felt the sting and dropped the chair onto the cement patio. I looked on the ground around the chair. Nothing there. I wondered what could have bit me. My finger was throbbing. I rushed inside the house and closed the glass sliding door. I looked at my swollen finger and called the operator for the Poison Control Center number.

A kind man answered the phone at the center. I explained what happened. He said, "What you're describing sounds like you were bit by a black widow spider. You need to go to the hospital and get a Tetanus shot immediately."

"Are you sure it isn't a regular spider."

"Yes, I'm positive."

I hung up the phone. Now what do I do? I had no idea where the nearest hospital was, nor did I know anyone in Mesa. Jerod was a paramedic at one time; maybe he could tell me where the nearest hospital is or what I should do. I dialed his cell and explained to him what happened.

He said, "I'm in Las Vegas. You need to ice your finger. I'll call my assistant, Tera, as she lives nearby and have her call you." Strange I never knew he had an assistant. Oh, Jerod and his secrets – especially lately.

I placed ice in a plastic bag and covered the bag with a paper towel and held it on my swollen finger. Tera called and told me not to worry that she would be at the house within ten minutes.

After Tera arrived she said, "I know exactly where the hospital is. It's not far." I immediately liked her; she had an open honest energy about her.

"Thank you so much for getting here so quickly." I showed her my swollen finger. I followed her to her truck and settled into the passenger seat. She drove to the hospital, which was about five minutes away. By now, not only was my finger swollen, the swelling had progressed to my hand.

"Great! I'm going to die before I get to Sedona," I worried to myself.

The doctor was kind and informed me I wasn't going to die. He gave me a Tetanus shot. Now I hurt in my right upper arm as well as my left middle finger. Tera drove me back to the house. I thanked her profusely and offered to pay her gas. She would not hear of it.

"I hope everything works out for you," she said.

"Thanks again, remember you and your daughter can come visit me anytime." She had shared with me that her daughter was asthmatic and had all sorts of allergies and the fresh Sedona air seemed to help her.

Once inside the house, I looked around at the packing mess. The movers would arrive tomorrow. I tried to pack as best as I could with my one hand. Thank goodness I'm right-handed. My throbbing left hand, I held up in the air! "Just keep going," I mumbled and packed another box with my right hand. I kept icing my swollen hand.

The mover called the next morning and when I explained what happened, he said, "You know it would be easier for us to come on Saturday. We have another load we could pick up. Would that work for you?" I could not believe he was so nice. What a special man– to be so accommodating.

"Thank you. Yes, I really can use this extra day."

With the extra day in tow, I managed to complete the packing one handed. The swelling had progressed to my elbow. I slept very little that night because I kept icing my hand. The movers arrived before 10:00 am and within a few hours had their truck loaded with my stuff. They had another pickup and would meet me at the Sedona condo around 4:00 o'clock.

After the big van left, I gathered my things, put a leash on Teddy, and left the garage remote and a note for Jerod on the counter. I waved and said, "Farewell" to this eerie house and locked the front door and put the house key under the mat. I was so relieved to be out of there.

I thought the black widow's bite was either from the negative energy in the house or the stress of leaving the relationship. I realized it was probably a little of both. Again, I need to let go of negativity and stress for it can be harmful.

My arm ached as I carried a big overflowing shopping bag, my full handbag and Teddy 's leash to the car. When I opened the car door awkwardly with my swollen hand, the door slammed shut, grabbing the leash – jerking Teddy's head as he was about to jump into the car.

"No!" I screamed. I quickly opened the car door and watched the leash fall to the ground. I picked up Teddy and checked him. I took off his leash. I felt better when I saw him jump into the car and lay down on the front seat. He could have broken his neck. I asked myself, why did this happen? Was this the dark house's last hurrah?

Once inside the car, I stroked Teddy's white furry head. As I pulled away, I started to cry, sob! Why is it so hard to leave a relationship? I knew this was the best- for both of us. I wiped my eyes and tried to keep my painful arm up as I drove towards Sedona.

I finally pulled into the condo's carport. I sighed deeply, opened the driver's side door, and slid out. The sweet air and flawless blue sky set against the red rocks was soulful. I took a deep breath as it felt like I was coming home. I opened the passenger door. Teddy bolted out and waited impatiently while I unlocked the front door. I walked into the living room and felt the quiet, peaceful atmosphere. I continued into each room, Teddy at my heels, checking everything out in his own way.

I went back to the car and brought more boxes inside despite my aching arm. I brought in my electric coffee pot, coffee and a carton of milk. As the wonderful coffee aroma drifted through the kitchen into the condo, I toasted a bagel in the toaster oven thankful that I had remembered to bring it with me. I filled Teddy's water bowl and his food bowl with dog bones and placed them on the kitchen tiles. I shared a half of my toasted bagel with him; he loves bagels. His tail kept wagging.

Going over to the patio door, I unlocked the latch, moved the sliding door over and felt a soft breeze amid the clean air. Teddy followed me out onto the small patio. I stared at the mountain, seeing her beautiful red body. I noticed that the three-foot black iron patio fence had open spaces, big enough for Teddy to squeeze through. I turned to Teddy. "I need to enclose this little area, so you don't get out," and made a mental note.

I breathed deeply and felt grateful for this tranquil place.

The mover called from the road. They would arrive in a half hour. After they arrived, the chaos kicked in. The two strong men were very efficient. "We grew up here and loved it," said Larry, one of the movers.

The other man, Dave, said, "Me too, I grew up here and loved it. You'll probably see us around town because we move most of the people here."

They were speedy and before long, they were done and gone.

Now my work began. I struggled to make my bed one handed, managed to get the sheets over the mattress, the pillowcases over the pillows, and fold the denim comforter over the end of the bed. I was happy that I remembered to bring these items for as soon as I completed the task, I lay down to take a nap. Teddy jumped up on the bed and laid his furry body next to mine. After we rested, I started unpacking as best I could.

My new neighbor, Alice, stopped by. "Welcome, I brought you some homemade banana bread. I hope you like it. I won't stay long. I just wanted to let you know that I decided to stay."

"Great, I'm so glad. The banana bread smells wonderful. How about going to breakfast Monday morning?"

"Okay," she answered, "that sounds good. Let me know if you need anything. Happy moving," she grimaced as she made her way out of the clutter. I laughed. Yes, moving is moving. I continued to unpack.

That night I slept well, even though my pillowcase was damp from tears when I awoke. I knew I was still sad and needed to let my emotions surface to heal.

After brushing my teeth, I heard Teddy. Something was wrong with him. He was barking and yelping. My sweet lovable guy was growling like a tiger. I got dressed, as fast as I could, and called a vet I found in the phonebook. The receptionist told me to bring him right in. I wrote down the directions hoping I could find the place.

Teddy followed me to the car and jumped in. I was going to pick him up, however, he would not let me. I drove the short distance to the animal clinic.

The vet examined Teddy and asked, "What happened?"

"I'm not sure. We moved here yesterday, and he got up this morning barking and carrying on like he was in pain."

"He sprained his neck. I injected him with a tranquilizer to help him with the pain until he heals. He'll be unsteady for the rest of the day."

"Thanks for taking him so quickly. Maybe I need the tranquilizer after the move," I teased.

On the drive back, I remembered the car door slamming shut: Teddy must have sprained his neck when the leash caught in the door.

The tranquilizer worked quickly, and before long Teddy didn't know where he was. He was weaving around the kitchen bumping into the cabinets like a drunken sailor. He finally settled down and went to sleep. I was glad because I was becoming concerned he would hurt himself.

Back I went to unpack another box. Every now and then, I would wipe a stray tear to remind me that the relationship was over. As difficult as it was, I needed to change my thoughts. I focused on my new home; new job, and breakfast with Alice.

In the morning, Teddy woke up more like his old self. I took him for a walk around the complex and saw Alice coming towards us. She had a broad smile and a twinkle in her deep dark eyes.

"Are you ready to go to breakfast?"

"Yes, as soon as I put Teddy back in the condo,

we can go. I'll drive because I want to get to know the area."

Alice said, "Let's go to Tlaquepaque, they have a new breakfast place there that's pretty good. I might order their blueberry pancakes. I ate them the last time I was there and enjoyed them."

"Perfect! That is exactly where I wanted to go today. I wanted to see how long it will take me to get to work." I felt myself smile.

As I drove, Alice kept track of the time for me and estimated the drive would be about seventeen minutes, depending upon traffic. "There are only two traffic lights in Sedona, so you can safely judge the time. Our population is about 11,000. The weekends bring tourists, so you may have to adjust your time accordingly."

"Good to know. How is your magazine doing? One day I want to write something and have it published. Who knows, maybe I can publish something in your magazine?"

"The magazine seems to be holding its own. I just received several big ads. I'll keep you in mind, if I need an article written. Right now, I've more than enough free-lance writers."

After breakfast, we surveyed the area and found a little store that sold crystals, gemstones and inspirational books.

She said, "I really like candles. I think I'll get a lavender one." She returned with the candle.

"I'm going to get these moonstone earrings as moonstone is a stone for new beginnings, inner growth and strength. I felt drawn to get this Rider Tarot deck as well. I've always wanted to learn tarot. Maybe this deck will teach me. I can't wait to play with it."

We walked on the cobble-stoned walkways through arched entryways, so I could become more familiar with the shopping center.

I said, "Look, how beautiful it is back here. I didn't know that Oak Creek ran through part of the property.

Alice said, "Neither did I. You found a beautiful place to work. I read somewhere that Tlaquepaque means best of everything."

Now feeling confident that I could find the store tomorrow, I drove us back to the condos. Alice pointed at some of the incredible life forms that were carved into the red rocks.

After I parked my car she said, "I've work to do for my magazine. Let's get together for breakfast again. I enjoyed this."

"So, did I. I'll call you after I get my schedule."

15
accept healing and transformation

Tuesday I got up with the sun because I felt ready to begin my new job. Teddy and I walked around the complex. I didn't have to be at work until 9:45am, so I stopped at a patio restaurant not far from Tlaquepaque.

"Sit wherever you like." I looked up at the tall earthy woman with gray shoulder length hair. She seemed like a wise owl with a no-nonsense manner. I figured that she was the owner. I sat outside on the open patio. A pleasant waitress took my order of coffee and a bran muffin.

Later after I became a regular, I would ask the server, "Lynn, which muffin is the freshest of the oldest?" She smirked because the owner was very frugal, and didn't throw away day-old, or, I'm sorry to say, sometimes longer than day old muffins.

After breakfast, I parked in the lot adjacent to the mall where the employees parked. I pulled my car into an open spot on the rough terrain and made my way across the deserted parking lot to a flowered path that led to the shops. I smelled the pungent brightly colored flowers tucked into their terra cotta pots, savored the quaint Mexican atmosphere and appreciated the builder's attention to detail as he created this picturesque postcard.

The door was locked so I tapped the window, and Elizabeth opened the thick wood door. As I entered the little shop, my new home, I smiled, I embraced the charm of this creative atmosphere from the unique designed earrings to the simple carved gourds, even to the handcrafted display cases.

"Good morning, "I said cheerily to Elizabeth. She smiled back at me. She wore a long denim skirt, a turquoise blouse and brown cowboy boots. Her large dangling earrings filled with different colored gemstones jingled as she walked over to me. Her striking features, deep searching baby blue eyes emitted a spiritual knowing; her calmness relaxed me.

She said, "I like your moonstone earrings. I want to show you around." She picked up an etched gourd and handed it to me. I felt the smooth and etched textures.

"This handcrafted gourd has information about this artist and his pieces," she said as she handed me his brochure.

She walked through the shop and told stories about the different artisans, so I could relate this information to the customers. She gave me information on each of them. She must have seen the distant look on my face.

"No worries – I'll be training you over the next couple of weeks. You'll never remember all this in one day." She handed me several sheets. "Read these and the brochures when you can."

Another employee arrived. Elizabeth said,

"This is Vicki. She works four days like you do." Vicki shook my hand. She had long blonde hair that was tied back in a ponytail. She was younger and shorter than me. I noticed a mischievous sparkle in her topaz eyes.

"Hi, glad you're here. I moved here from Indiana, right after I graduated college about a year ago. We have another person that works here as well. She is a high school student and works on Saturday and Sunday."

"Thanks, I'm excited to be here. There is so much to learn. Do we get a lunch break?" I looked at Elizabeth and Vicki.

"No," replied Vicki, "We don't take lunch breaks. We usually get guacamole and chips from the Mexican restaurant which is close by."

I figured 'when in Rome, do as the Romans do,' and that became my lunch as well. Good thing I stopped for a muffin and coffee before I came into work today. As the day progressed I noticed that I wasn't feeling well. I seemed unusually tired and out of breath most of the day. I could not wait to drag myself home. What is going on? I usually have an abundance of energy. I wondered.

Alice, my neighbor and I went to breakfast on Thursday, my day off. She wanted to go to a little restaurant she liked that was not far from our complex. The small place was very cozy, very clean, and very gingham.

A tall, thin-haired gentleman, I guessed one of their regular customers, came around the restaurant with a coffee pot. He was serving himself and decided to serve everyone else in the small room. When he came over to our table, I asked, much to my amazement, "Do you know a doctor?"

"Yes," he replied, "Dr. Paul Jamison," as he filled our cups with coffee. He jotted the doctor's name and phone number as well as his name on a piece of paper and handed it to me.

He said, "I went to him because I was ill. I called for an appointment and his receptionist told me they didn't have one available until the following week. I told her that I would be 'dead' by then. They managed to get me in that day. When Dr. Jamison examined me, he sent me immediately to the hospital. I had double pneumonia. He saved my life!"

"Thank you," I said, "I'll definitely call him."

After he left the table, I said to Alice, "Things certainly manifest quickly here. Ask for help and here it is! I've had low energy since I moved here. Maybe it's the altitude. I read somewhere that we are 4,500 ft. above sea level."

"Yes, some people have a hard time adjusting to this altitude," she replied.

Back at the condo I called and made the appointment.

The following Thursday I walked into the small lobby at the doctor's office and was greeted by a friendly female assistant. She ushered me into one of the Dr. Jamison's waiting rooms. I sat down in a chair in the middle of the room. What an odd patient room – just a chair.

An interesting man dressed in casual clothes with shoulder length dark hair came into the room, introduced himself and asked, "What brings you in today?"

"I'm not feeling well. I've been tired and dizzy since I moved here last week."

"Please stand. Let me see if I can detect anything," he said as he proceeded to scan my fully clothed body with his penetrating dark eyes. I could feel the love vibration glide through my body. It was as if I was being scanned through an MRI machine – only this love energy felt peaceful and comforting.

"Well," he said, "Your symptoms could be from high altitude because it does affect some people until they adjust to it. I did see some of your lower chakras are out of balance. I see something going on in your right breast. I'm going to recommend colonics; this should clear this up and give you more energy."

I spoke up! "What about the right breast?" suddenly alarmed that something bad was going on in my body.

"The colonics should clear this up as well. I'll see you again once you have completed the colonics."

Unbelievable that he could get all this information about my physical body through his unorthodox method. It was hard for me to fathom, however, I intuitively knew that he was remarkably gifted.

Before I left the office, I scheduled the colonics on my next day off, even though I had no clue what colonics were. I would read the brochure the nurse gave me about this procedure. Before I left the office, I stopped and looked at the doctor's plaque on the wall and saw that he had graduated from Harvard Medical School. He had a traditional education, and now he is an energy doctor. I thought I was seeing a traditional doctor - only in Sedona!

The colonics was done using a tube that was inserted into my rectum to cleanse and flush water through my intestines. After the initial session, I was not uncomfortable with this procedure. The colonics seemed to work as I was beginning to feel better and have more energy. I would need several of these. I was told by the technician that it would probably be a month to several months before I felt completely back to normal.

In the meantime, I thought I was *in love* with Dr. Jamison, however, when I went back for my checkup, I realized that while he was a very attractive man, I had no romantic feelings for him. I wondered how many of his patients felt this way as they connected with his powerful diagnostic technique - *love energy*. He again scanned my body and said, "Your chakras are back in balance."

Back at work, I glanced at myself in the mirror and saw that my thick short hair was too long and unruly and really needed to be cut. I asked one of our customers where she got her hair styled. I liked her haircut. She gave me Hannah's information. I called and booked an appointment.

Hannah's single-family house was easy to find, and it was not far from my condo. A tall raven-haired woman in her early 30's opened the door. I liked her even though she was a bit spacey. She seemed to have an eccentricity about her. I noticed that she had a great short haircut.

She led me into one of her bedrooms that she had set up as a beauty salon. I sat down in a comfortable swivel chair and glanced at myself in a large mirror. She did a great job shaping my hair following the lines from my previous hair stylist.

Something inside me prompted me to ask, "Do you read?" She was not surprised by this question and replied, "Yes, I do. I read stones."

"I've never known anyone who read stones, most readers read tarot cards," I said as I reached into my wallet to pay her for the haircut. "Could you read for me?" I looked into her dark violet eyes.

"Sure, I'll check my schedule and see when I've time to do a reading." I glanced into the mirror one last time. I was pleased. Not only was I living in beautiful Sedona, I just had a great haircut and met another friend. On the way out, Hannah introduced me to her tall muscular husband and their six-month old large pet.

"He's 80% wolf and 20% Malamute. We're training him." She showed me his iron chain and spiked collar that I would never think of using on Teddy. I looked at this giant animal and gulped. His intense eyes bore right through me. I did manage to stroke his massive head.

Many haircuts later, Hannah said, "I could read for you today if you'd like. I've some extra time."

I answered quickly, "That would be great!"

We walked into the dining room. She picked up a pouch filled with stones and motioned for me to sit next to her at her dining room table, which I did.

"I'll pray over the stones and ask them for an accurate reading." She began to chant as she flung the stones onto a dark brown cloth that she had placed on the table.

"Pick out five stones," she instructed me. I selected two large and three small stones. She looked at each of these stone and picked up the apache tear, "I see your tears have dried. You'll not be staying in Sedona." Touching the citrine, she said, "Your next move could be near water. This will be a positive joyful move."

With the carnelian stone in her hand, she informed me, "Many moves will happen for you in this lifetime. You'll learn how to use your personal power to help others. This could be through writing."

She held the garnet and studied it for a moment, "You'll have an unexpected visitor from your past. I think this is a male."

And lastly holding the smoky quartz, "You're in the process of healing and transformation. You're grounding yourself – connecting to Mother Earth. Trust that everything will work out as you release negative energy from this lifetime and past lifetimes." She then collected all the stones and gently placed them back into the pouch.

"Thank you, Hannah," I said excitedly, "for my first stone reading."

She said, "There is a gathering with a medicine woman at a private home next week. I'm going. Would you like to go to this as well?"

"Sure, I would love to."

She wrote down the date and the address, and said, "Be there before1:00 pm. I'll RSVP for both of us."

Before I left her house, I sent a telepathic message to the wolf, "Hi, how are you?"

When I walked over to say goodbye to him, I

could see he was very agitated! I looked at his clenched teeth, angry eyes and vowed never to send him any psychic messages.

16
forgiveness is a gift to you

On the day of the gathering, I could hardly wait to go and meet more of the Sedona community. The morning had quickly disappeared. I drove to the outskirts of West Sedona and turned onto a long dirt drive to a large rustic house nestled in the thick woods. There were cars parked everywhere. I pulled into the first open space I could find and walked to the house.

I entered the large foyer and saw a side table with a love offering bowl. I placed money into the bowl and proceeded to the spacious living room. There were about fifteen women seated in a circle including a Native American woman with long greying hair and leathered skin. She was dressed in a colorful tribal garment. I spotted an empty folding chair and sat down. I looked around the circle and nodded to Hannah, who was seated directly across from me. Two women were facilitating this gathering. They introduced the Hopi woman.

She lit a long wood pipe, took a puff and passed the pipe to the woman next to her. We each puffed on this pipe and returned it to her. She held the pipe and began to chant softly. I felt myself relax into the folding chair.

One of the facilitators, a woman around forty with short auburn hair said, "We'll go around the room. Please tell us a little about yourself." Each woman spoke about herself.

When it was my turn, I said, "I'm a writer, and I'm interviewing ordinary/extraordinary women who want to share their life stories for a book that I'm writing."

After the last woman, a nurse, had contributed, the auburn-haired woman said, "We were guided to do this gathering. Our guides told us that something special would happen while we were here. Now we're going to pass around a glass bowl as well as paper and pens. I want each of you to write on a piece of paper a word or short message, something that you want to benefit someone other than yourself. It can be to a person or a group of people. You don't need to name the person or the group."

Her tall, studious colleague added, "Write something that you want to bless another with." The bowl went around the room. Each woman wrote out her message, put the folded paper into the bowl, and passed it to the woman on her right.

When it came to me, I thought, what can I write? I know, I can write, *forgiveness,* for I want Jerod to forgive me for anything I may have done or said to hurt him. I was the one that left the relationship not him. I want him to have a good life and find another relationship.

After I wrote the message, I folded the little piece of white paper, placed it into the bowl, now practically overflowing with paper messages, and passed the bowl to the woman next to me. She was the last one to put her message into the bowl. She handed this full bowl to the facilitator.

"We'll take a short break. Enjoy the refreshments in the kitchen."

The facilitators walked into the large country kitchen. I followed and took one of the small paper cups of lemonade. It tasted cool and refreshing. I watched the two facilitators, each took a turn and mixed the papers in the glass bowl. Hannah and I hung out together until it was time to return to our seats.

After we were settled in our chairs, the scholarly facilitator wearing large tortoise glasses, probably in her early 40s, came into the room with the glass bowl and started passing it around again. She said, "Now I want you to pick out one of the papers and read your message out loud. This is your blessing."

"How fun," I thought! Each of the women reached into the bowl and read her message out loud and passed the bowl to the next woman: a fun trip, prosperity, $5,000.00, joy, peace.

When it was my turn, I reached in the bowl to pick from the two remaining papers and read out loud . . . *forgiveness*. I started to cry! Someone handed me a Kleenex. I wiped my watery eyes and composed myself as best as I could. As difficult as it was to speak, I managed to get out, "I can't believe that I'm blessed by my own blessing, *forgiveness*. I wrote this as my gift to my past relationship. I wanted him to forgive me and go on with his life. This is amazing!"

When the gathering was over, some congregated to talk. I waved goodbye to Hannah and walked to the door. A woman, her white hair pulled back into a tight bun, stopped me just as I was about to leave. She gave me a piece of paper with the name and phone number of a woman she wanted me to interview.

"Patricia lives in Oak Creek. She has lived there forever. Recently she took a writing class and wrote a book. She would be a great candidate for your book. I can let her know that you would like to interview her."

"Thank you. Yes, tell her that I'll definitely call her."

I thought about magic, synchronicity and messages! Sedona's enchantment was everywhere.

Patricia

The next chance I had, I called and spoke to Patricia.

"Yes, you can come over and interview me." We set a convenient time for the following day.

After following her explicit directions, I drove through Sedona, along the tree-lined Oak Creek to a long driveway that led to a little white house near the flowing creek. From my car, I could see the creek, and once outside, I could hear the moving water.

What on earth are all those things stuck to the side of her house? It looked like a garage sale attached to her house. I stared at the ceramic dishes, stones, candlesticks, you name it. I knocked on the door.

A plain woman in her late 70's, dressed in a simple printed dress, a hand knitted wool shawl thrown around her thick shoulders, opened the door. She had wiry grey short hair and a practical attitude.

"Come in. I made some tea. Sit down and make yourself comfortable."

"Thank you." I sunk into a dated light brown sofa. She sat next to me on a rough tweedy brown chair. That chair, I thought, is where she sits most of her time. She poured the brewed tea into two mugs and placed her tea pot on a lace doily on the antique coffee table.

"So, you heard I published my first book at the age of 70. Can you imagine me, a school dropout, a widow, and a grandmother to actually do this? I attended a creative writing class at our local high school. It's never too late, you're never too old to change - try new things - write a book. The book I published is about my travels as a thirteen-year-old in rural Arizona." She gave me one of the books.

"Life is not always easy. We lived during the Depression, during this time the smelter shut down; everyone lost their jobs. Because there was no work, we lived and even worked in a tent. Times were different then; people were different."

She continued, "Eventually my husband and I built a tar paper shack right near Oak Creek; we put in a wood stove. We had an outhouse on the hill. What a blessing when we were able to have water and electricity in the house. I honestly wouldn't want to go back before electricity."

"Years went by and we kept adding on, until the tar shack became this house. We raised our four children here. I added the finishing touches to the exterior. You see, I'm a collector, a 'junkie' that's what I call myself. I started collecting things. I needed a place to put them. I ran out of room in my house, so I cemented rocks, decorative plates, seashells, things from trips, even anniversary gifts that were given to us to the outside of this house."

She smiled mischievously. "My husband would tell me not to put another thing on the house. When he wasn't looking, I would slip something else on it. When I filled up our house's exterior, I went next door to my daughter's house and cemented things onto the exterior of her house."

"Times have changed. Today's world is much different than the one I remember as a child. Everyone is running here and there, dashing off in the car to take their children to some activity."

"Even though our family was poor, we would have time after our work was done to visit and spend quality time together: singing, talking, laughing, playing cards, and lots of games by the kerosene lamp. I owned two dresses, flour sack bloomers, and one pair of Boy Scout shoes. I never worried when I was a kid. I had no big problems because of the harmony within my family. I learned to be myself - and not pretend to be what I wasn't."

"I work on myself instead of trying to change others. I solve my own problems without hurting anyone. I keep my nose out of other people's business. I've had my ups and downs like everyone else, yet I wouldn't change my life."

There was a small *Twelve Steps*, Alcoholic Anonymous book on the side table alongside her sofa. Patricia caught my glance. "Yes, someone in the family was an alcoholic. I keep this book, so I can read it to know the best way to solve a problem without hurting anyone. You know anyone that has a problem might want to read the 'Serenity Prayer.'"

"Is there anything you would like to add to help others," I asked.

She thought for a moment and said, "Change yourself without trying to change others. You're never too old to try new things. You could even write a book!"

"Thank you Patricia, your inspiration has helped me, and I'm sure will help others. I'm working on this book and yes, it's not too late to have it published!"

Before I left, I followed her around the outside of her house and her daughter's house as she pointed to several unusual pieces such as a ceramic blue pitcher and sterling silver tea set that she cherished from her astonishing collection.

I stood outside my car and breathed in the aromatic Juniper and evergreen trees, listened to the gurgling creek as it flowed beneath the glorious red rock mountains. The view was so serene, so soulful. What a special place this pioneer woman had settled in.

17
know, love, and honor yourself

The unfinished book tugged at my heart. I felt the desire to continue to interview the women: seek their stories, and what they had learned. Now even more so, after meeting Patricia, if she could complete her book, why couldn't I?

I thought it would be a good idea to take photos of the women I interviewed and possibly create a tabletop book. I decided to hire a professional photographer. Asking around at work, a customer suggested that I meet Crystal and gave me her phone number. She told me that she was a gifted photographer and knew many of the residents in Sedona.

I still could not fathom how quickly things manifest here. I called Crystal and set up a meeting at a local coffee shop.

Several days later, while in the coffee shop, I intuitively knew it was Crystal when I saw her. She wore a medium length yellow cotton dress which hung loosely on her. Her pale face had many lines for such a young person. She was in her early thirties. Her blonde hair hung limply around her thin shoulders. Her soft aura had a glowing energy.

At the counter, we ordered cold drinks and took them to a small table outside the restaurant.

In her sing-song voice she said, "It's so good to meet you. I just love that you're writing such an inspiring book. Yes, I'd love to photograph these remarkable women." She showed me a presentation album of her photos. I was impressed with her work.

"Okay, I think this could work. I'll pay you for each woman that you photograph."

She answered, "Why don't I photograph the women using black and white film because color is going to be much more expensive?" I could see the excitement in her pale blue eyes.

I said, "Good idea. I totally agree black and white is the way to go."

"I can't wait to get started," she said. "I've several women in mind that would be great for you to interview. I'll contact them and get back to you."

"That would be great!" I said.

Within a few days, Crystal called to tell me that she had set up interviews with several women. I knew intuitively that she needed the money; this arrangement would work for both of us. I felt on another level that we were able to help each other. I could not wait to meet the Sedona women, interview them and write about them.

She made an appointment for me to meet with a woman named Caroline at her home in Uptown Sedona. She suggested that she come along on this interview.

I turned into the street and immediately saw Crystal standing next to her truck.

"Thanks for waiting outside for me."

She replied, "I wanted to make sure you found the place. It's not easy to find. I visit Caroline whenever I need a lift. I feel so positive and energetic when I leave, regardless of how I felt before I arrived."

"I can't wait to meet her," I said.

Caroline

It was nearly dusk. We walked toward a new one-level townhouse with a red tiled roof. Just as Crystal was about to ring the doorbell, a small woman with a deeply wrinkled face smiled up at us. She wore a loose-fitting floral cotton dress.

"This is Sera, the writer I told you about."

I felt the warmth and strength of Caroline's rough hand as she grasped mine. We followed her into her kitchen. I breathed in the intoxicating aroma of freshly baked chocolate chip cookies.

"I thought you might want some." She took the cookies out of the oven and placed them on a ceramic plate, which she set on the sofa table in her living room. Crystal and I began munching on the cookies.

"I'm an avid reader," she said as she noticed me looking at her array of magazines on her coffee table. "Ask me anything you like. I'm from Oklahoma originally. I'm 89 and ½ years old and have been crippled from a birth defect. My father, a single parent, taught me to be independent and that I can do or be anything I want and not to let my birth defect stop me.

When I was ten years old, wearing leg braces, he lifted me and placed me high up in one of our peach trees. Frightened, I cried out, how will I get down? He said, 'You'll get down, and I'll be here when you do.' So, I climbed higher and higher, and when I was ready, I came down."

"There were some people that thought I was a *poor thing* because I was crippled, and my mother was dead; she died when I was nine years old. I'd look at these concerned people and think to myself - you're mistaken. You see, I was and still am far from a poor thing. I make all my clothes. I even make my shoes."

"My husband Dennis and I knew each other for six years before we married. I can honestly say that there were no surprises about our personalities after we wed. You know he was far from perfect, but he was the perfect man for me."

"After graduating from high school, I worked for the government as a mapper earning $25 a week. When I married Dennis, I quit my job because my husband wanted to support me. I let him even though he earned less than me. His paycheck for a six-day week was $18. That was 37 ½ cents per hour. Bread was 10 cents a loaf. I believe it was just as damned hard then as now."

"Come with me," she said, "I want you to see my garden." We slowly followed her outside. Her beautiful flower garden was filled with vibrant roses, brilliant azaleas, and delicate hyacinths. A subtle breeze stirred the scented air; birds chirped in the nearby trees. It was an enchanting sight.

"I planted these beautiful flowers wherever I could around my place." She pointed to a small area of land beyond her house filled with colorful wildflowers. "That used to be a city dump. After the planting was done around my house, I dug in, weeded and planted wildflowers over there."

"Spring is my favorite time of the year. I live for spring for then I get to see my plants come up. I planted 600 bulbs last year. My salvation is working with my plants. Work is our salvation."

I saw her wheelchair parked by the side of her garden. She glanced in that direction and said, "If I get tired, I sit in it and rest."

"You're an inspiring role model," I said. "You have created a beautiful haven and I can see why you love to be out here."

We walked back into the house and before we left she smiled and said, "I'm extremely self-sufficient. Life is too short. I've never done something simply to have or make money - to hell with money. I derive more pleasure out of planting a flower garden than any amount of money could give me. Like my grandmother used to say, '*It doesn't matter how much money you have, there will always be things in life you can't afford.*'"

"Thank you," we chimed and each hugged Caroline before we left.

Outside I said, "You're right. Caroline's spirit and outlook on life is so uplifting! I definitely feel more energetic."

Amita

Crystal nodded and said, "I set up an interview with Amita at her house." She gave me a piece of paper with all the information on it.

In a few days, I was on my way to meet Amita. I drove to the outskirts of West Sedona and pulled my car in front of a quaint white house with a white picket fence. The handwritten sign on the front door read, "Please remove your shoes." I took off my sandals and put them on a woven matt outside her door and pushed the buzzer.

A dark-skinned woman, in her early 30's, greeted me and invited me in. Her brightly colored parrot was squawking at me from his large wooden cage. I sunk into a worn imitation leather chair. The room was sparse except for a sofa and a few chairs.

"Why do you want to interview me?" She asked abruptly as her dark eyes stared right through my soul. I was caught off guard.

"I, uh, thought Crystal explained that I was interviewing women on their life experiences and lessons learned. She thought you might have wisdom to pass on to other women." I felt uncomfortable - like I was being cross-examined.

Her expression showed she still was not convinced as she sat down on the sofa next to me. I decided to begin the questioning, "Where are you from? I noticed your accent."

"I tell you. I come from Fuji Islands. When I was 21 years old, my beloved mother died in her sleep. I awoke the next morning, and when I heard what happened, I immediately went into shock. My body shut down - I became paralyzed. After many months, I regained some movement. My sister, concerned about my well-being, told me to go to the Yogi Institute, not far from where we lived."

Her dark eyes looked off in the distance as she remembered and said, "Are you serious? I can hardly walk. I can hardly move without pain, and you want me to do yoga. I think you're crazy."

"My sister persisted until one day I consented to go to the Ashram. I remember the first Hatha Yoga class vividly as I couldn't even move my toes without extreme pain. Yet I continued to take the classes, because instinctively I knew - that if I did - I would get better."

"Through these daily classes using simple exercises, visualization meditations, and focused awareness, I was totally recovered within a month. I was so happy that I could walk and move without pain. I continued to practice yoga at home and at the Ashram. I met my husband there, a disabled war veteran, who was strengthening his mind and body through the practice of yoga."

"My husband and I moved to Gosford, Australia, and I continued my yoga at the Ashram there. I remember when the masters came around the room selecting the ones that were to be the teachers. I was surprised when the masters stood before me and chose me for this special honor. Later I asked my swami, why was I chosen? He replied, 'You have the gift – to teach and impart spiritual guidance to others no matter what is going on with them.'"

"Now I'm fulfilling my life's mission by teaching yoga to students here in my home. I teach one on one. I stress discipline, creative movement exercises and a healthy diet."

I asked, "What message do you want to share with others?"

"Know yourself, love and honor yourself. I know myself and can deal with anything that goes on with me. I truly love and honor myself and because of this deep respect for myself, I can love others."

"Thank you," I said, "You have inspired me. I want to take your yoga class. I like the idea of a one-on-one class for I think I could learn more this way."

Her spiritual eyes studied mine. She went across the room and picked up a notebook. After glancing through it she said, "I've an opening next Thursday morning at nine."

"That works for me as it's my day off." She noted this, then guided me to the front door and opened it. Once outside, I put on my sandals. I was very excited to learn yoga with this master teacher.

The following Thursday, I arrived a little early because I could not wait to begin the class. I removed my sandals and rang the doorbell. Amita greeted me warmly, and I followed her into her living room. Sweet incense filled the air.

There were two yoga mats next to each other on the wood floor. She pointed to one of the mats, "Sit down in a cross-legged position. I want you to relax, watch your breathing." She had a gentle way of teaching using deep breathing exercises and simple asanas (yoga postures).

At the end of the class, I laid down on the mat for a special healing meditation. I could hear her soothing voice, "Relax first the big toe, and the next toe." When each toe was relaxed, she said, "Relax the bottom of the foot, top of the foot, ankle, shin, knee, thigh, hip. Now relax the other leg." She relaxed this leg starting with the big toe.

"Relax all the body parts," she said. "Relax the front of the body - relax the back of the body - relax the whole body, the whole body, the whole body."

I mentally let go of any tension in my body from the soles of my feet to the fine lines around my eyes.

After a brief guided, and then silent meditation, I came back to her living room feeling like I stepped out of a refreshing sauna. I could barely get, "thank you," out of my relaxed mouth.

My yoga sessions were the highlight of my week. I looked forward to seeing Amita and doing the stretching exercises, and the deep healing meditation. I could feel my spiritual side expanding. Our friendship developed over the weeks to mutual trust.

Since we both loved eating breakfast out, I drove to her house, and away we went to the restaurant at the airport. We enjoyed watching the small planes fly in and out on the runway outside our window.

"You're a remarkable and gifted teacher," I said one day at breakfast. "My body is certainly a happy flexible one since I started your class. Hard to believe, I've taken your class for almost two months."

After I sipped my coffee, I asked, "How come you never learned to drive? You're an intelligent and free-spirited woman."

She replied, "I tried to learn, however my husband had no patience for me. I think he doesn't want me to drive and makes excuses not to teach me. He wants me to be dependent upon him. I think he's afraid that if I learn to drive, I'll become too independent and leave him."

"I can teach you to drive if you are open to this. I would not mind at all. You're too young not to drive. What if an emergency happened and you needed to drive?"

She said, "Yes, I agree. How about we trade yoga lessons for driving lessons? I can teach you yoga and you can teach me to drive."

"Okay, it's a deal. We'll start after my yoga lesson."

After the next class, we began the driving lessons. We did a protection ritual before each driving lesson.

I said, "I am putting protective white and gold light around my car. I'm also putting this light around both of us and the other drivers on the road as well."

Then she would get into the driver's seat and take us through a quick meditative prayer. I think we were both nervous at first. She took to driving just like I pictured she would. She was a very good driver. After many weeks of driving around the city, she progressed onto the busy freeway. I taught her how to park the car. Then I helped her study for her written test. She was an excellent student.

She passed her driver's test with flying colors, and received her driver's license, which led to her freedom and ultimately to her divorce.

18
life is a tough teacher

Crystal stopped at the gift shop. "Hi, here is Diana's name, phone number and address. I'll set up a time to photograph her after your interview."

I tucked this paper into my handbag. "Thanks for bringing this to the store. I'll call her on my break."

Diana agreed to meet the following day at her house.

Diana

On my way to Diana's house, I looked at my watch. It was almost noon. I felt this would give me plenty of time to get there by 12:30pm. Yet I kept getting lost, turning onto to one cul-de-sac, after another, until finally I rerouted myself back to where I started.

I finally gave in and asked for help from my Higher Self, that higher part of me that is connected to both the physical and etheric worlds. It was after one o'clock when I finally arrived at my destination: a charming story book cottage with a dark thatched roof. I was agitated and upset because I hate being late.

I knocked loudly on the front door. A statuesque blonde woman, 50ish, opened the door and instantly I felt - calm - peaceful. What!! How could this be? My mind could not comprehend this for just a moment ago, I was frustrated, angry and upset. I stared up into Diana's angelic eyes and sighed. "I can't believe this. This is surreal."

"I know," she answered, "this seems to happen to people when they come into my energy."

I still could not get over that I was feeling so peaceful - calm. I followed her tall frame into her living room, where I sunk down into a comfortable sofa. I took several sips of water from the water bottle she graciously handed me.

"Thanks," is all that I could say.

Then I found the words. "I can't understand this. I was so agitated and upset when I arrived, and now I'm *so relaxed*. I couldn't find your house and kept driving around in a circle, up and down dead-end streets getting myself more and more lost and more and more frustrated. I finally asked my Higher Self for guidance to your house. I still don't get it – I was so stressed when I arrived, and now I feel like I just came out of a sauna. How is this possible?"

Diana answered, "I've had this incredible gift of healing since I was a child, a spontaneity that allows me to remove pain and suffering from people's hearts. Some people actually fall asleep in my presence."

The water I drank seemed to clear my mind a little. "What drew you to Sedona?" I managed to ask in my floating state.

"I fell in love with the beauty, the red rocks. The Hopi think this is the home of God, that the city is surrounded by seven angels."

"What was your mother like?" I looked into her expressive eyes, perfect nose – a face that could be easily photographed.

"My mother, an alcoholic, was manic depressive and suicidal. She was a gifted psychic and healer who could not balance the two worlds."

"I've always been drawn to help others. I received my PH.D., as a transpersonal psychotherapist from the Institute of Transpersonal Psychology at Menlo Park, California. I've been in practice for over thirty years. A transpersonal psychotherapist views a person holistically. I'm also a neurolinguistics programmer and certified hypnotherapist, a professional intuitive, and a paranormal consultant."

"You're a remarkable woman." I took another long drink of water and put the bottle back on the table. I still was in a detached state.

"Thank you," she said, "however, at Menlo Park, I wasn't in touch with my intellect or my spiritual side. I viewed myself as a pretty young thing! Through my internship with Nathaniel Brandon, I learned that I needed to wake up and take note of my mind. I learned from Virginia Satir to become strong as a woman and to have a generosity of spirit."

"I studied with masters such as 16th Gwalya Karmapa (who has the same lineage as the Dali Lama, and is the spiritual head rather than the political head of Tibet), Fritz Perls, Laura Huxley, Jean Houston and others."

"I strongly suggest that it's good to study under people, but ultimately you need to go within, to the deepest place of your inner knowing and actualize that from the inside out."

Diana sat upright and said, "It's important for women to learn to listen to the sweet voice within that speaks to them energetically."

She continued, "From my days spent with the Buddhist teacher, I learned the true meaning of compassion and service. Beginning in 1979, my life was turned upside down: it involved the loss of my fiancé and my financial security. My fiancé walked across a busy street towards a telephone booth to call me and was killed by an oncoming car. We were to be married the following week. Everything I owned was tied up in his name, our house, even our bank accounts. I was devastated not only with his loss, but with my financial loss as well."

"From this loss and over the next nine years, I experienced the death of eighteen people that I cared about. I stood empty without landmarks as to who I was or who I thought I was! I lacked confidence in myself, my ability to follow inner guidance. It was only when I began to come into Divine Wisdom that I was able to get back to my intuitive gifts.

"I opened myself up to the pain. I became more loving, more helpful to myself and others. I began to see my losses as a profound gift to help others. Through my designated alone time, I opened to serenity, love, and compassion, which led me to become a grief counselor."

"Life is hard – it's a tough teacher. There's a notion out there that life should be joyful and easy. Personally, I don't know of anyone who hasn't experienced some suffering in their lifetime. There is a way to move through the suffering, cope with it, lessen it and get on with one's life. Instead of feeling reverence, we get into what I call 'small ego'. This happens because the means that we are used to identifying with are threatened at these times of crisis. To better prepare for the future, I teach my students to live in a condition of total love, total perfection, to feel good about themselves."

"Find time to be alone, listen to your intuition. Through this alignment, you can reap prosperity, harmony in relationships, success and your deepest desires."

"I've a favorite verse, 'Now that the barn has burned to the ground, I can see the moon.' Move through challenging life experiences - see the moon."

"I'm so grateful for this interview," I said. "You're an incredibly gifted healer!"

Driving back to the condo, I was confident that this route would be easier. I thought about Diana, her lessons, her tremendous gifts and how unbelievably peaceful I felt.

Back at work the next day, I met a friendly middle-aged couple who were visiting from Cleveland, Ohio. I said to them, "I'm from Cleveland. I still have family living there."

The husband asked, "What do you do besides work here? You look like you have a creative side to you."

I smiled, thinking it was probably my Sedona attire, long skirt, boots and big dangling silver and feather earrings. "I'm writing a book about inspirational women, ordinary, yet extraordinary women. The book seems to have a life of its own and is guiding me to the very women that I need to meet."

"I want a copy," said the interested tourist. "Wait, I want three copies, one for me, one for my wife and one for my exceptional daughter." He gave me his business card and wrote his address on the back.

"Thank you. Enjoy Sedona and have a safe trip back," I said as they were leaving the shop.

The next morning at work, I was busy polishing the silver jewelry, when the phone rang. Vicki answered it, "You have a phone call."

She handed me the phone. I said, "Hi this is Sera, how can I help you?"

"Do you remember me?" asked the male voice, "My wife and I were in yesterday, and we spoke to you about your book."

"Yes, of course, I do. You're from Cleveland."

"We were at an open house in Carefree, Arizona, yesterday and met the owner, a rather remarkable woman named Marilyn. She built her dream house, which she is selling. A year after she completed this house, she had a health issue and was in a coma. She recovered and now is actively building another house. She is an 86 years old dynamo." He rattled off her phone number which I wrote down.

"I think she would be an asset to your book. I

took the liberty and told her I was going to contact you and that you would call her."

"Yes, she sounds like an excellent candidate for the book. I would love to meet and interview her. I'll call her. Thank you. I really appreciate your doing this. Have a safe rest of your trip."

"That was totally unexpected!" I mumbled out loud after I hung up the phone. The book certainly has its own agenda or is it Sedona's magic? I repeated our conversation to Vicki.

I called Marilyn when I went on my break. Marilyn, however, was not really interested in being interviewed. "Why don't you pick me up, and we'll go to my club for lunch. Then I'll decide whether or not I want to be interviewed!" She said in her soft shaky voice.

"That is a great idea. I would love to meet you. Would next Thursday, at 11:00 am work for you?"

"Yes, that would be good." She gave me her address, and I figured it would take me about two hours to drive to Carefree from Sedona.

Marilyn

On Thursday, I was on my way to meet Marilyn. As I drove on the freeway, I thought about the book, the women, Sedona, and lo and behold, bright lights, siren blasting, a policeman was chasing me. No! I must have gone over the speed limit while I was deep in my inner dialogue. I pulled over, opened my handbag, pulled out my driver's license, car registration and waited.

"Don't get out of the car! You were speeding,"

the stocky balding policeman said in a menacing way.

"Here is my driver's license and registration. Do you need anything else?" I was as polite as I could be.

"If I do, I'll let you know," he retorted in a growling voice. I kept myself from saying anything, for I was sure whatever I said would not be to his liking! I took the ticket and carefully drove the car back onto the highway.

"What an annoying man! What is going on with him? He obviously doesn't like his job."

I tried not to think about his surly behavior because it only made me frustrated. Yes, my lesson was to be more aware especially when driving.

After I found Marilyn's house, I parked my car and walked through a black iron gate. Marilyn's wispy white hair hung around her craggy face. She was about five feet tall, very tiny, very frail. She wore a navy-blue linen dress and low heels. She was accompanied by an older gentleman. They slowly, very slowly approached me.

"This is my groundskeeper, Joe," she explained. I could feel her scrutinizing me to see whether she liked me or not.

"Hi, pleased to meet you," I said to Joe. Very carefully, Joe walked her to my car and waited until she was seated comfortably before he shut the door and slowly walked back to the house. He was not young either as I noticed his slow gait back to the house.

"Okay, I'll direct you to my club," she said in her whispery voice. The club wasn't far away, and within minutes I pulled up to impressive double doors of the white sprawling structure. I opened the car door for her. After she was safely on the sidewalk, I moved my car to an adjacent parking lot and returned. We walked through an ornate vestibule to the noisy bustling dining room.

"Hi Marilyn, how are you today?" said the hostess. She led us to a table nearby. Marilyn waved at the men, mostly golfers who walked past our table. She seemed to know most everyone there.

"I just got a speeding ticket on the way here! I'm really upset by it," I confided after we sat down at the cloth covered table.

"How awful," she said, "I think you need a drink."

I said, "A drink! I usually don't like to drink when I interview anyone, however - I think I'll make an exception today!"

When the waitress came over, Marilyn said in a kind way, "Gail, please bring this young woman a drink. I'll have my usual Bloody Mary."

"I'll have the same," I replied.

"Tell me about the women you have interviewed," she said. I explained how I seemed to be guided to the women. I shared several of the women's stories. She listened intently. I didn't ask about interviewing her, because I didn't want to offend her. Yet, I reminded her about the couple that wanted me to meet her.

Our drinks came. "Thank you, I think I needed this! Her eyes lit up and we clicked our glasses "to life" and sipped our drinks.

The salad was very good. Suddenly I realized that I was hungry and ate most of it. I could see that

Marilyn was a light eater. I looked around the table for butter for my roll. She looked at me, then jumped up, and found another waitress, who returned with butter.

To see her jump up like that, I was astounded, and after she returned I said, "Marilyn, you really are a twenty-year-old." She chuckled and finished her drink.

"Okay, you can interview me," she said suddenly.

"Great!" I took out my writing tools without saying another word.

She began, "At 86, I can attest that one is never too old to follow a dream, I did, I built the house of my dreams - when I was 84. So, I'm in my 80's - besides, who's counting?" She added, "No one dared tell me I couldn't or shouldn't, besides do you think I would have listened? As a child, I learned to stand on my own two feet, to think for myself. You see, I was an unwanted child - an unexpected child. My mother, already had two daughters, rejected me outright - refused to take care of me. I became an extremely self-reliant child."

"I learned to be serious, resourceful and to keep balance. I developed a sense of humor - that was my escape. I learned to look beyond, not behind."

"You know I use that old saying to remind me, 'That we come into this world alone, and we will leave this world alone. I am the captain of my ship. I am the master of my fate.'"

"This attitude helped me last year when I fell ill with double pneumonia, staph infections and lung cancer. I went into a coma. Certain that I was dying, my attorney began to execute the necessary procedures. After thirty days in a coma, I made a miraculous recovery. The first thing I saw was my doctor and this meant one thing - I was alive! I knew then that I had more work to do here, and I was anxious to get started."

"I took complete charge of my life. I contacted my attorney and ordered him to cease, stop all the legal work he had started. I contacted my former doctor for a second opinion, and ultimately, walked out of the hospital against the hospital's wishes. It seems, after a second look, that I didn't have lung cancer. I felt fine - saw no sense in staying - doing nothing."

"I like to believe that there is always a bright side to everything. One needs to stop negative thoughts from entering one's head. When they appear, I usually say . . . '*STOP*!' Things work out, they usually do."

Hum, I thought I need to release negative thoughts regarding that policeman and the speeding ticket. When these thoughts come up – I'll say, *STOP!*

Marilyn said, "See those men over there." I looked at a group of four older gentlemen who looked like they had nothing planned for the day.

"Look at their expressions, so bored complacent. No life in them. Too many people retire only to become dull. Start giving some thought to what you want to do. Your mind is an incredible device - use it! Get out of your coma. Use that mind of yours to explore yourself, others, different places, even different realms. There's excitement when you learn, plan for a new adventure. Go after your dreams - make them come true - it's never too late to do this. I did it!"

We left the restaurant and walked slowly towards the exit. Once outside, she said, "I want you to see my dream house, the house that is for sale. After the coma, I decided this house was too large and began to design and build a smaller house."

"I would love to see it."

Once she was safely inside my car, she guided me through various streets until we came upon a stately home among other lovely homes.

"What a magnificent house," I said as I parked my car in the circular drive. She unlocked the lockbox on one of the towering dark wood double doors.

We walked into a stunning living room with high vaulted ceilings. I looked at her petite silhouette dwarfed against the high ceilings, spacious open floor plan, and marveled at her tenacity to design and build something of this scale at her age, honestly at any age. She guided me through the four bedrooms, four bathrooms and into a paneled den. I noticed that the home had been staged with expensive and tasteful furnishings.

As I drove my car out onto the cul-de-sac I said, "You're an extraordinary woman!" She smiled broadly.

Back at her house, I said, "Thank you again for lunch. I'm so glad that I had this opportunity to meet you and see your beautiful home. You're such an inspiration." I opened the car door for her and was about to walk her through the gate, when her groundskeeper appeared and slowly, very slowly, I watched them walk back to the house arm in arm.

On the way home, I was very aware of my speed limit. I did see the unpleasant policeman on the other side of the highway. I was about to dwell on his bad behavior and my ticket. STOP - all negative thoughts. I mentally send him a psychic message to have a good day.

I thought about Marilyn and her words of wisdom and was comforted by them. I could forge ahead, create new things, not be afraid to conquer big projects at my age or any age.

19

accept the unexpected

In a few weeks, my parents were coming to visit me in Sedona. They wanted to drive to Laughlin, Nevada and stay overnight at a casino hotel there. Their cousins, a married couple from California, whom they had not seen for many years, would meet up with us in Laughlin. I was thankful that my mother wanted to fly the distance from Cleveland to Phoenix. Flying had become something she tried to avoid.

As I wanted to get an early start, I left Sedona at dawn and drove into Phoenix. I picked my parents up at the Phoenix Sky Harbor Airport. We stopped and had lunch before I drove back. As we neared Sedona, they were awed by the colors and red rock formations.

In the morning, knowing they would want to rest and have a leisure day after their long plane ride, I said, "Dad, why don't you drive me to work? You could explore the area with Mom. I've plans to go to dinner with two of my work friends and will get a ride home with one of them."

He answered, "Good idea. We'll relax and see the area later in the day." Before I left, I drew him a map of Sedona, with the condo's address and location on it, so he could find his way back to the condo. He dropped me off at Tlaquepaque.

After work, Elizabeth, Vicki and I walked over to the Mexican restaurant. We were about to order dinner when I looked up, blinked and saw Jerod walking towards our table. I could not believe my eyes! I immediately got up, hugged him, and asked him to join us. I introduced him to my friends.

"How did you know I was in this restaurant?"

"Oh, I stopped by the store and the young woman told me I would find you here."

While we were standing I said, "What are you doing here? I heard you were in a relationship."

He reddened a little and said, "It's a long story. I'm leaving for Wisconsin and wanted to say goodbye before I left." I sensed that he wanted to talk and was uncomfortable doing it here.

"I think we should go somewhere." I turned to the women, and they nodded in agreement. "I'll see you on Tuesday." I grabbed my coat and my handbag. Once outside I suggested, "Let's go to a restaurant that I like that is nearby."

I climbed into his familiar blue pickup truck and directed him to the restaurant. We walked into the busy setting that resembled a cozy library. High bookshelves were filled with all sorts of books. We were escorted to a booth near the back of the restaurant. It was quiet and cozy.

"We are friends, tell me what happened? I heard you were in a relationship." I repeated myself.

He was silent for a moment. "The relationship didn't work out. I decided it was time to go back home. I want to start a business there. Be around my son."

I thought: Jerod and relationships are not easy. I also intuitively knew that he didn't have a place to stay as this was his style, to run, whenever the situation became too difficult. My intuition told me that his relationship had ended - today.

His light blue eyes searched mine as he asked, "How are you doing?"

"I love it here. The people are friendly; many are spiritually aware. The red rock scenery is magnificent, magical - uplifting. I like work, the condo I'm renting." I told him about the gathering of women and *forgiveness*."

He said, "Oh, I forgave you a long time ago."

I was glad to hear this, yet somehow Sedona, Jerod, and forgiveness seemed grouped together.

"Oh, I forgot to tell you my parents are here, visiting. We are leaving tomorrow morning for Laughlin." He had met my parents when we went to Cleveland to celebrate their 50th Anniversary."

"We're meeting my mother's California cousins in Laughlin and will spend the night there." I looked at my watch and said, "Oh my, it's after eleven. It's too late for you to drive back to Phoenix. Stay over! You can stay at the condo while we're away and take care of Teddy; he would love it! I'll give you the phone number of the kennel to cancel his booking."

I could see he was going to refuse my offer and stopped. He knew I was right. He needed a place to stay, regroup until he went on his way.

"I'll call my parents and let them know you're staying over." He stood next to me as I dialed my number. My mother answered. I said, "Jerod is here. No, we're not getting back together. He will stay overnight, and then stay with Teddy while we're in Laughlin."

In the morning, I brewed coffee, scrambled eggs and toasted bagels for my parents. I microwaved rolled oats, cinnamon and raisins for Jerod and myself. I hugged his tall lanky frame before we walked out the door. "Keep in touch. I wish you success in your new adventure," I said as I left to join my parents in my car.

After we checked into the Laughlin hotel, we met up with the aging cousins. My parents had their own room, and I had mine. I enjoyed my quiet space. I did join everyone for meals. The time passed quickly.

Back in Sedona, I pointed out to them, "There is the Priest of the Red Rocks. I read somewhere that these rock formations have hidden spiritual messages to awaken our soul." Anything is possible, I thought, especially in mystical Sedona.

It was noon when I walked back into the condo pulling my suitcase to Teddy's happy barks. My parents followed behind me with their luggage. On the kitchen table was a scribbled note from Jerod. "Thanks for everything. I put chicken wire around the patio, so Teddy can't get out."

Great! I can check that off my list of to do's. I knew he wouldn't be there when we returned, yet I was glad that I kept my promise for us to remain friends. I was thankful that he forgave me and would go on with his life. I felt closure.
.

20
meditation clears judgment

After my parents left, Crystal scheduled another Sedona woman for me to interview, Lynn, a psychologist and writer. I asked her to meet me at the base of Cathedral Rock in the parking lot at 9:00 am on my day off.

Lynn

I drove to Cathedral Rock and waited for Lynn. I saw her drive up and get out of her car. Our cars were the only ones in the large gravel lot. She was in her 40s, several inches shorter than me with thick frizzy reddish hair.

"Hi Lynn!" I called out as she got out of her car. "Thank you for meeting me here. My dog and I walk this trail quite often. I know a perfect spot where we can talk."

The sun glowed around us until we hiked higher up the mountain trail, then it disappeared. Thick foliage darkened the trail. The Arizona clear blue sky would occasionally poke through the tall clustered trees. We reached my favorite viewing area high up the mountain, stood for a moment, and observed the vast red rock canyon before us. We sat on a red rock shelf which overlooked this magnificent vista.

"Let's go into meditation," I said, "as I want to become a clear channel and let go of judgment and limitation." My intuition was guiding me. When the meditation was complete, I spoke in a low tone, "Tell me about your mother."

Her jaw tightened as she spoke almost inaudibly. "My beautiful mother, my mummy, was mentally ill and depressed. She was a victim of her own tormented world, debilitated by drugs. She was not available to me or anyone. My father was an alcoholic and a strict authoritarian. He directed his attention to me and my physical development. The abuse and incest upset me, and when I complained, my cries for help were ignored. I became frightened and trapped, unable to express my rage and fears because he was always there."

"I remember when my brother and I were children, my father ordered us to place large rocks in a row. I could hardly lift the heavy rocks. He beat me when my rock wasn't placed exactly where he wanted it."

Her tears flowed as she said, "I ran into the house to my mother and grandmother to tell them what happened. They saw my torn clothes and bruises. They pretended they didn't hear me, see me. It was like I didn't exist." She stopped, wiped her eyes and said, "This incident was hidden away within me – until now."

She shifted her weight on the red stone ledge. We sat in silence for a moment, and then she continued, "All those years, it was like I was frozen.

It wasn't until I realized I had options that my blood began to circulate through me. Victims need to come to terms with the stark reality of what happened to them. We often develop guarded stances against painful experiences. Don't do this. Drop your guards - reveal yourself. As victims of incest we do have a future - a good future."

Lynn's voice grew stronger as she continued, "The key is not to focus on the past; don't rationalize what happened - change the present conditions of your life. There's something very central about all of us. Human nature has given us the ability to survive - to be resilient. Don't alienate yourself from others. End that isolated feeling that you're alone – that no one can understand how you feel."

I breathed deeply. A coyote howled in the distance. I connected to the red ground beneath me. I sat quietly and waited for her to continue.

Lynn's green eyes looked straight ahead at the vast canyon. She said, "At 40, bits and pieces of my tormented past began to reappear in my mind. These flashbacks and obtrusive thoughts were fragments of my unremembered childhood incest when I was 14 to 16 years old. I told myself that I wasn't going to be able to live if I didn't remember and remember accurately what had happened. I needed to discover the person I was from the beginning. "

"I took myself in hand and focused on my least traumatic experience – which to me was my father's drinking. I attended AA, Alcoholics Anonymous, and then ACOA – Twelve Step Program for adult children of alcoholics. My self-worth increased as did my spiritual connection - my relationship with God."

"I needed to know that I could still be myself - that I could create a good future. I needed to let go of the past – the abuse, the incest - and change the present conditions in my life."

"Through psychotherapy, I've learned to witness the reality of each person I meet. I'm prepared to view them in a way that I had never seen before – nonjudgmentally. I disowned every preconceived notion of self, my language, my appearance and my thoughts. I read everything available on the subject of incest."

Lynn continued, "I explored ways to heal using such methods as meditation and art therapy. I became active in yoga, running, swimming, hiking and climbing. I needed to try anything: anything that could stimulate me to feel I was alive. I kept on until I succeeded. The strongest thing is knowing that I did survive and that I'm still myself."

"I hold a master's in social psychology. I'm drawn to help other victims. I appeal to them to seek help now – don't suffer. Contact other victims who have had similar experiences."

She said, "We human beings are in ourselves so precious that we can come to terms with and through human resilience we can surmount almost any kind of experience."

When I stood up, I noticed my stiff legs, "Lynn, thank you for sharing. This has not been an easy journey for you." I hugged her. I followed her athletic figure down the mountain struggling to hold back my tears. I waved goodbye to her as she got in her car and drove away. I opened my car door, slid onto the seat and sobbed and sobbed.

What a brave soul. A healing had taken place, not only for her - for me as well. I felt it. Something deep inside me had healed. Perhaps I had been abused in a past life or many past lives. I resonated with Lynn's journey. I was connecting more and more to my powerful feminine side.

As I drove home, I sent love and healing to Lynn. I stopped at the local market for a few items and was putting them away at the condo when I heard a knock on my door.

"Hi," said Alice, "I saw your car in the carport. I've an appointment at a restaurant in Flagstaff on Monday and wondered if you wanted to go with me and write the article. My independent writers seem to be too busy or on vacation."

"Yes, of course, I would love to do this. I can't believe that I'm actually going to write an article that will be published in the magazine."

"You'll get paid."

"Don't worry about that. I know that you're struggling financially with the magazine. Besides this is something I've wanted to do, and I'm so excited about this assignment."

On Monday, Alice drove us to the charming Victorian-style restaurant in Flagstaff. One of the owners showed us through the restaurant, which was quite large and had many meeting rooms. Then another family member, dressed in a circa1900 outfit escorted us to a table.

After I sat down, I took out my writing tools and started jotting notes. I glided my hand over the smooth thick wood tabletop. Another waitress stopped by. "The tabletop was salvaged from the old Lumberjack barn. Help yourself to the salad bar."

I said to Alice as we both stood up, "That salad bar we passed looked impressive. I'm hungry."

"Me too," she replied, "I could eat everything off the salad bar; however, they want us to try one of their specialties. I told them to go ahead and prepare what they wished us to sample." We returned with our salads.

"Another server appeared and said, "Hi, my name is Kelly, and I'm a student at NAU. This is our specialty dish, homemade lasagna, and our freshly baked buttery rolls. Enjoy."

After eating a portion of the delicious lunch, I said, "I think I just ate lunch plus dinner." We each took a doggie bag with us. We thanked everyone on our way out. I slipped the menu into my handbag just to make sure I spelled all the names correctly.

Before she dropped me off, I said, "Thanks. That was so much fun. I'll enjoy the leftovers. I'll write this article tonight."

The next morning, I knocked on Alice's door and handed her the finished article. She read it twice and then looked up at me and said, "If I had known you could write like this, I would have given you more articles."

I felt my lips curve upward and said, "Thank you. I gave her a big hug and dashed out the door.

On my way to work, I thought; Sedona - grantor of wishes -how about that - I had fulfilled my wish to have something I had written – published!

21
a magical gift can appear

The bright sun pushed through my blinds. I awoke to its warm energy and immediately felt the urge to drive to Cathedral Rock and meditate.

I attached Teddy's leash onto his collar. He jumped up and down and into the car. The air felt fresh, and the reddish orange rocks glowed from the strong sunlight as we made our way to Cathedral Rock. Teddy barked at everything he noticed: other dogs, people, the wind through the slit in the back window.

After I parked the car, I opened the passenger door for him. I took off his leash, so he was free to roam. He was not going far from me. I hiked up the trail. I could see his white furry body darting here and there ahead of me. At one point, I could see my car, like a toy, in the lot far below. Finding my favorite spot, I sat down on the cool red rock shelve, and began to meditate. I listened to my breathing take me deeper within myself.

A raven's low croaky "kaw" brought me out of my trance. I looked over at Teddy lying on the ground near me. My hand went down to pick up my handbag, and there on the red earth next to my left foot was a dark green polished stone about an inch long. What is this? How did it get here? I wondered as I picked up the stone and felt its smooth surface. I knew it was not there before I went into meditation as I would have seen it. Teddy would have barked if someone came up the trail or near me. Sedona's magic was at work. "Thank you for this wonderful gift," I said.

As I fingered the green stone in my hand, I thought I can hardly wait to show this stone to Hannah. I carefully placed it deep in the pocket of my jeans.

In a few days, I went to Hannah's house for my haircut. I brought the stone with me. After she cut my hair, I showed her my treasure and explained how I found it. I placed the stone in her hand. She studied it and said, "I think this is jade. It looks like California Jade."

She went into the other room and came back with her gem book and read, "California Jade will relieve anxiety and will lighten any emotions developed from fear. This stone will never allow any negative energy or negative influences to affect you while you wear it. It will protect you as it radiates a cleansing and calming aura."

"Wow, that is amazing!" I said.

She said, "This stone, I feel, was given to you for your protection. I've a pinch bail lying around here that you can have. Then you could wear the stone as a necklace."

"Let me pay you for it," I insisted.

"No, I've lots of these." She rummaged through a drawer in her credenza and found the gold-plated pinch bail she was looking for and gave it to me.

"I wish I had some glue, so I could attach the stone to this pinch bail."

"No need, I'll take it to work. The owner's husband is the silversmith. Thank you again for the pinch bail." On the way out of Hannah's house, I thought about the pinch bail. I knew that gold is material; silver is spiritual. I guess this gold-plated setting is more material although this does not feel right. Both gold and silver are good metals. Each metal indicates a different value system.

The next day after I settled in at work I said, "Look what I found after I meditated at Cathedral Rock. This stone was at my left foot." My colleagues gathered around me and touched the stone. I put the stone, the pinch bail, and my tan leather necklace into a little paper bag with the instructions: *Please glue the stone into the pinch bail and add a bevel that will fit over the leather necklace. Thank you.*

When I arrived at work several days later, the stone necklace was back intact with a note that read: *Sorry, when I put this pinch bail in the cleaning solution, the gold-plating turned to silver-plating.*

How about that! This was to be silver all along. I fastened the necklace around my neck. I noticed that there were still some flecks of gold in the pinch bail. I thought why not? A little materialism can be a good thing.

I walked over to one of the long mirrors and stared into it, admiring the green stone. I whispered, "You look like you belong there. "

That night Tera, the woman that took me to the

hospital in Mesa after the black widow bite, called right after I finished dinner. "Can my daughter and I come for a visit? I think Sedona's healing energy would be good for her. I know this is short notice, but could we come next Saturday morning and leave Sunday. There is a restaurant in Jerome we heard about and would like to go to on Saturday for dinner. It's called, "The House of Pleasure."

"What a name!" flew out of my mouth. I thought no doubt about what this house was used for during the mining days.

I said, "Absolutely. You both can come and stay with me. Do I need to make reservations at this restaurant?"

"Yes, they only take reservations. That is the only way to get a table. They're usually booked weeks in advance as they're only open on weekends. The rest of the week, the owners are repairing the house as it hangs onto the side of a cliff. Thanks again for letting us stay at your place."

"Not a problem, I'll call the restaurant and make reservations."

The following Friday, Tera called to say that she was very sorry, but her daughter was too ill to make the trip. Immediately after I hung up, I dialed the restaurant and was about to cancel and instead said, "I made a reservation for three, however the other two will not be able to make it. Would it be okay if I came alone?"

"Wow, you're brave," the hostess replied, "Of course you can come alone. We'll have a special table waiting for you."

"Thank you," I replied and hung up the phone. Was I brave? I tried to figure out what she meant because I was just driving to Jerome.

On Saturday I gave myself plenty of time and drove through Sedona, past Cottonwood, and Clarksdale to Jerome. I looked down at the remnants of the United Verde open-pit copper mine and copper mining area as my car climbed the very steep incline. I had read that Jerome, now a touristy, arty community, was once known as 'wild and wicked.'

Once on flat ground I located the small white house among the other small shops and parked my car in a lot across the street from it. The sun was slowly lowering itself.

The smiling hostess was ready for me. She sat me at a little table for two: the only table in the small foyer. I hung my handbag on the back of the wooden slotted chair. She handed me the menu and said, "Everything is included from appetizer to desert. Enjoy."

While I ate dinner, the waiters and waitresses talked with me while waiting to contact their customers. A perky waitress said, "Jerome's personality has changed dramatically in the past thirty years. Now there are about two hundred of us that live and work in the restored buildings. The mining area and town has become a tourist attraction."

Another waitress shared, "This building used to be a brothel for the miners. The women lived in this house."

"Do you ever hear any strange sounds?" I asked her. I wondered if any of the women's spirits were still here."

"I haven't, but Tim, one of the busboys, swears

he heard moaning and banging one night when he was cleaning up. He was alone. It made him very nervous."

Several people were now crowded in the lobby waiting to be seated. I felt the energy of this special place that once held so many women and their stories. I thought about these women: surviving, resilient, some sad, some forsaken, yet their strong aura still present in this house.

The night surrounded me like a dark blindfold. I inched my way, as if I was wearing a tight kimono, across the silent street towards my car. I could not see my feet in front of me. Somehow, I managed to get to my car.

I drove around the small houses and little shops until I sped down the steep roller coaster incline. I screamed, "HELP!" My foot was on and off the brake pedal as I thrust forward. The headlights fought to shed light through the thick dark curtain as the car flung itself towards the bottom. I grasped the steering wheel. The car stopped right before the incline met the flat road. I stayed several minutes to recover.

"I made it!" I screamed. Now I understood what the hostess meant about being brave.

22
keep an open heart and mind

Vicki, my co-worker, stopped me one day at work and said, "I know someone I think would be great for you to interview. She's a friend of mine."

"Sure, I would love to meet her. What is her name and why is she a candidate for the book?"

"Her name is Terry. Wait until you meet her, she has led an interesting life. Also, she is a remarkably talented artist and her sculptures are shown at prestigious galleries in the USA. I'll call her and see if she wants to do this."

Vicki dialed her friend, and turned to me, "She suggested we meet for dinner tomorrow night at the little Italian restaurant in West Sedona. She wants to meet you before she consents to the interview."

Terry

"That works for me," I said. Vicki relayed the message to Terry. The shop filled with customers; the tour buses had arrived. We were off in different directions helping customers.

The following night after we closed the shop, I followed Vicki's car to an old-world Italian restaurant in West Sedona. I was looking forward to meeting Terry. As we walked together towards the restaurant, Vicki waved to a stunning, blonde-haired woman. Terry possessed the same sex appeal as Marilyn Monroe, dressed in simple black pants and a white cotton shirt with its buttons ready to pop. She was far from a quiet beauty, much too sexy for this description.

The young male host escorted us to an enclosed wood booth and then lingered around our table. The restaurant was nearly empty. Another waiter with thin-rimmed glasses took our orders, returned and hovered with the host as they blatantly stared at Terry. Then the chef in his chef's hat walked over to the table. Another waiter came over to the table, just to make sure we were taken care of. Terry ignored the four gaping men and finally they left.

I teased, "Terry, those men were captivated by you. You certainly possess some sort of magnetic charm. I hope our waiter remembers to place our order."

She smiled. I wondered, what could this beautiful, sexy, young woman have to share? She seemed to have it altogether. We talked about the weather, the women in the book, and how tasty our pasta and salads were. She alluded that she had learned from her past experiences.

Something in me knew that she had a story to tell. Intrigued, I asked, "How do you feel about being interviewed? I would like to set up a time to meet with you?"

"Yes, I would like that. Why don't you come to my townhouse on Thursday, how about one' o'clock?" She wrote her information on the napkin.

"Thanks. I'm looking forward to it."

Thursday came, and I was on my way to meet with Terry. I pulled into a parking area not too far from a two-story building. I heard dogs barking incessantly. The only way to get to the townhouse was past the thick chain link fence that enclosed the vicious sounding dogs. My heart felt like it was going to run away as I glanced into the yellow eyes of the two Dobermans as they attacked the fence. I am a dog lover, but these dogs looked vicious.

Almost out of breath, I rushed up the tiled stairs and knocked on the door. There was a handmade ceramic pot filled with pink and orange impatiens on the small tiled landing. Terry was dressed casually in a denim shirt and jeans. "Welcome. Sorry the dogs are so noisy."

Once inside I said, "Thank you for agreeing to this interview."

I could see she loved artwork as I observed small and large handmade vases, interesting paintings in her open, yet tiny space. She pointed out some of her clay sculptures and exquisite metal art pieces.

"I love this sculpture," I said as I stopped at a small molding table and studied an unfinished clay piece she was working on: a lovely Indian maiden, her slender arms extended to the sky. Terry had captured the Native American woman's essence, her sensitivity, her feminine spirit. "You're a very talented artist."

"I enjoy my work, my creative side. When I'm

finished, I'll send this to a gallery in LA that shows my work." She motioned for me to sit down on the loveseat.

I asked, "Whose dogs are those outside?"

"They are mine. They are great dogs and great protectors."

I said, "What would you like to share?"

Terry sat on the sofa. and said, "I'm thirty-one years old. I married a charismatic billionaire much older than me and moved to Italy right after I graduated from college. He was very supportive of my art career. We had been together for three and half years, when I became pregnant. We were aboard his yacht when a fire broke out. We needed to get off the burning yacht and jumped overboard into the rough sea and in doing so, I received serious injuries. I had a miscarriage when I was in my fourth month and I lost the only child I would ever conceive. "

"Soon I grew tired of the material things. What matters most to me, and still does, are people. People, rather than collections, really count and are difficult to lose. I didn't allow wealth as such to spoil me. I place more value on intangibles – things we cannot buy – such as inner peace. I believe you're rich when you're at peace with yourself. You can have everything, but if you lack inner peace, then I believe - you have nothing. "

"I lived an opulent life that included art, jewelry, vacation homes, and a fourteen-bedroom house. We divorced shortly after the miscarriage and my ex-husband suggested I remain in Europe and find myself. I stayed in Europe for three months, and then went to India. I worked with

Mother Theresa in Calcutta for a month. She said to me, 'Go home and get to know yourself by helping people. Help people one on one; help those with AIDS.'"

"This is something I'll always do. I knew I had to put to rest – the anger and bitterness of the loss of my child and my marriage. Releasing these feelings freed me to move on to the next stage of my life - to become a successful sculptor."

I said, "Thanks for sharing this part of your life and what you have learned. Your art shows your sensitivity, creativity and wisdom. Is there a message you want to share to help others?"

She thought for a moment and said, "What has helped me the most is to keep an open heart. Bad things happen. Everyone in their lifetime goes through some kind of hurt. Those of us who have been hurt tend to shut down and shut others out – don't do this. Have an open attitude towards healing, let yourself love, and let yourself believe there is still beauty in life."

"Terry, I'm so glad I had this opportunity to interview you. I would never have believed by looking at you, that you have experienced and learned so much. I know your story will inspire other women who are going through or have gone through rough times."

As she opened the door, I heard the frantic barking. I carefully descended the brightly colored tiled steps. I walked as fast as I could, my face turned away from the charging dogs. I could hear them banging against the chain fence as I rushed for the safety of my car.

Something in me was healing. It seemed the

interviews, while they were meant to help others, were healing me. I felt that something positive; something feminine was connecting and mending my spirit. I knew that I would never look at another woman as I had in the past. I would intuitively look beyond her façade and know that there was more to her: more than her physical appearance showed.

After I returned home, I checked my phone messages and heard Crystal's familiar voice, "Hi, I would like you to interview Laura." She left her phone number. After I called her, we agreed to meet at her home in Uptown Sedona.

Checking the address to make sure I had the right house, I knocked on the door and introduced myself to Laura, a tall willowy woman with a very confident air about her. She seemed to glow.

Her little black and white dog was yapping and jumping at my feet. She motioned for me to follow her into her living room. The room wasn't very large, yet it looked like a page in a designer magazine. I sat on a comfortable sofa that was covered in a soft floral pattern.

"Would you like some lavender tea?"

"Yes and thank you again for this interview."

She poured the tea gracefully into little china cups. The smell of lavender soothed me. I carefully sipped the delicious hot brew. "What do you want to share with others, what have you learned?"

"My husband and I were entrenched in an unfulfilling pretentious lifestyle in a suburb in California outside of Los Angeles. I owned a gallery, and he was a real estate developer. During that time, we began to read *A Course in Miracles* from the Foundation for Inner Peace. We felt the void and lack of meaning in our lives. We decided to give up our shallow existence, our attachment to our jobs, our things, and our commitments and go for our freedom. We decided to sell everything and move to France."

"Our yuppie California friends were mortified. They thought we were crazy! They asked us, 'Why would you give up everything and move to a remote place in France? You don't even speak French!' Yet, that is exactly what we did!"

"I'll brew some more tea," she said to me. I thought, she certainly lights up the room. Her energy is so strong and bright.

When she returned, she refilled my cup. I took a sip and said, "I don't know if I could do what you did, even moving to Sedona is not as adventurous as moving to another country and not speaking the language! I've let go of furniture and stuff, however, not like you did."

She said, "I want to tell you that selling *everything*, letting go of those things was the biggest, single, most challenging lesson in my whole life. I learned that material possessions don't make me whole and complete. My happiness is not dependent on possessions."

"In France, we had to learn many things - in particular trust. The morning after our arrival in Nice, we were informed that there was a mistake, and there were no rooms available that night at the hotel. We had booked this hotel months ago. Instead of panicking, we opened to trust: we were guided to an adorable couple, rental agents, who showed us a wonderfully furnished apartment. We leased it and moved in. All this happened in one hour."

"We traveled throughout Europe in our little Volkswagen and never called ahead for reservations. We just went on faith that the appropriate place would appear, and it did. From these experiences and others like it, we learned to surrender - to trust that all would work out - and it did. We truly became different people."

"We lived in France for five years until our funds ran low. We went back to the US and we thought about moving to Carmel, California, however, fate intervened. Friends in Sedona invited us to visit and to help them paint their house, serenity blue. We agreed and when our friends were called away on business for three months, we stayed on and fell in love with this lovely, spiritual area and decided to make it our home. "

"Life in general, for me, is what comes with my spiritual growth, my relationship with God. All these experiences encouraged me to see things and life very differently. I now have an appreciation for simplicity and see beauty in everything surrounding me. I understand that love is all that is real; it's a precious thing to give and receive love."

"Laura, thank you for sharing your journey and the spiritual lessons you have learned."

I thought I will be open to trust and see what happens. "

23

there are no accidents

Susan and Howie, my friends from Cleveland, had moved to La Jolla, California. Even though I had not seen or talked to them in quite a while, we seemed to pick up our conversation from where we left off. Something stirred in me to call them.

I dialed their phone number and Susan answered in her cheerful voice, "Hi Sera, great to hear from you. Funny, I was just thinking about you. What's going on? I heard you moved from Cleveland to Ft. Lauderdale. On my last visit to Cleveland, someone told me you moved to Phoenix."

"Yes, I've become a spiritual vagabond. My relationship ended. I felt guided to move to Sedona. How are you doing? How is Howie?"

"We're doing great. We always wanted to live in La Jolla, and now we are living the dream. It's been too long since we've seen each other. Why don't you come for a visit?"

"I would love to. Let me see if I can get vacation time." Susan and Howie are like old shoes; when you put them on they feel good, comfortable.

The following day, I asked Elizabeth for the

time off. She said, "Let me check the schedule." She walked to the counter and pulled out the schedule. "Vicki has been asking for more days. She will be happy to fill in. Have fun in La Jolla. It's my favorite place."

"Thanks, I'm excited to see my friends and spend time near the ocean." The store was filling with people, so we set off to help them.

I booked a flight to San Diego with a great low fare. I made a reservation for Teddy at the kennel. I was happy that everything fell into place: always a good sign. After this was done, I called Susan and said, "Hi. Everything is good to go. Can you pick me up at the airport? I get in at 4:30 pm on Sunday."

I heard her reply, "We'll be there."

The plane taxied to the gate at the San Diego Airport. I pulled my black suitcase behind me through the maze of people and the sliding glass doors to the curb. The scene was very busy: droves of people pulling their luggage or waiting to be picked up, cars honking, policemen ticketing. Warm car fumes choked the air, yet somehow a little breeze managed to float past me. It felt cool and inviting.

After a few minutes, I spotted Susan and her new look: her hair a reddish color was short and spiked. I noticed Howie's curly hair was graying. I waved as Howie drove their car up to the curb. Susan called out of her window, "Put your luggage into the back seat because the trunk is filled with stuff. Climb in. It's way too busy for us to get out of the car."

Once in their car, Susan and I caught up on our mutual Cleveland friends and our daughters. The green hills and thick vegetation flew past my window as we drove through San Diego. The houses looked like colorful buttons pinned on a crinkly green crinoline. I opened my window and breathed in the scent of the green landscape and its healing power.

Their house reminded me of a seaside cottage, white with black shutters and window boxes filled with pretty flowers.

Susan said, "We choose this location to live since it's in the heart of La Jolla. We can walk to shops or to restaurants from here."

I gave them each a hug. Howie took my suitcase out of the backseat and rolled it into the house. We followed him.

I said to Susan, "You both look fit."

"Yes, we do a lot of walking and running around La Jolla, especially down by the Cove."

Howie set my luggage on the floor in their second bedroom. The high antique bed took up most of the space in the tiny room. I thought this will be a challenge to climb up there. I placed my handbag up onto the vintage dresser and my book on the little antique nightstand. My friends like antiques, thrift shops and eclectic surroundings. Modern and contemporary are not in their vocabulary, however, it's in mine. While I prefer new rather than old furnishings and housing, I can still appreciate their love of antiques.

Susan called from the living room, "Come with me. I'll give you a quick tour."

"All the antiques you brought with you from Cleveland fit in. I like the red and green fabric on your sofa and chairs. You did a great job decorating the house."

I followed her into the dark green kitchen complete with an antique free-standing stove, dark cabinetry and wood floors.

"How about something to eat?" She quickly found a wooden board and placed Brie, crackers, and sundried tomatoes on it. She poured two glassed of red wine. "Help yourself. Howie has disappeared. He's probably in the garage. He set up a photography studio in there. It's his domain. I'm afraid to step foot in there, afraid of what I might find. You know it's enough that I pick up after him in the house. I can only imagine what the garage looks like."

I chuckled to myself. Even though she is complaining, she dearly loves her husband of thirty years or so. She once told me that the reason their marriage has lasted so long is that she finds him *interesting.*

"I miss you. You both feel like family to me."

I put my arms around Susan's waist and gave her a tight squeeze. After the wine and several appetizers, I went to unpack.

The wonderful aromas coming out of the kitchen drew me there. Susan was busy at the white antique stove top putting spices into the chicken marsala, while Howie was at the counter, cutting up romaine lettuce and tomatoes for the salad. I sat at the small kitchen table watching the two of them performing their culinary skills.

"Where are you working?" I asked her at the dinner table. She could never be a stay at home personality since she had worked from a young age mostly in her family's gift and jewelry business, and then in their own jewelry store, where I had worked part-time.

"I'm a card rep, and my territory is La Jolla, San Diego, and some adjacent cities around the area. Tomorrow I want to visit some of my customers and see if they need reordering. You'll come with me. This will give you a chance to see more of the area."

"Sounds good. After dinner and the day of travel, I felt myself yawn and said, "Good night, I'll see you both in the morning."

The bright sunlight flooded the room through the light curtains. The smell of coffee and scones drifted into the bedroom. Susan and Howie are like Eskimos. They like to sleep in frigid temperatures, so I came prepared and entered their kitchen in a thick sweat outfit and warm socks.

I picked up a currant scone that Howie made. He poured coffee into a mug and handed it to me. "Susan will be out in a minute."

"I can't believe you made these scones. They are really good and so is the coffee."

Susan said upon entering the kitchen, "Yes, I taught him how to bake and cook so he could take care of himself if something happened to me. One of our friends lost his wife. He didn't know how to take care of himself. She had done everything for him. He couldn't even boil water."

She took a bite out of her scone. "As soon as you're ready, we'll get going. I want to get an early start."

"Good. I can't wait to see more of the area."

Susan was waiting in the living room. She looked very professional: dressed in a patterned silk blouse, navy pants and navy leather pumps.

She said, "Let's get the show on the road. We'll stop at a shop in the heart of La Jolla first."

She drove a short distance, then parked on a side street in front of a little stationary store. The store's window display featured a handsome large mahogany desk filled with leather desk accessories and open catalogs with sample invitations.

After lifting the folding cart from the trunk, Susan set it on the ground and put several large catalogs in it and pulled it into the store. I trailed behind her.

We were greeted by the owner, Cindy. She had the most incredible ocean blue eyes, graceful mouth and a cheery personality. "Susan told me you were coming for a visit." She held out her strong hand which I shook. "I'm glad to meet you."

"Thank you. I love your shop. You did a great job displaying everything." I felt a strong connection with this woman with the amazing eyes.

Engrossed in conversation, the two gravitated to a large cabinet that held many thick catalogs filled with invitations and stationary items. They sat down on wooden stools in front of the cabinet. I heard Cindy call out the greeting cards she wanted to order, and saw Susan writing down the numbers.

I walked around the small shop and looked at some of the greeting cards, formal monogrammed stationary, and printed invitations for all occasions. Small and large desks were positioned around the store with elegant desk accessories.

A comfortable looking beige linen sofa lured me into it. I glanced through a catalog of printed invitations on the glass coffee table in front of the sofa.

"Okay, let's go," Susan motioned to me. "Thank you." She hugged Cindy.

"It was great meeting you," I said to Cindy as I followed Susan out the door. "I love your store."

The brilliant California sunshine highlighted everything in its path. I breathed in the cool moist air. I could feel the ocean, sense it. "We must be close to the ocean."

Susan replied, "We're a block away. La Jolla is surrounded on three sides by ocean bluffs and beaches."

After we were in the car she said, "I'm going to take the scenic route to Del Mar, another beach town to see another customer."

The lush green landscape on the left side of the road changed to sparkling blue green water. I saw the big ocean waves froth white at the shore. I opened my window and heard the crashing waves and felt the cool moisture soften my face.

Susan pulled into a tiered parking garage and parked on the second level. We walked into an elevator with the cart. The elevator door opened into a large plaza with bright orange lounges and oversized orange umbrellas. We walked across the plaza to a bookstore with a restaurant that had organic and natural foods.

A tall thin earthy woman with thin clear glasses walked up to us. Her long chestnut hair was tied back with a scarf.

Susan introduced me and said, "This is Mattie; the owner." I shook her hand.

"Nice to meet you.

They walked to a nearby table to look through the greeting card catalogs. I meandered through many aisles filled with all sorts of books and spotted the New Age section. I selected a book about psychic energy and glanced through it.

Susan found me and said, "Let's have lunch here."

"Okay. I glanced at the menu. Everything looks good – organic and fresh." After lunch, we waved to the owner as we left the bookstore.

On the way out, Susan said, "I've one more stop. We're going to another section of Del Mar away from the ocean." She drove us through newly built houses. These two-story, red tiled roofed houses looked like each other.

She parked at a two-story retail building. She carried a catalog. We walked up wood plank stairs to the second level and into a cozy bookstore. Its selection of books, and greeting cards looked appealing.

The owner, a middle-aged woman with a pleasant face, greeted Susan warmly. "This is my friend, Sera. She is visiting from Sedona."

"Nice to meet you," I said.

From behind her desk, she said, "I've been to Sedona. It's quite beautiful. My husband and I enjoyed hiking the red rock trails."

"Yes, I hike there as well. The mountain scenery is soulful."

Susan put the catalog on top of the checkout

counter. The owner quickly looked through it and picked out greeting cards she wanted to order.

Before we left, the owner picked up a book. "Susan, you might want to read this. I read it, and I'm sure you'll enjoy it. It's very well written about a woman and her red dog."

After Susan read the back cover and several of the pages, she nodded and said, "It looks interesting. I'll get it for Howie and me. We enjoyed the last book you recommended."

"Sera, you're a fast reader. I'll let you read it first," she handed me the book after she paid for it.

We left the bookstore and walked a short distance to a large coffeehouse located on the same level. We split a homemade carrot and walnut muffin with our coffees.

"Why don't you move here," she said.

"I'm happy in Sedona right now. I'm busy interviewing women for my book, working, and enjoying the sacred red mountains. Why don't you and Howie come visit me?"

"We may just take you up on your invitation. We visited Sedona many years ago and thought it was beautiful."

At their house, Susan said, "Howie wants to go to a Vietnamese restaurant for dinner tonight."

"Okay, I've never eaten Vietnamese food before."

We freshened up and left for the restaurant which was not far from their house. Susan ordered different dishes to taste, which we all enjoyed.

The next morning after breakfast, we left for the airport. As I savored the beautiful green landscaping I said, "Thank you for everything. I'll miss you both. I asked again. "Why don't you come for a visit? I've plenty of room for you to stay."

Susan said, "We'll think about this?"

The flight seemed quick. I found my car in the parking garage and began the long drive back to Sedona. I heard the ocean's breath roaring in my ears. It seemed to be calling, beckoning me to return. I wondered what that was all about. Then I forgot about this sensation. I picked Teddy up from the kennel. His wagging tail showed me how happy he was to see me.

24
it takes work to be a positive person

A month had passed since my trip to La Jolla. As I walked through the condo door with Teddy, I heard the phone ringing and ran to answer it. "Hi Susan, what's happening?"

Her voice rising in excitement, she asked, "How would you like to go to Santa Fe, New Mexico with us? Howie and I've wanted to get back there since our last trip a few years ago. The area is quite beautiful as is surrounded by the Sangre de Cristo Mountains. I think you would enjoy the Spanish influence, art galleries, and boutiques."

"Sure," I replied, "I would love to. I've never been there. I heard it's a beautiful, spiritual place. Funny, a tarot reader once told me that I was a potter, worked in clay and knew Georgia O'Keefe in a past life in Santa Fe." Susan, I could tell was half-listening to my conversation regarding my past life. While it's not necessarily her belief, she respects mine.

She said, "We could visit her museum while we are there. We thought we could fly into Phoenix, rent a car, and drive to your place. We'll leave early the next morning for Santa Fe."

I said, "Sounds great! When where you

thinking of going there? I'll have to ask for time off."

"See if next Thursday through Sunday works. Let us know."

The next day, after Elizabeth came to work, I asked her for the time off. She assured me that it would be fine. I called and booked Teddy into the kennel. Everything seemed to fall into place. Again, a good omen! Then I thought, maybe I could interview women in Santa Fe for the book. Howie could take photographs of them. Susan showed me some of his work while I was visiting them. His black and white photos were exceptionally good, gallery good.

After asking around, I was successful in securing an interview with Dr. Amy for Sunday morning. She is a director of an international school that teaches Chinese medicine. I was excited to meet her.

I called Susan with the good news. "Ask Howie if he would photograph a woman while we are there. I scheduled an interview with her for the book I'm writing. I am hopeful that I can find other women in the area to interview that he can also photograph."

She answered, "I'll ask him. I'm sure he won't mind. He is bringing his camera and lens."

I set about to getting the condo ready for my visitors. Work kept me busy. I was looking forward to the Santa Fe trip.

Susan called me at the store. "We just got into Phoenix."

"Great. I left the front door key under the mat. Make yourself comfortable. There are appetizers in the refrigerator. I prepared dinner, so you can relax at the condo tonight. I'll see you later."

The next morning, we left in their rental car: our luggage snug in the trunk, mugs of hot coffee, a bag of Howie's currant scones and Teddy, who we dropped off at the kennel, much to his dismay.

It was dark when Howie pulled into a guest parking space at a quaint small inn, close to the Plaza, near the center of town. After we checked in and put our luggage in our rooms, we were more than ready for dinner. The cold November night air made us walk fast. The streetlights showed the deserted sidewalk and dark stores as we trudged against the wind hoping to find an open restaurant.

I watched my breath become a white puff in front of me. I said to Susan, "It's a good thing that you brought an extra pair of earmuffs and a wool scarf for me." I could not stop shivering as the strong wind whipped at me. I was grateful when I heard loud country music and laughter spilling into the air.

The large restaurant was completely full. I mentally asked for a *runner* (an entity that comes to our aid when asked to do so, of course, this is always for the highest good for all) to help us secure a table, and lo and behold, we were escorted to a table in the back. The only available table in the restaurant. I occasionally ask for help to find a parking space as well. I mentally thanked the *runner* for the table.

Up early the next morning, I walked carefully down the open metal stairs adjacent to the hotel's coffee shop. The cold wind reddened my cheeks.

The restaurant felt warm and inviting. As I stood at the register with three hot coffees, I felt guided to talk to the friendly cashier that was processing my credit card, "I'm writing a book about women, ordinary yet extraordinary women who are willing to share their life experiences to help others. Do you know anyone I can interview?"

"Yes. You should interview Juanita, our manager. She's an amazing woman. She'll be here at two o'clock today. I'll let her know you asked about her."

"Thank you, I'll stop back later and see if I can meet with her." I took the coffees and flew up the stairs to share the coffee and the news with my friends in their room.

Later we left for the Plaza and ate breakfast in a small restaurant with an eclectic atmosphere. After breakfast, we walked down a long street. The older stately houses, each one different, unique, were set back quite a distance from the curb. The trees like giant green soldiers lined both sides of the streets. We walked along another long street filled with galleries including one dedicated to Georgia O'Keefe, which I really enjoyed. We browsed in and out of Southwestern jewelry stores, retail shops and galleries along our way.

Around lunchtime, we trudged up a steep sidewalk on a long street to small restaurants and shops near its peak. We chose a restaurant with a large courtyard and sat outside among colorful flowers. It felt toasty sitting out in the direct sun. I took off my heavy jacket.

We walked back down the steep street towards the Plaza. I glanced at my watch and said, "See you later," and walked to the Inn hoping to meet with Juanita.

Juanita

The coffee shop was empty when I arrived. I asked a hostess to direct me to Juanita. She pointed to a corridor that led to a very spacious meeting room filled with round unclothed banquet tables and chairs. The unlit room was quiet. A woman in her early 40's, dressed in a black and white starched uniform, was straightening a drapery that hung over one of the French doors.

"Hi, I'm looking for Juanita."

"I'm Juanita; my cashier said that you wanted to meet me."

I held out my hand to gently grasp hers and sensed a sturdy, self-assured energy. "I am writing a book to empower women and would like to interview you. I was hoping that you'll share your story, your wisdom, and whatever you have learned."

Her dark prudent eyes studied me before she made her decision. I waited silently. She spoke softly, yet clearly, "Please have a seat. "

We sat on two white banquet chairs near an impressive unlit fireplace. Sunlight filtered through the large French doors at the rear of the room creating some light in the dark chilly room.

"What was your mother like?" I asked.

She paused and then replied, "Innocent, quiet, an unassertive woman who had a difficult, unfulfilled life. Even though she had tremendous strength, she died angry."

"I'm a Pueblo Indian. My Hispanic family dates back three hundred years to the Re Conquest of Santé Fe, New Mexico. My family lived in the Pueblo community outside Santa Fe. My father, an alcoholic with a machismo belief system, wanted a son. When his first daughter was born, he accepted his fate. After his second daughter was born, he became outraged, intolerant as he felt cheated. I was the second daughter. He rejected me; verbally abused me, tried to make me feel inferior. He told me I was useless. He kept this up until he succeeded - my self-image was low."

"When I was twelve years old, I worked at a nearby hotel ranch. I was respected for my work. I worked very hard and never missed a day. I taught myself that I'll do what has to be done to the best of my ability. Through this work experience, I flourished and became self-reliant."

"In the 1960's, I was caught in the middle between the hippy generation and my mother's subservient generation, I chose neither; instead I marched to a different drummer. When I didn't walk three paces behind the man or behave like the other women, I became an outcast in my community. Yes, our macho traditions are archaic, yet difficult to change, even in the 60's."

"Despite my father's cruel remarks that no one would marry me, I did marry and have two children. I've told my daughter and my son the truth - they could count on this. Life is not fair; it takes hard work to be a positive person. You don't have to submit to a role - just be true to yourself, even if you pay a different price – it's worth it! I know, for I paid that price: by the avoidance of my female friends and relatives and disapproval by the men in my community for my independence, my assertiveness, and my different ways."

"On this isolated path, I felt out of sync with the time - with other women. There was no one to turn to, no one to relate to. I began to read self-help books and came across Scott Peck's book, *The Road Less Traveled*. This book made me realize that there was nothing wrong with me."

"After my twenty-year marriage started to deteriorate, I questioned - why be alone and be married - why not just be alone? I wasn't willing to compromise anymore; I stood my ground. I'm important. I'm a person of worth and worthy of being loved. I deserve to get the best that I can achieve. As I became stronger within myself, my marriage became stronger: it took on a different direction, a more satisfying one. We eventually moved back into the Pueblo community."

"I continue to strive for self-improvement. I now don't accept guilt that is not mine. I don't accept responsibilities that are not mine. From Tai Chi, I learned to allow the force that would destroy me - go past me and destroy itself."

"My hard work and determination have promoted me to becoming the restaurant manager at this Inn. My success continues in my life as I meet everyday challenges head on, positive, following my intuition."

"What do you want to share to help other women?"

"I encourage you to be true to yourself. You cannot love anybody until you love yourself. Release the need to conform and your fear of rejection or isolation."

"Thank you for this interview. You're such a courageous and inspiring woman. I know that you'll be an advocate for change in your community."

Before I left, I asked Juanita if Howie could take a photo of her for the book later that day. She agreed even though she felt that she was not attractive. As I gazed into her dark eyes, I saw her inner reflection, her outer loveliness – a beautiful flora. Is one flower more beautiful than another?

I met up with Susan and Howie at the inn. We decided to eat dinner in their dining room. After dinner, my friends wanted to retire early. I stayed as I felt drawn to the upbeat music at the piano bar. I slid into an empty seat around the ebony piano and ordered an apricot brandy. A charismatic slightly balding man was playing many old favorites and talking to his seated guests around his piano. I felt comfortable, relaxed. One conversation led to another and I found myself talking about the book to the interested pianist.

After a woman left, a young man in his twenties jumped into the seat next to me. He said, "Hi, my name is John. Tell me about your book."

I related some of the stories and wisdom from some of the women, I had interviewed, including Juanita. His courteous manner and worldly air made me think that he was much older, wiser than his years. I guessed he was Hispanic probably from this area.

His dark eyes locked into mine. "You should interview my mother. She is an incredible woman. She was a concert pianist performing her first public concert at the age of eleven and later became a music teacher. She has a great attitude and view of life. She would be a great candidate for your book."

"I would love to meet her," I answered. I wrote down her information in my little notebook, and carefully put it back into my handbag.

He said, "I'll call her tomorrow morning and let her know that you'll contact her." He bent over and kissed my cheek. This young man, a junior at the University of Albuquerque, seemed wise, spiritually aware for someone so young. I felt a profound connection to him.

"Can I walk you to your room?"

"No, thank you." Even though I felt this strong connection with him, however, he was much too young for me in this lifetime. "I look forward to my visit with your mother. Good luck at school," I said as I stood up and quickly left the noisy room.

I was in awe of how fast the Universe works when you're open to receive. Now I had another candidate for the book. I could not wait to meet her.

Pauline

In the morning, I called Pauline, John's mother, and set up an interview with her for that afternoon and mentioned that Howie would take photos. After I hung up, I called Dr. Amy and confirmed our appointment for Sunday morning and explained that I was bringing along a photographer.

I called my friends and we decided to go back into town for breakfast. We hiked up a very steep street stopping at several busy restaurants to review their breakfast menu until we found one that appealed to us: a restaurant with a large outdoor patio so we could enjoy the crisp sunny day. Because it was Sunday, tourists, locals, and families with hungry children walked past us eyeing our table in their search for an empty one.

With breakfast over, Susan left to revisit some of the shops. Howie and I walked to Pauline's house. We found the modest white house surrounded by massive Ash trees. The house was set back from the busy street. A stout blonde-haired woman wearing a dark blue dress with an embroidered poncho over it greeted us at the door. She appeared to be in her late 50's. She towered over both Howie and me. After a brief introduction, Howie quickly took the photos and left.

I said, "Thank you for this interview. I am glad John suggested I interview you for the book about inspiration women. He is very proud of you."

Her face took on a radiant glow as she smiled and said. "He is a wonderful son." She sat down in the chair next to me.

"John told me that you had a musical career."

"Yes, I was trained as a concert pianist, and later I became a music teacher at a prominent music institute of tone and techniques. I received my music degree from the Royal Academy of Music in London, England. At age eleven, I performed solo in England and the United States. I won honors in Sonata performances, contemporary music and was a three-time winner in contrapuntal performances."

I asked, "What was your mother like?"

"My lovely, serene mother died when I was seven years old. My former piano teacher became not only my instructor - she became my surrogate mother as well. She taught me to pursue excellence, search for quality, and look behind music to what meanings I might find. She taught me to never, never give up. I could fall on my face a hundred times . . . *it is the getting up that is important.*"

"She helped me recognize the beauty and energy inside of me and to share it with others. All of us have creativity within ourselves, whether it is in music, painting, literary arts or another form of our artistic expression. There is a reservoir inside all of us. We need not be afraid to tap an untried skill at any age. Discover yourself - these skills are there; you only need to find them."

"It was during the international convention in Santa Fe that I met my husband-to-be. We soon married. Within time, we adopted two children to complete and share our happiness. However, fate struck a hard blow to us after we adopted our son, John. The six-week old baby was not well and was soon hospitalized. I stayed with him in the hospital night after night sending him love and hope. When he was a year old, he weighed fourteen pounds. His chances of survival were not good, yet I refused to succumb to pessimism. I needed to ride out this storm using faith, energy and every ounce of hope for his survival."

"I remember standing tall, keeping my spirit and optimism strong, even at a time when the outward situation seemed so out of control. As I watched my son fight for his life, I began to draw on that same inner strength and the strength of my former performing days. I remembered my piano teacher's advice to 'never, never give up.' This advice is what sustained me through long periods of anxiety. My son, also determined never to give up, fought for his life and won. As you could see, my son turned out to be a remarkable young man, healthy, and vibrant."

"I'm so grateful that I met your son and now you. You're a wonderful role model and a wonderful mother. No wonder John is so proud of you and wanted me to meet you." I pictured her charming son in my mind, his charisma, his aliveness, and his deep wise soul.

I walked back toward the inn and thought about synchronicity, first Juanita and then meeting John and his mother. I had wished to interview others in Santa Fe and I did.

Susan and Howie were at a historical hotel and renowned bar next to our inn where we were to meet up.

I opened a thick rustic door and entered a large room with high ceilings that I presumed was the lobby. The dark polished floors and the sparse antique chairs and benches outlining the walls made the room feel like a monastery instead of a hotel.

I moved toward the loud chatter into the crowded room. I saw my friends near the end of an ornate brass bar deeply engrossed in conversation with the bartender. I forged through the crowd to where they were standing. After a warming Sambuca and good conversation, we walked out into the frigid night for hot Mexican food. This sadly was our last night in this amazing place.

After breakfast at the Inn, we checked out and stowed our luggage in the trunk of the rental car. Howie drove us to the Healing Institute, so I could interview Dr. Amy and he could photograph her.

On the way there I said, "The place we are going to is an international school that teaches traditional Chinese medicine including acupuncture and Chinese herbology."

Susan turned to me, "I'm going to stay in the car for it won't take him long to take the photos. I want to go back to some of the stores. We'll pick you up after your interview and head back to Sedona."

"Okay, sounds like a plan. I'll meet you out front after the interview."

Dr. Amy

Once in the lobby, Howie and I introduced ourselves to Dr. Amy, a mature Chinese woman, who peered up at us through clear framed glasses. A pretty silk scarf was tied around her neck and a patterned cardigan sweater set hung over her black wool pants. Her dark hair was cut short around her pleasant face.

She introduced her husband and co-director of the school, Dr. David, who was also Chinese. He was slightly taller than her, dressed professionally in a well-tailored dark suit, white shirt and tie. He had a strong handshake. Howie speedily took photos of the doctor right there in the lobby and left.

It was Sunday, the school was closed. I followed the doctors down a hallway to an empty classroom. The large bright classroom was filled with blond wooden chair desks. I maneuvered into one of the chairs in the front row.

Dr. Amy sat next to me. I found it interesting that she brought her husband with her for the interview. Odd, none of the other women I interviewed brought their spouses or significant others; they attended the interview alone.

After I took out my pen and paper, I said to her, "Thank you for letting me interview you. What would you like to share to help other women?"

Her husband started to speak on her behalf. "I'll do this," she spoke up, as she turned around in her chair to alert her husband, who was seated several rows behind us. He remained silent, yet totally present for the rest of the interview.

She looked at me and continued, "I think I want to begin by telling you about a series of events that brought me from China to America and how these events dramatically changed my life."

"My father-in-law, a governor with the Old Government of China, was given political asylum in America. There was no communication at that time with him, so the family had no idea where he had settled in the United States. Years later, after an extensive research, my husband located him. He visited his father and became enamored with America. In 1980, he also moved here with the plan that I and our sons would follow in due course."

In 1983, my husband sent me an urgent letter requesting that I come to America and assist him at the International School, where he was the director. After I reread his letter, I knew that my life would never be the same. I didn't speak a word of English. I thought about the negative changes in China, how concerned I was about the controls the government had regarding my children's education and family life."

"My family is very important to me. We are very tight. I wanted all of us to be together, yet I feared living in America. I really thought this was a violent country and was concerned about all the terrible things I had heard about the United States such as the drugs, alcohol, free sex, and the killings on the streets. I carefully studied my choices knowing that my decision not only affected my life but my husband and two sons as well. With mixed feelings, I chose to leave my prominent position as chief physician, Chinese Herbologist and Acupuncturist at the hospital and College of Traditional Medicine and its teaching hospital in Changzhou."

"I was successful in China; all the students liked me. When asked by the students, who was the best teacher? They would select me. Leaving my country, my home, my practice, my colleagues, and my students was very difficult."

"From being very busy, teaching, treating, and researching, I found myself in New Mexico at a complete standstill. I couldn't do anything because I didn't know the language. I was totally unprepared for this sudden loss. Not knowing a single word of English was a bigger disadvantage than I could ever have realized. From a totally independent woman, I was now forced to become dependent on my husband, even though we were both professionals, and held the same degrees."

"I enrolled in a basic English class for foreigners for three months, where I struggled to learn my A, B, C's, which were so hard for me to understand. I was worried that if I didn't learn the language, I couldn't do my life's work, the work that I was trained and loved to do - teach."

"I wanted to learn from my unhappiness and focused on myself. I 've always had compassion for others, now it was my turn. I directed this caring, energy to me. I began to regain my self-esteem. My unhappiness taught me to have kindness for myself."

"The first class I taught at the Institute was on a subject that would have been simplistic for me to teach in China. I spent one week preparing, relearning all the names of the herbs in English. This process was very difficult and upsetting. In the Chinese language, there are no n's or l's. and it's hard to determine the s's and z's in the English language. My students helped me during the class. I used my hands and my face to help them understand me. Together, we made it work. I was so happy that I was teaching again."

"I now teach my students to have compassion for themselves. I instruct them to direct the same loving energy you give to others - to yourself especially during difficult and stressful times. Study your unhappiness to learn happiness."

"Thank you, what an inspiration you are!" I told her.

After returning to the lobby, I said, "You should be very proud of your wife." I caught his pleased expression as I walked out the door.

Susan and Howie were waiting outside in the car.. We left for Sedona.

I said, "What a fun trip! Howie, thanks again for taking the photos of the women." I shared Dr. Amy's inspiring story with them.

25
eagle energy brings higher wisdom

Right after Susan and Howie left Sedona, I received a call from Teresa, my friend from Tempe. She and her husband, Jack, wanted to come for a visit. We decided that the following weekend would work. I loved that my friends wanted to visit. I sensed it was Sedona's special charm, her red beauty drawing them to her.

My neighbor, Alice, stopped by the condo for coffee with banana bread. She said, "Fresh out of my oven. "How is everything?"

"Work is good. My friends are coming in town. I don't know where to take them other than the usual hiking spots. I wish I had something special planned."

"I've a great idea," said Alice. "There is a local tour company, Sedona Tours. Their jeep tours take people through Sedona's sacred areas beginning at dusk. They call this - a *Vision Quest*. The tour owner told me that some people have a spiritual awakening in the vortexes located high in the red mountains."

"That sounds like a great idea. What will it cost?" I said quickly.

"Nothing, he traded me a Vision Quest Tour for

four people as payment for an ad featuring his company that I placed in my travel magazine."

"Are you sure you want to give up this adventure?"

"Yes, positive, I'll never use it."

"Okay, I love the idea of going on this tour, and I know they will too."

"When will your friends be in town?"

"They are coming in Friday and will leave Sunday."

She set her coffee mug down and called the tour company, "Hi Ted. It's Alice. I would like to use my Vision Quest Tour for one of my writers. Is next Saturday evening going to work? It will be for three. No, I won't be there. Yes, her name is Sera. Okay, I'll tell her to be there at six at your office. Thanks."

"Are you sure you want to give me this outing? Why don't you come along?" I asked again.

"Listen, I really appreciated the article you wrote and your friendship. No, I really have no desire to do this; this is more your thing than mine."

"Thanks." I gave her a big hug.

I could hardly wait until the weekend. Teresa and Jack called after they arrived in Sedona. I gave them directions to the condo. Teresa loves Teddy, and I knew he would be happy to see her. We agreed to meet for dinner at an Italian restaurant right after I finished work.

That night I walked into the busy restaurant. The ambience was inviting: red and white checkered vinyl tablecloths, decorative wine bottles with dripping candles and landscape paintings of Italy. The large open room was filled with locals and tourists amid bustling servers.

I spotted my friends at a table near the window. Teresa looked the same; her thick blonde bangs still hung over her dark eyes. Jack's dark hair was well groomed; he looked trim and fit. They seemed happy.

"You both look great!" I said. Jack stood up. I gave each of them a hug. "Did you find the condo without a problem?"

"Yes, you gave us good directions. We drove around Sedona after we settled in. I love the area and the condo. You did a great job in finding this."

"Thanks. I've something exciting to tell you. Tomorrow night at six, we're going on a special jeep tour, a Vision Quest. I can't wait to share this adventure with you. My friend, Alice, gave me this gift for an article I wrote for her travel magazine. Do you want to do this? I can cancel this tour if you aren't interested."

She looked at her husband and said, "We would love to. It will be a new experience for us."

"For me as well," I said. "I've never been on a Vision Quest."

The next morning, bright and early, they left to go sightseeing. I had laundry to do in town and a few errands to run. We would meet back at the condo in the late afternoon. They arrived back around five. I had set different cheeses, crackers out on a wood cheese board as I knew we would be eating late.

At a quarter to six, I drove the three of us to

Uptown and parked my car near the jeep tour office. We walked upstairs. I knocked on the door. I pulled at the door; it was locked. I peered through the window and saw it was dark inside. We walked back down the stairs and waited at the bottom of the staircase.

Several minutes later, a tall distinguished looking man, his dark hair sprinkled with silver, came towards us. His hair was shorter than most of the men in the Sedona area. His female companion looked much younger than him. They were warmly outfitted and looked like seasoned campers.

"Hi, you must Sera," he said. "I'm Ted; this is my friend, Liz." Teresa and Jack introduced themselves. and followed our guides to their parked jeep.

Ted said, "Hop in." The three of us snuggled into the back of the open jeep. Ted gave each of us a Native blanket. "It can get chilly in the mountain air. You'll need these."

"Thanks," we said in unison.

Then I asked, "Where are you from?"

"Boston." he replied, "you probably detected my accent," as he started the jeep. "I was fed up with the corporate day-to-day survival. I was divorced and wanted a totally different lifestyle. I came here for a visit, resonated with the red rocks, went home, packed my belongings and never looked back. I bought this jeep company shortly after I moved to Sedona about four years ago."

He guided the jeep up and down different residential areas with breathtaking scenery. We were bouncing around in the back of the fast-moving jeep. I silently absorbed the beauty of the darkening red rocks, the thick dark green foliage, and the sweet-smelling wind. Ted, like an experienced Native American scout, guided the jeep through rough and smooth terrain.

"Sedona is known for its four main vortexes. Right now, we are near the Airport Mesa Vortex. Other vortexes are at Bell Rock and Boynton Canyon; later we'll end up at the one of my favorite spots, Cathedral Rock Vortex."

Teresa asked, "What is a vortex?'

He said, "The vortexes are swirling centers of subtle energy that come out from the earth's surface. Some say the vortexes are portals where the extraterrestrials can enter our planet especially near Boynton Canyon. Others seem to think that that Sedona is a vortex: it draws spiritually minded people. The subtle energy that exists at these locations interacts with your spiritual nature. This energy vibrates and strengthens the Inner Being of each person that comes within a half mile of it."

After I listened to Ted, I said, "There is no doubt in my mind that Sedona is a mystical, healing place. I think people are vortexes: energies whirled together to a place, to meet, interact for a higher purpose, higher learning and then move on taking what they need with them. "

"I agree," he said as he drove the jeep up and down different scenic roads until he turned sharply and finally, I was in my familiar territory, Cathedral Rock. He drove through the vacant parking lot and started up the rough trail, past my favorite meditation spot, higher and higher. I had never ventured this far on the mountain.

"We are near the Cathedral Rock Vortex at Red Rock Crossing. You may or may not feel this strong energy. Just know it's here."

He stopped the jeep near the edge of the red rock crevice. The panoramic view from this high peak was breathtaking, soulful.

He said, 'Bring your blankets as you'll need them." Ted, with Liz's assistance spread the large woven blanket on the hard ground close to the crevice. We sat on the rough blanket, crossed our legs to face the grand vista that spread out before us.

The silence interacted with me as it blended with the incredible beauty that surrounded us: the darkening red orange colors of untouched land as it met the heavenly blue sky. I felt the cold hard ground beneath me and felt connected to it. I pulled the Native blanket around me tightly.

My friends wrapped their blankets around them as well. The temperature had dropped considerably. The glorious sunset exploded like a gigantic firecracker into a dazzling array of reds, purples, and oranges, and slowly faded into black. I could barely see my hand in front of me.

We turned around and formed a circle. Ted began to chant. My eyes closed as well as my mind as I listened to his low rhythmic sounds. I followed my breath as I sensed myself going within, connecting. Then he was silent. I relaxed and allowed the relaxation to take me even deeper. Time stood still. I was present and not present.

His loud chanting brought me back. I squirmed on the cold hard earth beneath me, and felt a cool breeze tighten my face and hands. I zipped my cotton hoodie up to my neck and tucked my hands under the blanket. I waited while the others came back from their sacred inner journey and opened their eyes.

Ted said, "I saw a black raven. I was seated next to him, high on the mountain. He is my spirit guide and usually comes through my dreams. He creates synchronicity as he can bend and fold time. He told me that we were to be together to experience this night. He brings the message of transition, change and healing for all of you. Be open to his magic."

He asked, "Who wants to share their experience?"

I knew Teresa and Jack would not share their experience or their feelings. They were very private people. I respected this.

I broke the long silence and said, "I'll share my vision. I saw a large eagle appear before me in my mind's eye. His yellow eyes looked directly into mine. I'm not sure what this means."

After a moment, Ted said, "You have eagle energy. This is your power symbol. Your destiny is to be a carrier of higher wisdom. You bring these higher messages from other worlds to this world. You'll be guided to write and speak about this. This is your sacred journey."

The soft moonlight outlined our silhouettes. Ted motioned for us to get into the jeep. Ted with Liz's help rolled up the large blanket and placed it in an opening behind us. He started the engine, turned on the headlights, and maneuvered the vehicle down the uneven trail.

I looked at my watch; it was almost eight. No

one spoke as he drove us back to his office. I could hear the other cars on the road. I felt the cool wind encircle me and shivered.

"Thank you. That was amazing," I said as I put my arms around his thick sweatshirt and gave him a hug.

He said, "Say hi to Alice."

"Of course," I replied. "I'll tell her she missed a grand adventure."

Turning to Liz, I hugged her and said, "Nice meeting you." My friends embraced them both.

I turned on the heater in my car as fast as I could. "The restaurant I want to take you to is right down the street."

We entered the eclectic restaurant, which was extremely busy. Fortunately, we were seated right away for we were very hungry.

Teresa said, "That was quite an experience. Neither of us has ever done anything like this. Thank you."

"I was hoping that it would be meaningful to you." I knew they would not discuss their experience with me. I hoped they would share their messages and insights if they received them.

My guests left early the next morning without breakfast since they wanted to get an early start. I realized after they left that Teresa and I never discussed the book.

I drove into West Sedona to run some errands and browsed in one of the metaphysical bookstores. I bought a small amethyst stone to meditate with because it awakens higher consciousness. As I drove back to the condo, I could not believe my eyes as I looked through my car window: the white and dark clouds had formed an enormous eagle within the pale blue sky. I stared at this spectacular sight and turned my head to see if any of the other drivers around me were aware of the gigantic eagle.

No one noticed. Was I the only one to see this? Look up, look up! I wanted to scream as I viewed this spectacle in the sky. The bearded man in the red truck drove past me, his eyes straight ahead; the dark-haired woman in the grey car next to me was deep in thought, the balding postman was intent on delivering the mail; none of them saw what I saw. No, they were too preoccupied, in their world and their thoughts.

Driving back to the condo, I remembered what Ted said about having eagle energy and that this was my power symbol. This was an amazing confirmation to see those clouds!

26
develop a philosophy of harmlessness

Crystal wanted to meet in town to give me the film of some of the women she had photographed so I could have them developed. I saw her seated at a table waiting for me. I waved and said, "Hi, I'm going to get an iced tea." After I joined her, she handed me the film.

I said, "Thank you. You've been doing a great job capturing the personality of each of the women." I put the rolls of film into my handbag. I wrote out a check and paid her. She very carefully put the check into her wallet.

"This money is helping us. My boyfriend hasn't been working due to his illness."

"I'm so sorry. I'll send him green healing energy. I'm sure you're doing that as well." Crystal nodded for she has a medical background and is a gifted healer.

She said, "I've two more women for you to interview: Elaina and her mother, Arlene. I told them you would call."

"I'll call her later today." I looked into her clear blue eyes. "Thanks for getting these interviews." She nodded. We hugged briefly.

Several days later, I set out with Elaina's instructions in hand, yet getting to her cottage was not easy, as her street was located off a hidden drive. I did manage to find the drive and was there on time.

Elaina

She opened the door as soon as I pulled onto her driveway. Her dark hair fell around her shoulders; she was in her early thirties, earthy. She wore a denim jumpsuit, sleeves rolled up. I followed her through her hallway laden with large green plants into her living room filled with an assortment of flowering plants.

"You have beautiful plants."

"Thanks. I love my plants. Plants have energy." Elaina moved to a large green leafed philodendron, "Put your hand close to this leaf."

I did this. "I felt a tingling sensation. That is amazing."

I followed her to a sofa in her rustic living room. I took out my writing tools and listened.

She began, "I was raised in private schools in the US and Europe. My Jewish parents are liberal and sent me to a Waldorf school based on Rudolph Steiner's educational philosophy. This school develops skills in a holistic manner, cultivating imagination and creativity, as well as empathic understanding. Rudolph Steiner was an Austrian philosopher, an original thinker, who founded Anthroposophy."

"When I was growing up, my father was a

screenwriter. He had many jungle animals on the sets, and I played with lion cubs, jaguar cubs and monkeys. I fell in love with a beautiful jaguar cub. After that I became a vegetarian because of my love of animals - I could not eat meat. When we lived in Beverly Hills, California, a friend of our family was going through a divorce and she wanted us to keep her seven lions. My compassionate parents built a compound on our acre of land. The lions were there for nine months. We love animals and loved having the lions there."

"Here is a photo of me when I was ten years old." The photo showed Elaina sound asleep snuggled between two lion cubs: each cub sucking one of her thumbs. As you can see, I stand firmly for animal rights. People need to think of animals as feeling, thinking beings, that have an interest in living and are just as afraid as we are of pain, suffering, and death."

"My philosophy is one of harmlessness. I want to live my life without ever intentionally hurting or harming a living soul. This is most likely why whatever I need seems to come to me. I don't seem to do much searching."

"I try to keep an open mind towards things in my personal life like never resisting new ideas, and not being afraid to try something new – not being afraid to fail. I've tried many things, wore many hats in my life from owning a film company to teaching belly dancing to bartending. I love helping people. My goal is to lessen the suffering in this world."

I said, "Thanks for the interview. Who knows maybe you can put the two together, your passion and your goal. You have such a kind nature. You made me aware that plants have energy and that animals have feelings. I'm so glad I met you. I look forward to interviewing your mother," I said as I walked out the door.

I thought about what Elaina said regarding animals and their feelings. I wondered about Teddy, my little dog. Yes, I felt he could have feelings. I'll give him extra attention when I get home.

Arlene

After I hugged Teddy, I phoned Arlene and explained the nature of my call. I heard a sweet voice with a European accent on the other end of the phone say, "I've been expecting your call."

"Great. I just met with your daughter and cannot wait to meet you. Yes, next Thursday morning at eleven would work. See you then."

The week disappeared and there I was in front of Arlene's cottage knocking on her black painted door.

I was surprised when I met Arlene. She didn't resemble her daughter. She was much shorter and rounder than Elaina, wore makeup and seemed to have an aging movie star quality about her.

"Come in," she said. Her living room conveyed old-world charm and was filled with relics from many countries, mostly from Africa. I sat down on a comfortable sofa. She sat next to me in a chair and said, "I look like such a mess. I've been nursing this cold and didn't have time to get my hair done."

"Don't worry," I replied. "Crystal will give you plenty of time to get ready before she takes your photo. Thank you for meeting with me." I looked at her features, tiny nose, expressive dark eyes and thought to myself, I bet she was a striking woman when she was younger.

I took out my notepad and said, "Your daughter is amazing - so sensitive and caring." Arlene smiled as a proud mother would do.

She asked, "Would you like some coffee?"

"Sure, I take milk or cream if you have it." She left to get the coffee. I noticed the large portrait of Elaina, and several smaller photos of Arlene and her husband surrounded by jungle animals. Some photos were with Hollywood celebrities. Many photos were with African dignitaries.

After taking a sip of the steaming bitter coffee, which reminded me of the freeze-dried stuff, I said, "What would you like to share?"

She replied, "My husband and I met and married in Palestine during World War II. We went to England where we both joined the British Army. I joined the Intelligence Core because I speak many languages. I made large maps of the desert. I was in Cairo for two years then sent to South Africa on a ship to the northern part of Ethiopia."

"In Nairobi, I boarded a paddle ship. I was dressed in civilian clothes. I was on this ship for two weeks and saw hippos and crocodiles. A cyclone hit the boat and turned it bottom side up. We were forced to shore. There I met a tall, seven-foot Dinka, who was nude except for a bracelet. I'm 5'2"; I kept averting my eyes. He wanted my cigarettes, 50 cigarettes for his pipe. I wanted his pipe for my husband. I bargained to give him 20 cigarettes. I boarded another ship. He followed the ship through three villages where we continued to barter and develop a comradery. At our last stop, I gave in, gave him 100 cigarettes, and he in turn, gave me his pipe and his favorite bow and arrow."

I said, "What an adventure!"

She sipped her coffee and continued, "My boss was worried about me; he sent parties out to look for me. After I was able to contact him, he asked me to remain in Africa for another year. "

"My husband and I returned to England in 1944. We stayed a year after the war ended. Neither my husband who was an actor, nor I, could find jobs in our fields, and besides my husband had fallen in love with Africa and wanted to go back there. He applied for a job as Chief of Police in Dill Adwa, part of Somali close to Ethiopia, and was hired. I became the First Lady of the Land. We supervised twenty miles of desert and lived there for thirteen years."

"In Kunduchi, Africa, the land of fertility, at 38 years old I became pregnant with my daughter, Elaina. We moved back to England and then moved to Los Angeles, California. My husband became a prolific writer in Africa and a successful screen writer in Los Angeles writing scripts about animals."

"When Elaina was seven years old, she came home from Catholic school in Los Angeles and told me that she had to say seven Hail Mary's. I decided to take her to Hollywood to see a synagogue, a Buddhist ashram, a mosque, and a Hari Krishna temple. We even went to a Catholic Church in Venice. Even though we are Jewish, I wanted my free-spirited daughter to explore different religions and choose one that she would be happy with."

I said, "That is remarkable that you held your daughter's interest so high and let her explore these different religions and her spirituality."

She said, "We have a special bond with our daughter. Now where was I? Oh, yes, my husband and I moved to Sedona to be near her and her boyfriend. We visited Sedona ten years before we started making movies and remembered the beauty and red rock sculptures."

"What wisdom do you want to share?" I asked.

"There is an awful lot of hatred here on this planet. I don't believe we are equal. Everything is individual. There are different levels of intelligence, some more talented. We need to help people, animals, and plants. We need to be tolerant and understanding of each other – let go of anger - because kindness is very important."

"Thank you," I said. "You have led an adventurous life. You have reminded me to be kinder and more sympathetic to others."

27
one is never too old to try new things

The gift store kept me busy. I enjoyed interacting with the customers, who were from all over the world. I appreciated the friendship of my fellow co-workers.

The drive to and from the gift store on Hwy 179 was beautiful and soulful. I passed Bell Rock, one of the large rock formations and a popular tourist attraction. Little by little, his spirit energy began to reveal more of himself. As I drove past him in the morning on my way to work, he showed me his handsome reddish orange profile with his favorite soft derby hat on top of his massive head.

On my way home near dusk, I would see a different side of him: his handsome face now shadowed appeared rougher, jagged and intimidating. He was allowing me to see the dual sides of his complex nature. I made a habit of waving to him regardless of his appearance.

"Hi Mr. Bell Rock," I would say out loud as I drove past his mammoth edifice. One night on the way home, I waved at him and said my usual greeting, and heard a deep male voice, "Hi Sera!" I looked up at his rugged profile in shock. I looked around my vacant car. Did I just hear that? I laughed out loud - only in Sedona! I waved again. What else is going to happen here? I could not help but wonder.

On Saturday morning, I drove to work and parked as usual in the lot adjacent to the shopping center where the employees were required to park their cars. I walked across the main parking lot to the entrance of the shops.

Halfway across the lot, I saw two couples looking in the opposite direction. I could not believe my eyes for one of the men, the shorter of the two, was standing on a ledge. I could see his black platform shoes. I knew without a doubt that it was Ken, my brief affair from Ft. Lauderdale. I could feel myself go weak. I really had no desire to encounter them. I didn't want Ken back in my life. My breath was coming fast. I could see as I got closer that his plump wife looked just like her photograph in their Florida condo. I didn't know the other couple.

I veered way off to the right and still had to pass them within a short distance. Quickly I grabbed my sunglasses from my handbag, placed them over my eyes, and ruffled my hair around my face. I changed my walk slightly and made it through the entrance and out of their vision. Once in the clear, I ran as fast as I could into the shop. It took a while for my panting to settle down. I thought they might come into the shop; I felt if they did do this– then I would deal with it. They never did.

Wow! I thought – this is karmic closure. I realized I was to see them, here in remote Sedona of all places – not for *them* to see me. I chose to direct my own destiny and avoidance, at this time, was my way to move forward with my life - unencumbered. This was *my choice.*

My list of karmic closures was growing: the designer sportswear manager in Cleveland that threatened me on the phone because she thought I took her job; Jerod, forgiveness and closure in Sedona and now Ken with his wife. I was glad that I had chosen not to play an ongoing part in Ken's life scenario. I was happy that this couple was still together - without me!

Eunice

Crystal had left a message on my phone. She wanted me to meet with a woman named Eunice. I called her and scheduled a time for the following week. Eunice sounded excited about the interview. I looked forward to meeting her.

Several days later, Eunice called with terrible news. "I'm in the hospital. I was involved in an automobile accident. I sustained internal injuries and as a result I had to have a hip replacement. Now I keep asking myself, "What do I need to learn from all this? Is it patience - with people, things - events? I still want you to interview me. I'm so sorry to have to cancel our appointment!"

I answered, "Of course we can reschedule whenever you're ready to do this."

Eunice said, "How about coming over to my place next Thursday afternoon around one? I'll be home and looking for something positive to do."

"Okay, that would work. I wish you a speedy

recovery and look forward to meeting you. I hung up the phone and thought she was adamant about the interview. Good for her!

A week later I stopped along the way and bought a flowering plant for Eunice. I rang the doorbell. A tall gray-haired man answered the door. "I'm Eunice's husband, Dan. Thank you for coming over. She has been looking forward to your visit." I followed him through the carpeted hallway to their bedroom.

"Eunice, thank you for meeting with me. You look good for someone that went through such a terrible ordeal." I could tell she had prepared herself for the interview: her short curly auburn hair was arranged neatly around her freshly made-up face. She was propped up in bed surrounded by layers of covers. "This is for you." I handed her the flowering plant which she placed on her nightstand. I sensed that it was hard for her to sit still, let alone be confined to her bed.

Her hazel eyes stared into mine as she said, "Thank you. I still can't believe this happened to me. I keep trying to figure out what I need to learn from all of this."

I looked around the bedroom which held a king bed, a mahogany double dresser with a large brass mirror over it, a tall antique cabinet and two nightstands. There was very little room to walk around.

She motioned for me to sit down on the side of her bed. I managed to sit near the edge of the bed and pulled out my writing tools and waited.

She said, "Sedona was where my first husband and I, both retired teachers, were going to retire.

He died right before we were to move here. I decided to sell everything that didn't fit into my Pinto and continue towards our dream. I left several days after his funeral - alone. My love of antiques and vintage clothing led to open my store in Uptown Sedona. I didn't need to possess the antiques. I just loved the scavenger hunt, finding the precious treasures, buying and selling them. In fact, I was on my way home from a great find, a jeweled tiara, when I had the accident. I was thinking more about the tiara than my driving."

"What would you like to share to help others?"

She replied, "I was teaching math and science in high school when I was chosen as one of the vanguards to showcase a new way of teaching throughout the United States. A team of teachers would jointly schedule, plan, and teach as many as 100 students in an unstructured environment without bells or walled classrooms. I encouraged my students and challenged them to think for themselves. Be an individualist - don't be afraid to be different - you don't have to conform. Be open - reach out to new people - new experiences."

"I've always loved to learn. My parents and grandparents encouraged me to use my mind and to respect knowledge. As a child, I would spend alternate summers with my grandparents on their farms in Maine. My grandmothers' lives were parallel; both were hard workers, rising at the crack of dawn. Neither of them had running water or electricity. It was really something, their capacity to be creative, to make do with virtually little or nothing. They used fabric from grain bags for slips, aprons and underwear. With all they had to do, their houses were kept spotlessly clean. There was little money left for feminine luxuries: jewelry, lingerie, or makeup. Yet they thrived on the deep satisfaction of their labor. I inherited their stamina. I must confess that I'm also a workaholic. Even now I'm anxious to get back to work, to enjoy life, every golden minute of it!"

"If I could unravel one of the strands of my life and trace it back to the beginning, then I would have been able to see the important event, and how gigantic it was at the beginning: moving to Sedona, taking risks, becoming active in the community, meeting and making new friends. I fell in love, which I thought would never happen again, and remarried."

I said, "You've such a positive outlook! You'll be up and about before you know it! Thank you for this interview. You've inspired me to take more risks, open up more."

She said, "Thank you for coming here and for the plant." I hugged her gently. I could sense that she was ready to take a nap. I left quickly. I was amazed she consented to the interview so quickly after her surgery. What a strong and determined woman she is. She had inherited the tenacity of her grandmothers.

Doris

Later that week, I had an interview with Doris, a director of a research foundation in Uptown Sedona. Her assistant guided me to her well-designed office. Seated at a chrome and glass desk, Doris stood and came to greet me. I grasped her hand and said, "Thank you for meeting with me."

Doris was a sight to behold! She wore a Kelly-green cowboy hat that covered her golden hair. Her mature figure was dressed in a Western style Kelly green pant outfit. She gazed at me through large sapphire eyes. Her makeup was impeccable. She seemed self-assured.

She said, "Please have a seat."

Her desk had stacks of files and papers, all neatly arranged. I sat in one of the tan faux leather and chrome chairs facing her and asked, "Where would you like to begin?"

"When I was a teenager and very much in love, I wanted to get married. My wise mother advised me, 'once you make your decision to marry a man; make sure he is the man you want to spend the rest of your life with.' I thought about what she said and decided to marry my teenage boyfriend. I felt our marriage would last as we had everything in common and still do. We just celebrated 46 years of marriage and are still in love."

"I stayed home and raised our two sons. As the boys grew older, they didn't need me. I needed something constructive to do to fill the void. Attracted to a cosmetics company, I thought this would be a wonderful way to create income and help other women raise their self-esteem. When a woman looks good, she feels good, she feels more confident, and this confidence benefits her in her career and personal life as well."

"I told my husband about my desire to join this company. I remembered when he was a young bridegroom, how he had announced, that 'no wife of mine is going to be the main support of this family!' Because through the years, we grew with mutual respect, he reconsidered his youthful statement and said, 'I know how badly you want to do this. You have my blessings. If this is fulfilling for you, it will be fulfilling for me. Your success is my success as well."

"I awakened my creative side and my career spiraled upwards: promotions within the cosmetic company to a buyer for a jewelry chain. I was offered a position as a Marketing Vice President in charge of a newly invented health product. I traveled to health food stores across the United States."

"My greatest lesson was learned from a business associate, who betrayed my trust. This was not just a business colleague - he was like a brother to me, and I trusted him like a brother. His betrayal totally shocked and hurt me."

"Consumed with negative thoughts for over a year, I gradually came to terms with myself. I was beginning to doubt everyone's actions. I needed to know that my inner value was still the same. I had always felt that my trust in someone always brought out the best in that person. I wanted to continue to trust others and feel that most people are basically honest. My belief is that if you're a warm, loving human being and sincere in your feelings, you'll attract people with the same qualities."

"I ultimately forgave this man. I needed to give up this consuming hatred for I knew it could only harm and ultimately destroy me. Once I gave up this anger, I could continue with my life. My deep conviction is that everything that happens to me is good – even this experience. Yes, in the end, good did come out of this. You see, I found the courage to go into business for myself and create my own cosmetic company."

"Years later, looking for a smog-free place to live, my husband and I settled in Sedona. My desire to help humanity led me to become the director of this non-profit research firm that supplies universal information on health and environmental issues."

I said, "Thank you for sharing your life-changing lessons and wisdom. You have accomplished and learned much in this lifetime. I am glad I had this opportunity to meet you."

I thought to myself, to ultimately forgive and let go of debilitating negativity towards a harmful person is very freeing. It cuts the bonds that holds them together.

Cheryl

After I left Doris's office, I set off on foot to try one of the local restaurants in West Sedona that one of my customers suggested for dinner. It was owned by a married couple: the husband was the chef and his wife was the hostess. I found the cozy restaurant easily.

An energetic dark-haired woman dressed in a stylish black pantsuit with quite a few gold and silver necklaces and jingling bracelets guided me to a small cozy table.

"My name is Cheryl. Let me know it you need anything." She handed me a menu.

I could see a gray haired distinguished looking man who I assumed was her husband cooking in the open kitchen. Whatever he was cooking smelled delicious. A whiff of garlic and fresh fragrant herbs permeated the air. I ordered the special: mussels with linguini. I ate more than I usually would.

After scanning the room, Cheryl came back to check on me. "You didn't finish your meal. Didn't you like it?" She scanned my table and the busy restaurant as she waited for my reply.

"No, I loved it. I'm a light eater. I ate more than I usually do. I'll take the rest home and savor it for dinner another night."

I watched Cheryl speak easily with the customers and settle her incoming guests into their chairs. Yes, I knew instinctively that she would be an excellent candidate for the book. I wanted to know how did this sophisticated, fashionable New Yorker get to rural Sedona?

She came back to my table with a box for my leftovers. I took a deep breath and said, "I would like to interview you for a book I'm writing about ordinary, yet extraordinary women."

"I would love to be interviewed," she said without hesitation.

"When can we meet?"

"Let me check my schedule. I'll be right back."

After she returned she said, "Next Monday morning around ten would be good. We could meet at my house." She wrote down her address and home phone number on one of the napkins.

"That works for me as well. I look forward to the interview. The mussels and linguine were delicious. Tell the chef!"

Her face lit up and she said, "Tony, my husband, will be happy to hear this." She hurried off to check on other customers.

When Monday came around, Cheryl cheerfully greeted me at her door. I followed her into a comfortable living room with bookshelves lined with cookbooks. She saw me glancing at them. "Yes, my husband is always trying out new recipes. The other day he made one of his new creations for lunch for my neighbor and me to taste. He loves to get our feedback."

She went into the kitchen and returned with a tray filled with homemade pastries and steaming coffee. I pulled out my pen. "Where do you want to begin?"

"When I was in my 40's, I lost my first husband after twenty-four years of marriage. I was devastated. We had shared an affluent lifestyle together. When the mourning period was over, I needed something to do. I hadn't worked in twenty-four years. I knew I needed some structure in my life, so I enrolled in a community college in New York City. My plan was to update my secretarial skills, to learn the electric typewriter. Eventually, I received my two-year degree and felt competent to enter the working world."

"My circle of friends said to me, 'why are you wasting your time looking for a job? Employers are looking for young women, you're too old, no one will hire you.' I refused to believe them and trusted my intuition which told me that I would get hired - that I wasn't too old."

"I did get a job as a secretary at a collection

agency. After working there several months, I realized that this job was not right for me. Now what was I going to do? A co-worker overheard a frazzled employer in an elevator; he wanted to hire a 'mature woman - a responsible woman.' This man's young secretary was not working out. Aware of my discontent, my co-worker informed me about the job. I quickly applied for the position as Executive Secretary of this charter service company."

"'Why do you want to work?' the owner questioned, as I was all dressed up, and didn't look like I needed a job. I told him my story and that I wanted something to do for my mind. Even though I had very little secretarial experience, he decided to give me a chance and hired me. He said he would train me. I quickly accepted and worked there happily for many years."

"Having gained self-confidence and assertiveness through working, I took the next step and ventured out into the single world. I was seated with some friends at a posh meeting place in New York City, when this attractive, smartly dressed gentleman entered. It was my Tony, a Manhattan attorney. Newly divorced, he too, felt it was time to start going out. He came right over to our table and introduced himself to me. I jokingly asked him, 'What took you so long?' The rest is history," she smiled.

"How was the apple tart?"

"Absolutely delicious."

She said, "Would you like another one? Tony made these pastries this morning."

"Thanks, no, I'm still savoring this one. How did

you get into the restaurant business?"

"My first husband, even though he was an excellent businessman didn't 'lift a glass'- that was my job. Tony changed my belief system about the roles men and women play. He is a totally different kind of man; he loves to cook and do the dishes. We decided to combine our talents and go into the restaurant business in San Diego, California. He gave up his law career and became the chef. I, of course, became the hostess dressing the part in fun outfits. Our little restaurant thrived."

"How did you get here?"

She replied, "On a spiritual retreat, we visited Sedona, fell in love with the area and decided to make it our home."

"What have you learned?" I asked.

She thought for a moment and said, "I've learned that the past does not exist anymore. If I go into the past, the old tapes come back, and I'll be judgmental and unyielding. By being here - right now - in this moment - I avoid pain, anger and lack of self-worth. This moment is all that counts. If I feel someone has hurt me, then I feel down and bad. I realize that this is from my perspective, coming from me, I chose to see it that way. I also learned that when one relationship ends, whether through death, divorce or mutual consent, there can be another loving one - life goes on."

"Thank you, Cheryl. You're such an inspiration. I agree with you about letting the past go. I'm working on this. You took risks and it paid off. You moved forward with your life and found love and happiness."

After the interview, I thought about Cheryl and

her strong messages: to trust your intuition and that one is never too old to try something new. This resonated with me. I felt change coming and knew I was to leave Sedona, this safe healing haven. La Jolla and the ocean, that beautiful flowing creature, were summoning me. Susan, my friend in California, was right. It was time to move to La Jolla.

Back in the condo, I looked through the women's profiles, and the many rejection letters from the publishers and agents to whom I had sent query letters. No, I was not going to get discouraged. I made up my mind that I was going to continue to interview women, ordinary yet extraordinary women in California. Why not? "Life is a journey – not a destination" is a quote I read somewhere. Time to explore more aspects of me in California.

28
live in the now

The next morning, I took several deep breaths and called Susan. "Hi, I thought about it, and it's time to move to La Jolla. Can I come down in two weeks for the weekend, and stay with you while I look for a place to rent?"

"Sure! Good for you! We'll pick you up from the airport. Let me know the details."

I stopped by Alice's condo before going off to work and rang the doorbell. "I've something to tell you."

She laughed and said, "I've something to tell you too. Okay, you go first."

"I'm leaving Sedona and moving near my friends in La Jolla."

She said, "I'm leaving as well. I've friends in Denver, Colorado, and will stay with them until I, like you, find a place and more importantly, a job. I just don't want to run the magazine anymore. A couple from Prescott approached me and offered to buy the magazine. I'm so relieved to let it go. Isn't that interesting? We are both leaving Sedona at the same time."

After I arrived at work, I gave my two-week notice to Karen, the owner, who was in the shop dropping off some jewelry repairs. Before she left, she wished me well. I took my co-workers aside and shared the news with them. We would miss each other for we had bonded during our time together. I was confident that they would find someone to replace me. It would now be their turn to experience this fun little shop. I hugged each of co-workers and then off we went to help customers.

I trusted that all would work out for me; after all, I was not moving from Bucharest to become an American doctor like Dr. Tamara or to live in France like Laura and her husband, or leaving China to come to America, like Dr. Amy did. Nor did I need to learn a new language as they each had to do.

Well, this will be my last hair appointment with Hannah, I thought as I drove to her house. Looking at my reflection in the mirror as Hannah cut my hair I said, "I 'm moving to La Jolla."

"Good for you. La Jolla is a beautiful place. My husband has a job opportunity in Birmingham, Alabama of all places. We may be moving as well. See what happens."

"Hannah, thanks for my great haircuts. Good luck in Birmingham." I walked through the house towards the front door making sure I didn't encounter the wolf, nor would I mentally send him a goodbye message.

When I was back in the condo, I called Crystal and told her of my decision. Her voice sounded choppy as she said, "I wish you the best. I'll miss you and Teddy. I really enjoyed working for you."

I replied, "You did a great job. Thanks for the

getting the interviews and taking the photos. We'll get together before I leave." I knew I had been a financial lifeline for her, but now it was time to complete this chapter in our lives.

The following morning, I went to the little breakfast place in West Sedona for I wanted to relax on the patio, have my last day-old-muffin and coffee.

Chloe

A tall woman was diligently sweeping the wood deck.

"Hi, I haven't seen you before," I said as I walked up the plank stairs onto the outdoor patio.

"My name is Chloe. I'm helping the owner. She's been a friend of mine for years. I'm staying at her house, doing odd jobs to pay for my room and board until I go back to California. I've no permanent home. I love the freedom."

She had such vitality even though I guessed she was older than she looked – maybe her late 60s.

"I love physical work, it makes me feel good," she said to me as I walked toward one of the picnic tables. I could feel the coarseness of the bench as I sat down. A motorcycle's popping noise broke through the air. The lovely pink bougainvillea clung to the white painted trellis behind me. The morning air smelled fresh.

"Do you need a menu, or do you know what you want?"

"A blueberry muffin and coffee would be good." I took a deep breath and said, "I am a writer and would like to interview you for a book, I am writing about women who want to share their life experiences and wisdom to help other women. I want to know how you seem to be so present, so positive, and so free."

"Sure, I would like that. Let me get your muffin and coffee. I'll be right back."

She brought the muffin and a mug of hot coffee and sat down on the bench opposite me.

"Okay, let me tell you, I live totally in the 'Now,' no future, no past, with no permanent address. I travel all over the West visiting friends or staying at small hostels along the way. I wasn't always like this; I lived a structured life. I married my high school sweetheart during World War II. After his service, we moved to Yuma, Arizona. I was unhappy in this marriage yet remained because no one divorced in those days. My reward was my three wonderful sons."

"After eighteen years of marriage, I found the courage to divorce my husband. I moved to Baja, Mexico and started a business buying and selling burros with a friend."

Chloe stood up, "You need a refill." She took my mug, refilled it and brought it back to the table. She brought a glass of orange juice for herself.

"Thank you," I said. I picked up my pen.

"Where was I? I know. . . I remarried and sold the business to my partner. My new husband and I moved to San Diego. There I began my life's work as a handwriting consultant. I'd completed the year's study and became certified. I've helped many discover their inner personality traits through their handwriting. I've found through their handwriting that many women have low self-esteem. They are taught to take care of others, to be wives and mothers; their needs are not fulfilled. At one time, I was exactly like these women; my self-esteem was low. I had to learn to ask for what I wanted. If I didn't let my needs be known, how would they ever be met?"

Her eyes looked deeply into mine, "Explore the potential you have - don't expect others to take care of you." Something inside of me connected with this.

"In 1979, I conquered my fear of heights by becoming an airline pilot! To conquer your fears, challenge them, don't ignore them. I became a partner in a flight school. My mentors, she smiled affectionately, are Charley Lindbergh and Amelia Earhart. They showed me that they dared to go for their dreams and inspired me to go for mine."

I watched Chloe move effortlessly off the bench to give menus to a young couple that sat a few tables away. I could not get over her positive attitude, her youthful appearance. She was dressed in a pink tee shirt and khaki shorts that showed off her long legs.

She returned to the table, drank some of her orange juice and said, "My second marriage didn't work out. I'm single, divorced again. I live day to day, completely independent; I take care of myself. I don't fear people or things. I simply do my own thing – to follow my quest to assist others - to find their purpose. See the tan Buick parked out front? That is my home whenever I need it." I looked at her weathered sedan, then back at her. I was awed and inspired at her fearlessness, her zest for life.

"Thanks for this interview. I'm moving to La Jolla and I needed to be reminded to let go of fears. I'll try my best to live in the 'Now,' to be positive, and not be afraid to move forward into the unknown. This is certainly not an accident that I met you today."

She said, "I may run into you in San Diego as I travel there a lot."

"I hope to see you there," I said.

She waved goodbye as she went over to help another table.

The two weeks since I gave my notice seemed to go too quickly. After we closed the shop, Elizabeth, Vicki and I celebrated my bon voyage at the Mexican restaurant with margaritas, quesadillas and of course, guacamole and corn chips. I knew that it was time to leave, and I also knew that I would miss my work buddies. I looked at Elizabeth and could not help but admire how chic she looked with her new sterling silver earrings that were enhanced with gemstone and feathers. They showed her strong creative side.

I turned to gaze at Vicki, her kind eyes met mine. I would miss her openness, her caring nature. They insisted on treating me. I accepted because this is what they wanted to do yet I knew how hard they worked for their money. We hugged each other and silently left the restaurant.

Back at the condo, I stood outside on the little patio with Teddy. I thought about Sedona, this mystical, magical, and breathtakingly beautiful place. I could feel her warmth, like a loving presence engulf me. I felt humbled and inspired by her.

I knew that whenever I wanted to I could invoke the presence of Sedona and the messages of the women into my heart. These women, as well as the Phoenix women that I had interviewed, touched my soul, and I'll never forget them. I felt stronger, ready to face the future because of them. I stroked the green stone hanging from my neck. It felt warm and protective.

The next day, I telephoned Crystal and asked, "Can I leave Teddy with you for the weekend. I hate to put him in the kennel while I'm in La Jolla."

"Of course, I would love to watch Teddy."

It was dark when I dropped Teddy off in the morning. His incessant barking and jumping showed his delight when he saw Crystal.

"We'll have fun together." She said to him as she carried him into their house. I could see him licking her face through their glass door as I drove away.

29

take Sedona's magic with you

The darkness shaded to grey as I drove the empty freeway. I was nearing Phoenix, when the sun peeked through the grey sky, creating a splash of brilliant orange and red. Mother Nature was at work painting the sky. The traffic had increased considerably. I was glad to get off the busy freeway and relieved when I found the airport shuttle parking area. I waited with a few other travelers to board the shuttle bus to the airport.

Susan and Howie picked me up from the crowded San Diego airport. What can I say? I was nervous and so excited at the same time about moving to La Jolla. I could hardly sleep that night in the high antique bed in their guest room. I kept stopping the worrisome thoughts. Would I find a place to live? *STOP!* Would I get a job? *STOP!!* Would I be able to afford to live in La Jolla? *STOP!* It's much more expensive to live here than in Sedona. *STOP!*

In the morning the smell of freshly brewed coffee brought me to their kitchen. Howie had left early and returned with newspapers and fresh bagels. The three of us scanned the rental ads as we drank our coffee and ate toasted bagels. I spotted an ad in the La Jolla Times: *a one-bedroom house for rent in Wind N Sea, part of La Jolla* and showed it to Susan.

After she read the ad, she said, "This isn't that far from us. See if we can see this place."

Many phone calls later, I finally reached the owner. He would meet us in one hour at the rental. My spirits soared with anticipation.

Howie parked the car on a residential street filled with tall trees and blooming flowering foliage. A well-dressed man with salt and pepper hair arrived and introduced himself as the owner.

He said, "The house that is for rent is directly behind this house. I could tell he was a professional by his mannerism.

Howie asked, "What do you do?"

"I'm an attorney. My wife and I bought both properties for investment. She takes care of the remodeling and management. We redid these houses slowly because of the cost. "

We followed him through a black wrought iron gate next to the charming house. He led the way along a long narrow cement walkway to an adorable pink cottage. We walked up pink plank steps onto a large pink deck that continued around the side of the house. He unlocked the front door and we entered a miniature living room, a tiny kitchen, a small dining area, one bedroom with a walk-in closet, a tiled bathroom, and a den without a closet. There was a small washer and dryer combination in a closet.

We walked around the house and noticed that the den at the back of the house was held up by wood stilts. The owner said, "I've a painter working on the interior as well as the exterior. He is nearly finished."

"I like it; I'll take it!" I heard myself say, even though the rent was steeper than I would have liked. I knew I had to do this. It felt right. I immediately pulled out my checkbook to give him the required first month's rent including the security and pet deposit.

"I can move in on the first of February." As I spoke, I realized that this was only ten days away! Here I go again!

"My wife has rented the place to a couple, but you can have it," he said rather abruptly.

I was caught off guard. I wondered what this is all about. What is going on here? I questioned why he bothered to show me this rental property in the first place! I started to ask him about this, then stopped - just accept. I hurriedly wrote the check and handed to him.

Susan said, "This is a determined lady when she sets her mind to something she wants." We followed the owner out the path to the cars. He left in his new black BMW.

As we drove away, she said, "It's hard to believe you found this little treasure so quickly. These places are not that easy to come by in La Jolla. You don't know how lucky you are. You did good!"

"You mean the garage! I bet they converted the garage into that little house," I said.

"No, it looks like someone built this house to rent out. Many residents in La Jolla and San Diego have back properties that they rent for extra income." She changed the subject and said, "Why don't we get something to eat? I'm hungry. Let's celebrate with lunch at the Mexican Café in Old Town in San Diego. We love to go there, have lunch and walk around."

Silently I wondered whether I really had the house, or would I receive a phone call from the owner. After all, they would have to contact the other potential tenants. I finally relaxed and just let all my inner chatter go. I saw a beautiful rainbow in my mind and focused my attention on it. Whatever happens, happens. I did invoke my Higher Self, *"May this be for everyone's highest good."*

Susan guided us to the busy restaurant. We stood and waited in a long line until the hostess sat us at an outside table. It felt so good to be outdoors on this glorious sun-filled California day. I took a deep breath and filled my lungs with the cool fresh air.

After lunch, we strolled around the bazaar, walked in and out of some of the interesting shops crammed with gifts and souvenirs. Some of the small shops were just too crowded, so we window shopped them.

Once back at Susan and Howie's, my thoughts turned to the little house and wondered how I was going to fit my furniture, and my clothes into that tiny place. There was only one closet, however, it did come with a stacked washer and dryer. This was a luxury! Well, I'm going to have to scale down again. I pictured Teddy happily running around the fenced in yard and felt a little better. I let out a big sigh.

Susan and Howie had previous plans for dinner with a group of their friends at a restaurant in Del Mar. They insisted I join them. Howie drove through the dark night along the water's edge. I remembered the blue green water off to the left, only now everything was black. I could catch a glimpse of white froth as the ocean heaved itself to the shore and opened my window slightly to hear the liquid giant inhale and exhale. I breathed in the ocean air.

Howie managed to find a parking space inside the crowded parking garage and took a parking ticket from a metal box.

We walked into the elevator. Two couples were awaiting our arrival at the doorway of the restaurant. Susan introduced me to everyone. After what seemed like a long time, we were escorted through the Saturday night crowd to an elegantly set table against a wall. The noise was elevated. The restaurant was completely full: a good thing we had reservations.

The women were quite newsworthy and discussed current events around town. Their husbands were from a different fabric, quiet, reserved. I was seated comfortably between Susan and Howie, half listening to the animated conversation around me. I meditated silently listening to my breath. Then I looked around the upscale restaurant at its chic ambience and interesting clientele. There seated at a nearby table was my new landlord and his wife with another couple. I blinked. I could not believe it!

"Excuse me! I think I see my new landlord," I said as I squeezed around Howie's chair to get out and walked to their table.

"Hi," I said to the surprised man, and then to his wife, I added, "I'm your new tenant!"

"*So, you're the new tenant!*" The raven-haired wife bellowed in an extremely loud agitated tone, "Do you know I had to call and cancel the other couple after *he* rented the house - to *you*?"

I chose to ignore her elevated tone and this delicate question. I simply smiled and said, "Thank you. Your place is lovely. I'm glad I found it." I silently thought, yes, I do have the house, and they obviously have communication issues.

The wife changed her tone, "Please let me know if you need anything before you move in. I'll be happy to help you."

"Thanks! Enjoy your dinners," I said and hastily left their table. Seated back between Susan and Howie, I said, "What are the odds of this happening?" They both shook their heads.

On the way home, we laughed at the serendipity. Then I thought, isn't that interesting. Here I am so far from Sedona, where serendipity seems the norm, where things manifest so quickly. Was I taking Sedona's magic with me - or was it always there for me? Did Sedona just highlight it?

The next morning at the San Diego Airport, I said to Susan, "If you hear of any job opportunities, let me know. I really like the owner of the little stationary store in La Jolla. Now that I've a place to live, I definitely need a job!"

She replied, "I've asked Cindy. She isn't hiring."

"You're way ahead of me. Oh well, something will come up. I'll call you and let you know when Teddy and I'll be there."

Sedona! She looked even more beautiful than when I left. Her purples, oranges, and burnt sienna skin appeared to be glowing. Were her outstretched arms awaiting my return? Mixed feelings struggled within me. This had been my Brigadoon, this small isolated spiritual place for the past ten months.

I picked Teddy up at Crystal's house and thanked her. I think he could have stayed with her for I had to coax him to leave with me. Once in the car he was happy to be going home.

Howie called several days later. He sounded excited, "Susan wanted me to call you. Guess what, Cindy needs a part-time person at her stationery store in La Jolla. You have a job waiting for you!"

"Oh, this is wonderful! Tell Susan and Cindy thank you." I hung up the phone. I could hardly believe it! Wow! Everything is falling into place! My thoughts turned to the La Jolla house. If I don't downsize, I'll never fit into that space. I need to get rid of things, clothes, furniture, and stuff.

I put an ad in the local paper. I hung a large painted cardboard sign with the big bold words, MOVING SALE, onto the outer post at the entrance to the condos and put another sign on the condo's front door.

People came and as each piece left, I struggled: did I really want to let go of my glass coffee table, the marble floor lamp, that sweater outfit? I felt a part of me leaving with each item. "Goodbye," I whispered to the old friends – "thank you!" I was cutting away at the thick umbilical cord of my possessions that I thought defined me.

I placed the unsold items in my car and took

them to Goodwill. I opened my car door, and two men appeared and began taking the items into the store. Away went my golf clubs. Those were my special golf clubs. Stop! I had to stop myself from quickly taking them back! Soon all the items were gone. As I drove back to the condo, I could feel the difference. Everything is energy. The atmosphere in the car felt lighter, peaceful.

After I gave notice to my landlord, I called the Sedona movers. The same two movers that moved me to Sedona would take my things to La Jolla. One of the men came to the condo to estimate the cost of the move.

After going through the condo, he said, "You've lightened your load quite a bit."

"Yes, I sold a bunch of things. The place in La Jolla is small." It was uncanny that he remembered what furniture I moved so many months ago. Only in Sedona!

The van will get to your new place on the first. If we're going to be late, we'll call you."

"Thank you. I am so relieved that you can move me on such short notice."

Moving day arrived and the large moving van pulled into the small community by mid-afternoon. They had two other loads in the van. The two professional movers were quick and efficient as usual. Before long, they and my things were gone. The condo was empty, silent. I thanked the condo.

I opened the closet in my bedroom to get my little brown tweed overnight suitcase and my new Italian leather jacket. It was a birthday present from my daughters. I had worn it just the other day. *Where could it be?*

I stopped for a moment and remembered that I had put the jacket in the back of the car as it was warm the morning before I went to Goodwill. I had forgot about it! I piled the other things on top of it. The jacket was taken with the rest of the things. *This was to be my ultimate letting go!* I knew as hard as this was, I needed to release this loss and negativity - let it go! I shut my eyes and breathed deeply several times.

Teddy was a jumping white fur yoyo. His sheltered lair was gone, with all his familiar things. When I opened the front door, he ran out and jumped into the open car. I shut the car doors, opening the windows slightly. He ran back and forth intently watching every move I made with his black troubled eyes. I cleaned up and checked again to make sure I didn't miss anything.

I pulled out of the drive of the condo for the last time and sighed. It had been a great place to nest for a while. I drove into West Sedona to meet Crystal at a local health food store.

I could see Crystal's thin form in her cotton dress waiting outside the store.

"Hi," I said as I got out of the car. Teddy was barking and jumping wildly inside. She crawled in and patted his furry head. After she scooted out, I shut the door and locked it. Teddy continued to bark.

She walked into the store with me and waited while I purchased some water and healthy snacks for the road trip. On the way out, she handed me a brown bag and said, "I brought you some apples, energy bars and dog biscuits for Teddy."

"How thoughtful! Thank you for the goodies and again for finding the women and taking their photos. I'll miss you."

She hugged me tightly. "I'll miss you too."

I drove out of the parking lot. Teddy began crying, sobbing loudly heaving his little body like an accordion. Big tears streamed down his furry face. I could not believe it! He was sobbing like a human. I moved him towards me, put his little furry head on my lap, and gently patted him like I would a crying toddler. I wiped his tears with a tissue. What is going on? I had never seen a dog cry before. I never knew dogs could cry. I had just experienced another Sedona phenomenon. My awareness about animals, all animals, especially Teddy, changed in that moment. Elaina was right; animals do have feelings and concerns.

In a soothing tone, I spoke to Teddy, "We are driving to Phoenix and will stay with Teresa and Jack overnight. You remember Teresa. You love her." Whenever he would hear her footsteps at the Tempe house, he would run to her. He calmed down as he listened to my voice. "Teddy, you're going with me. Don't worry! I 'm not leaving you. I love you."

I gently stroked his fur. "After we leave Teresa's house, we'll drive to Susan and Howie's house for a few days until the movers unpack our things."

He cocked his head back and forth, sighed and settled down. He seemed to understand me in some way. He fell asleep.

I thanked Sedona, the beautiful enchanted kingdom. I would remember her beauty, her healing and her magic with love and gratitude.

I was grateful to the Sedona women for sharing their hearts and stories. Through their life experiences and wisdom, I knew I was ready for whatever lies ahead. Back on the highway, I witnessed the last of the majestic red orange mountains fade from my mirror view.

Afterword

Kari closed the journal. Her grandmother's fragrant floral perfume drifted through the air. She took a deep breath and felt Gramma Sera's energy like a soft warm blanket surround her. She knew without a doubt that her grandmother's energy would be around her in this lifetime and beyond. This comforted her.

Kari shut her eyes. The women her grandmother had met and interviewed, each sharing a part of their life and their wisdom with such generosity of spirit appeared in her inner vision.

Kari felt different, connected to everything. She felt alive, more so then she had felt in a very long time. She clasped the journal tightly in her hands and knew that she would reread it again and again. She set it on her end table and looked around her modern apartment to center herself. She felt comfortable with her material possessions. She could enjoy them without having them define her – they are just things. They are a part of her journey here.

She observed how the snow gathered into little white flakes that were crocheting her window in a beautiful lacey design. She watched this for a quite a while. She remembered reading somewhere that no two snowflakes are alike. Yes, she mused, each is different, yet from the same source.

She thought maybe she could learn to become silent, to meditate. She knew she would view herself - others – everything - from a more open, loving and grateful perspective. She would listen and trust her intuition.

She searched through the boxes on the wood floor until she found the tarot deck she was searching for, The Rider Tarot. She took this to her chrome and glass dining table, opened it, and thought this is a good place to start as she pulled out the deck and shuffled the cards.

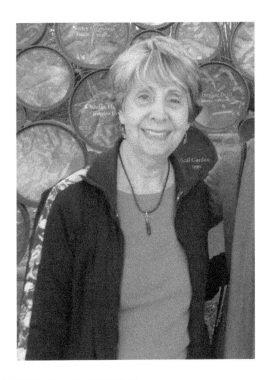

SANDRA SYDELL is a writer, artist and a gifted Spiritual Counselor. She uses tarot and oracle cards, psychometry, and gemstones to assists her clients to empower themselves. Through deep meditation, she facilitates their connection to their spiritual guides. She is a Medium and communicates with entities telepathically. She lives in Scottsdale, Arizona with her family, four dogs and five cats.

CPSIA information can be obtained
at www.ICGtesting.com
Printed in the USA
BVHW030249011021
617907BV00007B/62

9 781544 241296